God Bless the Church Folk

Just Jewel

Copyright © 2015 by Just Jewel
Published by Think Into Existence Ink

ISBN-10: 0991052110
ISBN-13: 978-0-9910521-1-0

Library of Congress Control Number: 2015917494

Book cover illustration by Tay Dubois
Book cover design by Jesh Designs

Printed in the United States of America

CHAPTER 1

She could hear and feel the gravel crunch beneath the tires along the bumpy ride. They'd been driving for what seemed like forever, but it was really only about twenty minutes. All of a sudden, she felt the van come to a stop. She heard the front driver door swing open.

"Stay here!" He instructed then, SLAM! The door shut and there was silence.

She sniffled and whimpered. She wiggled, tossed and turned but to no avail. Her hands and feet had been bound together hog style with flexi cuffs. She shook her head feverishly until she felt a headache coming on. The brown potato sac that was placed over her head wasn't coming off. It wouldn't matter anyway since her eyes were duct taped shut. The corners of her mouth were sore from the gag tied tightly around the back of her head.

Weak and helpless, all she could do was lay there and cry, bleeding from her breasts where she'd been sliced several times. Her thigh ached from the bite marks, but her rectum bore the most pain. The screwdriver hurt and so did the broomstick, but the bat … the bat is what left the splinters and agony.

The physical pain was bad, sure, but it was the waiting that became the worst part. Tears streamed down the corners of her eyes and into her hair as she listened to the sound of a shovel digging into dirt in the distance. She began to recite the Lord's Prayer in her head as she waited to meet her destiny.

1

Suddenly, the digging stopped and the side door slid open. "The less you fight death, the easier it will come. Don't fight it." He said to her softly. Then she felt herself being hoisted up onto shoulders. She winced from the pain of a shoulder pressing into the wound on her rib where she'd been stabbed. The night air sent a chill over her nude body. The drop felt like a long way down and that's when she knew. It was over.

She shook her head back and forth, "Mmm! Mmm!" Her pleas were muffled and gagged. The last thing she felt was cold dirt hitting her bruised and battered body one shovel full at a time. Larissa continued crying until the dirt reached a level too heavy for her face. Some even started to trickle into the bag where her only choice was to snort it into her nostrils, until she could breathe no more.

CHAPTER 2

"And here are your keys, Mrs. Mackey," their new apartment superintendent said proudly as she dangled two sets of keys with a wide smile on her round face. Cara seemed like a nice lady. She was way more pleasant than other supers they had dealt with while living in New York. When Vivian Mackey explained to Cara that she wouldn't have the full security deposit up front, she talked to the landlord for her and worked it out so she could pay in two parts once she had the rest of the money.

"It's *Ms*. Mackey, actually, but you can call me Viv." Vivian responded as she returned the smile and collected the keys from Cara's hand.

"Oh, I'm so sorry." Cara said, quickly feeling embarrassed.

"It's okay. Really. Thanks so much for everything." Vivian extended her hand to Cara.

"You're welcome. You two don't be strangers. If you need anything at all, you have both of my numbers there, okay?" Cara shook Vivian's hand then headed towards the door.

"Here, babe, don't lose 'em." She cautioned her fifteen-year-old daughter, Cinnamon.

Cinnamon Mackey was Vivian's only child. Only fifteen years younger than her mother, they were close, more like best girlfriends than mother and daughter. Looking like an exact carbon copy of her mother, they were mistaken for sisters all of the time. They both had a honey-brown complexion and sandy hair. Cinnamon was filling out nicely, mirroring her mother's same stacked frame, that coke bottle shape with curves in all the right places. Both had the same slim face with a cleft chin and high cheekbones. Cinnamon was catching up to her mother's height quickly, though still just a few inches shorter, standing at about five foot five. Vivian could see her daughter maturing quickly, and she worried about those juicy, cranberry-colored full lips that she had passed on. *Boy those lips are gonna get her into some trouble,* she always thought. The only indication of her father's traits were Cinnamon's dark brown eyes, where Vivian's were light brown.

It was January of 1997, and the Mackey women were getting a fresh start for the New Year. Leaving behind their rollercoaster ride of a life in New York, the two were just settling in nicely in their new two-bedroom apartment in the small town of Gracious Meadows, Delaware. Also only a teenager when she was born, Cinnamon's father didn't stick around for long. By the time he and Vivian graduated from high school, things between them were unraveling quickly. He left the city for college out West never to be heard from again. Vivian did what she had to to raise her daughter by herself, vowing to never fall in a position where she'd be forced to part from her only child. This included a life of crime, odd jobs, living from pillar to post, and a never-ending list of men she'd hoped could be Cin's "new daddy".

Now in her thirties, Vivian was finally maturing and ready to be done with that way of living. Moving to Gracious Meadows was going to be a new beginning for the two in her mind. She was ready to live a life on the straight and narrow and set a better example for her daughter, who was now approaching adulthood herself.

"Where do you want this, ma'am?" One of the movers asked.

"Oh, that can go in the bedroom down on the left." Vivian instructed.

"Well, alright. That's the last of it, Ms. Mackey." John, another one of the movers, said. He was the boss of the small, three-person crew.

Since Vivian and Cinnamon fled New York in somewhat of a hurry, they only had time to bring a few items of clothing with them and whatever could fit in Vivian's car. The two came across John's furniture store their first day in Gracious Meadows, and Vivian wasted no time spending the little bit of cash they had to make sure they'd be comfortable in their new place.

"Thank you guys so much," Vivian started. "I'm sorry I don't have any cold beers or water to offer you. As you know, we're just moving in, so there hasn't been time for grocery shopping just yet." She explained apologetically.

"That's okay. Don't you worry about that. Once the guys finish assembling that last bed, we'll be right out of your way." John removed his cap, running the back of his hand across his forehead to wipe away the sweat that was forming. It was the second week of January. The temperature was cold outside, but the heat was on full blast inside the small apartment. John grinned as he eyed Vivian up and down.

Vivian smiled back politely, "Oh there's no rush. I just appreciate you working with me on the price, Mr. John."

"My pleasure, my pleasure. I like to do what I can to help. And please, don't be so formal. Just call me John, ma'am."

"Okay, *John.*" Vivian flirted as she leaned on the kitchen counter, exposing the top of her full bosom while fanning herself, "But if I'm gonna call you John, then you're just gonna have to call me Viv."

Cinnamon rolled her eyes as she watched her mother's performance. She knew exactly what she was doing. Vivian just couldn't help herself. By now, she'd figured out that John owned the furniture store. Vivian saw dollar signs. If she saw a man with money, she couldn't help but turn on the charm. *I bet she doesn't even like him*, Cinnamon thought to herself. Cinnamon knew her mom was buttering John up to add to her "just in case" roster. The "just in case" roster was a term Cinnamon made up in her mind to categorize the men her mom kept on hand just in case she might need or want something from them later down the road.

There was the "just in case" team, the "blip-stick" men, and the "iron fist" crew. The blip-stick men were the bums. They didn't work, own anything, or have any type of income. Leeches and slackers, they were only good for sex. They didn't have blip but the stick between their legs. The iron fist guys usually took care of business. Some were legitimate businessmen, some drug dealers, but these types always made sure Cinnamon and her mother didn't want for anything. The only problem with these men was that they enjoyed using her mom as a punching bag. They had tempers and Vivian always seemed to know exactly what buttons to push to get them started. Cinnamon was so use to seeing all these different types of men come and go that she pretty much had it down to a science. Within fifteen minutes of being around a man, she could usually tell which category he would fit into.

John didn't even try to hide the fact that he was staring straight down Vivian's top. As she leaned on the counter, bent over with her butt poked out, he couldn't help but visualize yanking down her tight stretch pants and taking her from behind right there in the kitchen.

"Mmm mm! Miss Vivian, you sure don't look old enough to have a teenage daughter. You still look like a baby yourself." He said, eyeing her thick, toned thighs.

Vivian giggled, "Oh please, stop it."

"I'm serious."

"Well thank you," she replied, flashing a bashful smile; a smile that Cinnamon knew was fake.

Cinnamon couldn't take anymore of her mother's embarrassing performance, so she grabbed her jacket and excused herself to step outside. Also wearing stretch pants and a V-neck top, she walked into the sunlight, took a big stretch, and sat down on the stairs leading to their apartment. She leaned back with her elbows resting on the steps behind her.

"Excuse me," she heard a voice from behind.

She looked up and scooted to the side, allowing the other two movers to get past. They were bringing out empty cardboard and plastic wrapping from the furniture. One man looked to be around the same age as John, early forties. The other looked around Cinnamon's age or maybe a few years older. He was cute. They finished loading up the truck with the rest of the remnants. Then they sat on the back of the truck with their feet dangling, talking with their breath dancing in the air as they waited for John to come out.

The boy wore a white T-shirt that was now soaked with sweat, clinging to his toned frame. All he wore over that was an unzipped hoodie. He was tall, maybe around six feet. His brown sugar-colored skin perspired in the sunlight. He wore his hair in a short afro with a black pick sticking out. You could tell his facial hair was just coming in good, with a faint mustache and a small goatee. He had a serious, stern look on his face as he talked to the older man.

Just then, he locked eyes with Cinnamon who quickly glanced away. She felt silly realizing she'd been staring. She looked down the street, in the other direction, anything not to look back at this boy. She turned her attention to three girls playing hopscotch as if it were the most interesting thing she'd ever witnessed. She tried to casually sneak a peek out the corner of her eye to see if he'd stopped looking. He hadn't. His lips were still moving while he conversed with the older man but his eyes were locked on Cinnamon as he studied her from head to toe. A half smirk crept across his mouth and she blushed. That's when he said something to the older man, who looked in Cinnamon's direction. He then hopped off the back of the truck. He blew air into his cupped hands that wore gloves with the fingertips cut off. She got nervous as he made his way over.

Just as he opened his mouth to make his introduction, he was cut off. "Okay fellas! The truck ready to go? Let's roll out!" John yelled. Then he turned to Vivian, "And I'll see *you* on Friday… mm mm mmm woman, you too fine for your own good! Lord have mercy!" He took one last look at Vivian before turning back towards the street, shaking his head back and forth as he headed onto the sidewalk. The boy spun on his heels and headed back to the truck too.

Vivian grinned her fake grin as she waved goodbye. As soon as the truck pulled away, she dropped the fake smile. "So should we head to the grocery store and cook or go exploring and eat out somewhere tonight?"

Cinnamon shrugged without looking at her mother, "I don't know. It doesn't matter."

"Oh c'mon, Cin. I know you're sad about leaving New York, but this is gonna be good for us, a nice, fresh start! We need it, don't you think?" Vivian crouched down behind her daughter, hugging her.

"I don't know. I guess."

"C'mon, let me go grab the keys. We'll find the grocery store, and I'll make your favorite tonight. We'll have a girls' night in." With that, she rubbed Cinnamon's back and dashed back into their apartment. Cinnamon hugged her knees tightly to her chest as she thought about leaving New York behind. Everything she knew and loved was there: her friends and family. She missed them already, but she knew her mother was right. They did need a fresh start.

After going to the grocery store, mother and daughter returned just after the sun set. Vivian was breaking in their new kitchen making baked ziti, Cinnamon's favorite, with garlic bread. As they waited for the garlic bread to finish, Vivian poured two glasses of red wine. Even though Cinnamon was only fifteen, her mother allowed her to drink with her on a regular basis.

Vivian took a sip as Cinnamon swished hers around in the glass. "So...?"

"So what?" Cinnamon asked.

"So what do you think of John?"

"Mom, I have no idea. We just met him and he barely said two words to me." She said, eyeing her mother up and down.

"What? Why you looking at me like that?" Vivian asked with a big smile.

"You know why."

"I don't. What?" She repeated.

"Mommy, you know good n' well you don't like that man. Why you stringing him along like that?"

"Hey, that's not fair. I don't know if I like him yet. Sure, he ain't much to look at. I'll give you that. But he owns his own business which means he probably has money and he got a nice set of wheels too." She explained like she was proving her case in a debate.

"So?"

"So *what?*" she replied.

"So what does any of that have to do with anything? I thought you wanted something different this time. This is supposed to be a new start for us. Remember?"

"You're right. You're right. You're right, *Mom.*" She said sarcastically. "But look, we don't know anybody here. It won't hurt to make a friend or two. I'm just saying..." She said as she took another sip of wine and rolled her eyes.

"Now you know that man is not interested in being your friend. *'Mm mm mmm woman, you too fine for your own good!'*" Cinnamon mimicked John's earlier comment. "I was worried I might have to come in here and get you two the way y'all was both carrying on. Sickening." She made a face to show her disproval.

Vivian couldn't help but laugh at her daughter. As close as they were, sometimes it was hard to believe this stick in the mud came out of her own womb. "Worried for what? Please, ain't nothing going on over here but the rent!"

"Yeah, well, you might want to make sure he knows that. I'm sure he got other plans on his mind." Sometimes Cinnamon really did act like she was Vivian's mother.

"I just agreed to go on one date with him. That is all. He's taking me to his church and dinner after that. Ain't much trouble we could be getting into at church, Miss Cini-Cin-Cin." She put a potholder over her hand, waving it back and forth in front of Cinnamon's face before opening the oven door.

"*Church*? Oh Lord, Mommy you ain't been to church since......since......I don't even—have you *ever* been to church?" She asked, not taking her mother seriously.

"Yes, for your information, I have. We both have been a couple times. You were just too young to remember." Cinnamon grunted. "This'll be good, Cin. Maybe I'll meet some good, honest folks. Who knows, maybe it'll rub off on me. You never know." She winked at her daughter as she removed the garlic bread.

"I guess..."

As she looked at her mother in her stretch pants, Cinnamon couldn't even picture Vivian going to somebody's church. *I'm glad I won't be there to witness this*, was all she could think.

***

"Lord, I'm runnin', try'na make a hundred, ninety-nine n' a half won't do!" The choir belted out as they clapped and stomped their feet inside of Greater Saints First Baptist Church. They wore blue and red robes. The percussionist wailed on the drums and the organist plunked on the keys. The church was small but it was in full swing. The congregation nodded, clapped and sang along, some standing, some sitting. Vivian could hear tambourines banging and her eardrums had to adjust to the loudness as an usher escorted her and John up a side aisle to a seat.

Vivian smiled and excused herself as she climbed past members who were already seated in order to squeeze into the tight row. One by one, each one frowned or huffed at the inconvenience of letting them by. Vivian grew self-conscious, wondering if the frowns were from her disrupting the service or from their disapproval of her dress. She spent quite some time digging through her suitcase to try to find something suitable. She knew the dress was a little low-cut and form-fitting, but it was the only one that came past her knee. Once they were seated, John squeezed her hand and smiled, trying to make her feel comfortable. It worked, and Vivian sat up straight with her head held high, returning the smile before she turned her attention to the choir.

After a while, the sounds of the choir and the music got so good to her, Vivian stood up to clap along. It had been so many years since she found herself at church, and she was proud of herself for making the move to come. Her smile beamed as she clapped along off beat. She didn't care. She was in the house of the Lord, and in her eyes, this meant one step closer to having the relationship she always wanted with God. She could feel the eyes of different members looking her over. Some looked curious, some jealous, and the men just lustful.

Once the song was over, the preacher, Reverend Grienbachs, approached the microphone in the pulpit. "Praise the Lord, saints!"

"Praise the Lord!" The congregation responded. Vivian looked around, not realizing she was supposed to respond.

"Praise the Lord, saints!" he repeated. The congregation answered again, and this time Vivian responded right on cue with them. "Praise the Lord. I thank the Lord on today for the choir and that beautiful selection. The song says ninety-nine and a half won't do … *ninety-nine* and a half … won't do. Amen?"

He paused briefly for the congregation to acknowledge with a variety of "mmm hmms," grunts, and "amens".

"Ninety-nine and a half won't do, church. The song says, 'Lord I'm runnin', try'na make a hundred 'cause ninety-nine and a half … WON'T DO!'" he hollered the last part for emphasis, and the church erupted with more grunts and some handclaps. "And church, this applies to all areas of your life. We can't just be giving God ninety-nine percent. It is our duty to give one hundred percent. Amen?" This time he didn't wait for a response before continuing, "Some of us in this sanctuary only been giving ninety-nine percent, saints. Shoot, some of us only been giving fifty or forty percent, but that ain't what he

SAAAAID!" He hollered into the mic. "The song says one hundred! Oh-shamalamasha-colosholada-comada," he banged his fist on the podium and began to speak in tongues, but only for a moment. He took a deep breath before continuing, "Church, as we prepare for offering, I want you to remember the words of the song. We want to build and lift God's kingdom, and the only way to do that is to give, not ninety-nine, but one hundred percent. Amen? Some of us 'round here spending one hundred percent on pimpin' out our cars, one hundred percent on jewelry, one hundred percent on hair weaves." A few snickers and giggles could be heard throughout the church. "But we ain't giving one hundred percent to our God! Please bow your heads and let us bless the offering. Ushers?"

Two ushers and two deacons gathered at the front of the church, holding offering baskets as Reverend Grienbachs went into prayer. After the prayer, two ushers came up from the rear to guide people from their rows. Vivian clung to her five-dollar bill proudly as she stepped down the center aisle. Money was tight, and she hadn't even found a job yet. To her, that five dollars was a big deal. She dropped it in the first basket she came to.

After the offering, a woman from the first pew approached the podium to give the welcome address. She asked for all the visitors to stand. Vivian glanced at John, and he nudged her to stand up. Once she and a family of three toward the back stood, the woman asked them all to give their names.

"Hi, I'm Vivian Mackey..." The church was silent as they waited for her to say more. She just looked around and took her seat. John started clapping and the rest of the congregation slowly joined in.

"Praise the Lord, everybody. Giving honor to God who is the head of my life and my Lord and savior, the reverend and first lady, deacons and saints of the church, my name is Ana Brown. This is my husband, Andre Brown, and our two children, Shayna and Shaniah. We bring greetings from our church home, Christ Baptist Church in Raytown where the pastor is Reverend Troy Collins, and we're just so happy and blessed to be here." The woman in the back spoke for her whole family and the congregation clapped in return.

Dag, I didn't know I was supposed to give a whole speech, Vivian thought.

"We thank each and every one of you for joining us today. We hope you enjoy the service and please, please, please come back and visit us anytime." The welcome lady finished her spiel, and the church applauded some more.

The Reverend gave the sermon after that. Vivian enjoyed his word; although, she didn't understand a lot of it. It didn't matter. She was still in good spirits just being there. Something about being in the building just made her feel like she was on the right track in her new life.

"May the grace of God, the love of Jesus, and the sweet communion of the Holy Spirit rest, rule and abide now, henceforth and forever. Let us all sing together..." Reverend Grienbachs gave the benediction, and the congregation ended, singing "Aaaaaaaamennnnn," in unison.

As members greeted each other with hugs and handshakes, John placed his hand on Vivian's back, "Come on, I want you to meet the reverend and first lady." He guided her to the front of the church towards the pulpit as gawking eyes stared at this stranger in their church.

"Maybe I'm just being self-conscious, but I feel like all eyes are on me," she whispered.

"No, you're not being self-conscious. Don't worry about all these women here. They just love to have something or some*one* new to gossip about. By next week, you'll be old news, I'm sure." He said while lending a comforting smile. Vivian copied his smile and followed suit, lending hers to two of the gawkers.

They returned fake smiles and nods, "How you doing? God bless you, sister."

"God bless you," Vivian responded as she continued walking.

Once they approached the pulpit, they could see the reverend was talking to two of the deacons. They waited nearby for him to finish. The first lady was wrapping up a conversation with another member, then turned her attention to John.

"Brother John, good to see you. How are you?" She gave a big smile and a warm embrace to John. "And Sister Vivian, was it? Welcome, welcome." She gave the same warm embrace to Vivian.

"Yes, hi. Thank you, I really enjoyed the service."

"Vivian, this is First Lady Grienbachs, the reverend's beautiful wife." John introduced the two.

"Moni Grienbachs, but everyone here just calls me First Lady." She offered.

"Vivian just moved here from New York." John said.

"Oh is that right? How nice! Do you have family here or did you move here for work or something?" she asked.

"No, my daughter and I moved here sort of for a fresh start. I'm actually looking for work."

"Well glory be to God! We're glad he brought you to us. We know that with his help anything is possible. Anything!" She beamed.

"Amen," John added.

"So you said you and your daughter? How old is your daughter?" she asked.

"She's fifteen, going on forty." Vivian joked.

The first lady laughed, "I know what you mean. I have two of my own. My daughter, Generosa, is sixteen and my son, Gabriel, is fourteen. I guess they'll be going to school together over at Meadows High."

"Oh wow, I'm sure Cinnamon will be glad to have at least one person she knows going into a new school. I know she's really missing her friends back home, you know?"

"Awww, poor thing. I'm sure she is. Well you should bring her to service next Sunday. It's youth day, and she can meet the kids here. We have a lot of activities for them, and we have our teen bible study on Thursdays. We also have our regular bible study on Tuesdays. You should think about coming for yourself. Get to know some of your neighbors here in Gracious Meadows, and it'll be a good place to put the word out that you're looking for a job."

"Wow, that would be great! Thank you, I'm definitely looking forward to it." Vivian responded.

Reverend Grienbachs approached, "Brother John!" He said, excitedly. They exchanged a hearty handshake. "Now who is this beauty in our midst?" He asked while taking Vivian in lustfully from head to toe.

"Honey, this is Sister Vivian," First Lady Grienbachs answered.

"Mm mm um! The good Lord knew what he was doing when

he created you, sister." He said as he shook Vivian's hand, holding it for a few seconds before letting go. Vivian chuckled bashfully, but it was all an act. She definitely wasn't shy, and she was use to attracting men like a magnet.

"I was telling First Lady that Vivian just moved here a few days ago. She bought a couple pieces of furniture from the store." John explained.

"Oh really? Where'd you move from?" he asked.

"New York."

"*NEW YORK!*" He blurted out loudly. "The big city! Oh, so you a city girl, huh?" he laughed.

Vivian shrugged her shoulders, "guilty."

"I see. So just you, by yourself? No husband?" he asked. John shifted in his stance and glanced down at his feet. He didn't like the way the reverend was flirting with Vivian. He knew good and well she didn't have a husband, otherwise she wouldn't be out with him. First Lady Grienbachs just stood there with a painted smiled fixed on her face. She didn't seem bothered at all.

"Uh, no. Me and my daughter. And John here was so helpful and really worked with us on the furniture." She replied, lightly rubbing John on his back to let him know he shouldn't feel threatened by the reverend's flirtation. The smile returned to John's face.

"I was telling Sister Vivian that she should bring her daughter, Cinnamon, out for the youth service this coming Sunday and to swing by bible study. She's looking for a job. So if you hear of anything…" She drifted off.

"Yes. Yes. Most definitely. Moni, why don't we have Vivian over for dinner after service on Sunday? We can get better acquainted. You can even bring a copy of your resume. I deal with a lot of different people, all from different fields of work." He said.

"Oh, we don't want to tie up all of the sister's time, honey. I'm sure she might have her own plans for Sunday dinner." First Lady Grienbachs replied.

"She doesn't have any plans! Do you, Sister Vivian?" he asked, insistently. Before she could answer he continued, "First Lady just being lazy, try'na get out of cooking!" He shot the first lady a look and then a smile broke out as he started laughing. His belly jiggled.

Reverend Grienbachs was a tall man with a huge gut that poked out. He was well dressed beneath his robe, wearing a grey suit with a burgundy shirt. His grey and blue striped tie was affixed to his shirt with a silver clip tie. Every inch of his suit was neatly pressed and his shoes, shiny. Everything about him was neat—his freshly lined haircut and beard, eyebrows, manicured nails, and perfectly folded pocket-handkerchief. After his robe was removed, you could see the big-face, gold Rolex boasting from under his sleeve. On one hand, he wore his wedding band and a big diamond pinky ring on the other. Judging by the one small patch of grey hair that adorned his hairline in the front, he looked to be in his mid-forties.

The first lady smiled and looked down at her shoes like she was embarrassed. She was a pretty woman, but she looked tired and aged. She wore heavy makeup and cheap press-on nails. Even her hair looked tired. She had a lot more grey coming in than her husband. It was died black, but her roots were relentless. You could see that through the part she wore on one side. The strands lay flat, straight, and scraggily, coming to a frizzy halt against her fair neck. It didn't look like much effort was put in, and she could use a deep conditioning. Her outfit wasn't much better, such a contrast to her husband's. She wore a blue nylon suit that hung on her body with a beige blouse beneath. Her pantyhose were off white. The black shoes she wore were pleather slide-ins. Fake clip-on pearls clung to her ears and a matching necklace hung from her neck. She looked small and frail in her suit, especially standing next to such a large and boisterous man.

"Well, if you really don't have any plans, Sister Vivian, you and John are more than welcome to stop by after church on Sunday for dinner." First Lady Grienbachs said with a smile. "Oh, and your daughter too, of course."

"Okay, you sure? I don't want to impose. I know how it is just trying to feed two, never mind four plus!" Vivian waved her hand as she spoke.

"It is not a problem. We insist, and we just won't take no for an answer." Reverend Grienbachs chimed in.

"Well, okay then, it's a date! Can I bring anything?"

"All this right here, that's all you need to bring, sister." Reverend Grienbachs gestured his hand around and around in a circle in front of Vivian with a wide grin. Although this certainly wasn't the first pastor to flirt with her, or the first married man, Vivian was still surprised at how blatant he was in front of his wife. And his wife, she didn't seem fazed at all, keeping her same painted smile intact.

"Okay, Rev, we'll see you for dinner Sunday afternoon. We really enjoyed the service, as always. Right now we're gonna head on out for dinner. I'm taking Vivian over to The Carmichael." John said, trying to end the conversation and the reverend's uncomfortable flirting.

"Oh, *The Carmichael*, how nice! I can't remember the last time we've been there." First Lady Grienbachs sounded excited for them.

"Alright then, Brother John. We'll see you both on Sunday. Don't you be a stranger now, *Miss Vivian*," Reverend Grienbachs said with a half smirk.

The two walked towards the back of the church where the exit was. Before they could make it out of the door, a lady grabbed John's arm.

"Brother John, can we still count on your contribution for the fundraiser?" She asked, batting her lashes. She seemed very comfortable and familiar with John.

"Of course you can, Sister Connie. I gotta run right now, but I'll be sure to put my pledge in next Sunday."

"Okay, aren't you going to introduce us to your lady friend?" She asked, almost like she was a little girl teasing him.

"Oh, I'm sorry. Viv, this is Sister Connie and Sister Kim. This is Vivian Mackey."

"Hi, nice to meet you," Vivian said with a smile while extending her hand.

"Nice to meet you too. Hope we get to see you again, Vivian." Sister Kim said, warmly.

"Of course you will. She'll be back for the youth service on next Sunday." John answered.

"Well, you never know with you, John." Sister Connie tapped his chest playfully and winked at Vivian. Vivian just smiled, unfazed.

John chuckled nervously, "Alright, alright Connie. Don't scare her off, now. We gotta go. We have dinner reservations. We'll see you Sunday, ladies." He grabbed Vivian's hand before either woman could respond, making his way to the exit.

Vivian waved at the ladies, "bye bye."

Once they hit the parking lot, John said, "Don't mind those women. I already told you they ain't got nothing better to do than to gossip. I hope Connie didn't offend you."

"*What?* No way! Please, it takes more than that to get to me. I'm sure once they get to know me better, they'll be nicer." Vivian really did want to try to fit in Gracious Meadows. She would just have to win those women of the church over. *It won't be so hard*, she thought.

CHAPTER 3

"Ugh, Mommy, why we gotta go by John's store today? Didn't y'all just have dinner together last night?"

"Stop whining. We're only gonna swing by for a hot second. I promise." Cinnamon huffed and rolled her eyes. "I want to show my appreciation for the dinner last night. I'm just gonna drop off this basket, and we'll be on our way." Vivian tried to assure Cinnamon. Today she wore her hair cornrowed going back in two braids, giving her a young, innocent look. That's exactly what she was going for.

They entered the store and John was near the dining section talking to customers. He spotted Vivian as soon as they walked in. She smiled and waved. He held one finger up, signaling that he'd be right over. Cinnamon plopped down on one of the sofas as Vivian strolled around the store browsing. That's when she saw the same boy with the afro from moving day come through the double doors that led to the back. He stopped in his tracks, surprised to see Cinnamon again. He quickly regained his cool, straightening his back and lugging some boxes over to a corner for unpacking.

He lifted each mug out of the box in slow motion, stealing quick glances of Cinnamon. He took his time working on a kitchen display as he mustered up the courage to approach her again. Once he was done, he picked his afro out some and made his way over.

"Hey, didn't we do a furniture delivery to your house the other day?" He asked, pretending like he wasn't sure.

"Yeah," Cinnamon smiled shyly. Unlike her mother, she really was shy when it came to boys.

"Where did y'all move from?" he asked.

"Brooklyn."

"Oh, New York. I have an uncle and some cousins up there. I haven't seen them in years, though." He said.

"Really?" That was all Cinnamon could think to say.

"Yup! I don't know if they live in Brooklyn or another part…" The boy wasn't really sure what to say either as he stood there in a brief awkward silence. "Oh! I'm Raheem by the way. Sorry, I forgot to introduce myself." He said, extending his hand.

"I'm Cinnamon, nice to meet you."

Raheem chuckled, "*Cinnamon?* Is that your real name?"

"Yeah, don't ask…" Cinnamon said, rolling her eyes. She was so use to people asking her that by now. "Most of my friends just call me Cin for short, though."

Vivian caught a glance of the two and started inching her way over to the couches. She didn't want to embarrass her daughter, so she kept enough distance. She was trying to listen in without being so obvious.

"Oh okay, Cin. So how do you like it here so far?"

"I don't know. It's only been a couple days. We haven't done much since we been here." She answered.

"Oh, duh. I forgot it's only been a few days. So y'all back here to buy something else?" He asked, surprised.

"No, my mom just wanted to see John." She rolled her eyes again and sighed in annoyance.

Raheem chuckled, "What, you don't like John?"

"No, it's not that. I barely know him. I just know my mom." She explained.

"Oh … well, John is a good dude. He's been like a father to me. He gave me this job when nobody else would even hire me. Your mom is in good hands."

"How old are you?" Cinnamon asked, changing the subject.

"Just turned eighteen. How old are you?"

"Fifteen."

"Wow, you still a baby," he grinned.

"Boy, please. If you only knew…"

Vivian smiled to herself watching her baby in action. *That's right. You tell 'em, Cin.* She thought to herself.

"Well, I would like the chance to get to know." Raheem said, confidently. "Can you give me your number, so I can call you some time? Maybe we can go to the movies or something."

"I don't know."

"What'chu mean you don't know? What is there to know? Either you want to give me your number or you don't." Raheem said matter-of-factly.

Go 'head, girl, he's cute. Give him the number, Cin. Vivian urged on internally, wishing she could say it out loud.

"To what do I owe this pleasure?" John's voice boomed as he joined Vivian.

"Me and Cin just stopped by to say 'hi.' Right, Cin?" Vivian gave a phony smile, prompting Cinnamon to do the same.

"Hi, John," Cinnamon plastered a faint smile across her face, turning on the couch to face John and Vivian in the next row.

"Is this for me?" John asked.

"It sure is! I just wanted to thank you, again, for taking me to church and dinner last night. There's a couple pieces of fruit, and I made you a turkey n' cheese sandwich for lunch with a bag of chips. I hope you like turkey—and one slice of my sweet potato pie." Vivian said while she dangled the basket in front of John.

"Mm mm mm! Woman, you spoil a man like this and you won't be able to get rid of 'em!" John said after taking the basket and rummaging through with one hand. Then he turned his attention to Raheem, "Raheem, what'chu doing over here? Cinnamon, is he bothering you?" He asked, jokingly.

"No," she smiled.

"Well, them boxes ain't gonna unpack themselves," he raised one brow at Raheem.

"Sorry, John. I'll get right to it." Raheem scrambled back through the double doors to the back.

"Well, I know you're working, so we won't keep you. Plus, I promised Cin I'd take her over to the mall to fill out a couple of applications." Vivian said.

"Applications?" John questioned.

"Yeah, she wants to start looking for a part-time job now before I sign her up for school."

"Oh, is that right? Well, we could always use some help here if you're interested, Cinnamon." John offered.

Cinnamon raised her eyebrows and searched her mom's face for an answer. "Well, Cin? What'chu looking at me for? John said he could use some help here."

"I have to help move stuff?" She sounded unsure about the idea.

John laughed, "No, you'll be working the register, ringing up customers. When it's slow, you'll be out on the floor answering customers' questions or setting up displays, light stuff."

"Well how much do you pay?" Cinnamon blurted out.

"*Cinnamon!*" Vivian scolded.

"No, it's okay, Viv. I can see she's about business. I'll start you off at six dollars." He said, proudly. "But be prepared to work for the money, no slacking here."

Cinnamon thought it over quickly in her head. *Well that's a dollar more than I was making at Grazies* — a small clothing store she'd worked at in Brooklyn. *Plus I'll get to see Raheem more without Mom being all up in my business.* "Okay!" She said with enthusiasm.

"It's settled then. Walk with me up to the front, so I can give you an application to take home. You can start after the holiday and bring it back with you then. Things will be calmer then." He said as Vivian and Cinnamon followed his lead towards the front of the store near the register. "And you can wear khakis and a nice blouse. Make sure you wear some comfortable shoes too."

"Okay, thanks so much John!" Cinnamon smiled widely.

"Look at that, Cin! That was easy. Now you don't even need me to take you to the mall."

"Yah-huh! I don't have no khakis, and I need to get some new shoes too, so I can be comfortable. You heard John." Cinnamon said, purposely over exaggerating her needs.

"Girl, all them shoes we lugged from New York. I know you have to have something in there!"

"All what shoes? You know we barely brought anything with

us! C'mon, Mom. I still wanna check out the mall anyway, see what it's looking like in there. I know you do too." Cinnamon said, wrapping her arms around her mother's arm while she leaned her head on her shoulder, giving her the most innocent puppy dog expression. Vivian just opened her mouth, momentarily at a loss for words. She smiled at her daughter's sly attempt at a plea.

"Looks like she got you there, Viv," John laughed.

Vivian rolled her eyes, "Alright we'll go—but only to look around." She added with emphasis. "And *maybe* we'll get you a pair or two of khakis—only 'cause you need 'em for work now."

"Yes!" Cinnamon exclaimed while pulling her fist down and in towards her stomach.

"I guess we should get going and let you get back to work, John." Vivian said.

"Okay, thanks for stopping by and making me this tasty lunch." John said as he handed Cinnamon her application.

"Well, you ain't tasted it yet," Vivian chuckled.

"That's okay. You made it, and I know it's got to be good." John replied, eyeing Vivian from head to toe as though he was talking about her and not the food. "I'll still see you both on Sunday for the youth service, right?"

"We wouldn't miss it! Right, Cin?" Vivian nudged her daughter.

"I guess," she replied with less enthusiasm.

Just as they headed toward the door, Raheem reappeared with another box in tow. Cinnamon glanced back, making eye contact. Then she smiled shyly and waved goodbye.

Once outside, the duo was stopped by a woman. Dark circles framed her eyes and her lower lids sat on a stack of bags, her expression somber. "Excuse me, have you seen this girl?" She asked, holding up a flyer.

"No, sorry we just moved here." Vivian answered while Cinnamon shook her head.

"Please take a flyer. Take a couple and give to your friends." The lady sounded exasperated.

"No, that's okay," Vivian waved her off, not wanting to take the flyer.

"Please, please just take it. This is my daughter. She's been missing since Wednesday. She was last seen right across the street there at Dooley's Ice Cream Parlor. We're offering a ten thousand dollar reward to anyone who gives any information that leads to her return." The lady turned her attention to Cinnamon as she insisted. "You look about her age. Please give some to your friends. If you or anyone you know sees her, please contact this number. *Please*."

"Oh my God, I'm so sorry. I didn't realize she was missing. Sure, sure we'll take some. You're gonna find her. I can only imagine…" Vivian sympathized. Cinnamon glanced at her mother, wondering if she was sincere in her efforts or if the reward money had peaked her interest.

The lady handed them a few flyers and dashed back across the street to rejoin another lady and a man who were posting flyers and stopping passer-byers as well. Cinnamon studied the flyer as she held the stack on her lap once they were in the car and on their way to the mall. The girl was fourteen, just one year younger than her. She felt a chill as she thought about the possibility that a teen girl, just like her, may have been abducted right across the street from where they had just been, and where she would now be working.

***

"At this time, we'd like to open the alter up to anyone who needs prayer. Just come on down. Don't be shy. Don't worry about who's looking at you. The Lord has something special in store for you, and what is for you *is* for *you*. We welcome you. Choir?" Reverend Grienbachs was coming towards the closing of service. He cued the children's choir to chime in, singing lightly in the background.

"We wellllcome you, oh my brother. We wellllcome you, oh my sister," they sang like little angels.

Slowly, one by one, members of the congregation began to rise and make their way up the center aisle. Each one wore a look of grief on their face by the time they'd made it to the altar. The reverend whispered something into each person's ear when it was their turn, and they each responded, whispering back. Then he turned up a small bottle of oil to his fingers before placing his hand on each person's forehead as he prayed. Deacons stood on either side of him, chiming in on the prayers. Two ushers stood guard behind each person as they received prayer, one holding a box of tissues and the other something that resembled a table cloth.

Cinnamon didn't quite understand the whole ritual at first. She was uneasy as she studied each person's face while they returned to their seats. They all had twisted expressions like they were in pain or agony but they were clapping and thanking the Lord, some with tears rolling down their cheeks, some sniffling into tissues. She jumped once a woman started hollering. Long, shrill outbursts pierced the air as the latest woman being prayed for slammed her palms together, clapping hard. Cinnamon looked at her mother with worry written across her face. Vivian smiled in response.

The more the reverend prayed, the more excited the lady became. She started stomping her foot, accompanying her handclaps and yelps. As if they'd been signaled, the musicians switched the music up instantly to something a little more fast-paced. The drummer banged hard on the drums and slammed his foot against the kick drum pedal in tempo. Instantly the whole church caught the vibe and began clapping, dancing, and shouting. One lady that was waiting in the prayer line kicked off her shoes and took off running, doing laps around the church. That's when Cinnamon grabbed hold of the pew in front of her, afraid of whatever was about to break out. Vivian couldn't help but giggle a little at her daughter's first church experience. She reached over and stroked her daughter's arm, letting her know everything was okay and she could let go of her grip on the pew.

The floor bounced beneath them as everyone did their own individual versions of a holy ghost two-step. When the marathon runner ran out of steam, she doubled over in the middle of the aisle then broke into a shuffle, wobbling her hips around in circles, alternating clockwise and counter-clockwise in motion. Some continued clapping while others held their hands in the air and talked towards the ceiling. Once things calmed down some, moans, groans, whimpering, sniffling, random outbursts, and whispers of "Thank you Jesus" could be heard coming from all different directions throughout the church.

The same woman was still being prayed for. The reverend had his hand on her forehead, and her head was tilted back as though he was applying pressure. She stumbled back a couple of steps before falling down. Then she just lay there, and one of the ushers threw the tablecloth over her legs while the other fanned her. The next woman in line walked around her like she was just an object in a road. The reverend continued praying.

"Mom, what's wrong with that lady? How come she don't get up?"

"*Because*, Cin," Vivian whispered.

"Because what?"

"I don't know. That's just what happens sometimes when you get in the spirit." Vivian said, not quite sure herself. Sure, she'd seen people get slain in the spirit before but she didn't really understand it enough to explain to someone else. "C'mon," she instructed, grabbing Cinnamon's arm.

"Where we going? We leaving?" Cinnamon asked, hoping the answer was yes.

"No! We going up for prayer. C'mon." She repeated, inching her waist up to the edge of the seat, preparing to stand.

"Why?" Cinnamon whispered loudly. A man and woman sitting in front of them turned around with looks of disapproval.

"*Shhh*! We need prayer. That's why. Now hurry up before it's too late and they finish."

"Uh uh, Mommy, I ain't going up there! They gon' push us down like they just did that lady!" Cinnamon sounded scared. Vivian clasped her hands over her mouth to smother her snicker.

"Fine, move!" She said, rolling her eyes at her daughter as she stood to head to the front.

"Don't let 'em push you down, Mommy!" Cinnamon whispered from her seat to her mother's back, now wearing a smirk. Her fear now turned to amusement at her mother's bravery, and she wanted to see how she would look falling out on the floor too.

Vivian stole all the attention again as she strutted to the prayer line. When she and Cinnamon went to the mall, she bought herself three new dresses that she thought were more modest for church. Apparently some of the other women didn't agree as they looked on. A big grin spread across Reverend Grienbachs's face once she made it to the front of the line. He was all too happy whispering in her ear to ask what type of prayer she needed. John looked on from the pew with disgust. The prayer was brief but the embrace Reverend Grienbachs gave Vivian wasn't. Cinnamon was a little disappointed he hadn't tried to push her mother down.

After the service ended, John introduced mother and daughter to the youth pastor that had given the sermon that morning. "Pastor Leonards, I want you to meet Sister Vivian Mackey and her daughter, Cinnamon. They're new to Gracious Meadows."

John couldn't wait to show Vivian off to him. Pastor Leon Leonards was the man that all the middle-aged women in the church had their eye on. He was tall, dark, and handsome. One could just tell by his strong hands and the way his dress shirt clung to him that he was a man in good shape. His skin was smooth all over and his shiny bald head drove the ladies crazy. He had those big, dreamy bedroom eyes. Sure, John was a successful businessman, but he couldn't compete. He was average in every other way: average height, average build, and average looks. He felt threatened by Pastor Leonards even though the pastor didn't seem to have a clue.

"Is that right? Nice to meet you. Welcome, welcome." He replied with a bright white smile that set Vivian ablaze inside.

Look at those cute lil' dimples, she thought. "Hi, nice to meet you too." She shook his hand. Then Cinnamon smiled and did the same.

"Cinnamon, that's a pretty name." He said.

She smiled shyly in return, "Thank you."

"Cinnamon, how did you enjoy the youth service today?"

"It was nice."

"Have you met any of the other girls yet?" He asked.

"No."

"Well, we'll just have to get you acquainted before you leave. You aren't in a rush are you?" He turned towards Vivian to ask.

"No, not at all," she said, eyeing him slowly from top to bottom. "Take all the time you need. We got all day." She said seductively as she lightly tapped his arm.

"Well don't forget the Reverend and First Lady are expecting us for dinner after service." John cut in, his ego hurt by Vivian's obvious flirtation.

"Oh really? First Lady ain't invite me and she know I love her cookin'! Now I'm gon' have to talk to her about that." Pastor Leonards said, jokingly.

"Aw you poor thing. Well we'll just have to have you over to our place for dinner then once we get settled in." Vivian offered, turning on the charm.

"Thank you, Sister Vivian. See how they treat a brother around here? Can't even get no grub after preaching a hearty sermon." He looked down and shook his head theatrically, still joking. "C'mon Cinnamon, let me introduce you to some of the kids. I promise to bring her right back." He said as he placed his hand on Cinnamon's shoulder, looking back and forth between John and Vivian.

"So Cinnamon, what do you like to do? We have a lot of different activities for you to get involved in here."

"I don't know," she shrugged timidly. "I like to play double-dutch and listen to music."

"Well, we don't have a double-dutch team, but we do have the praise dance team. You like music. Do you like to dance?"

She laughed nervously, "I guess … sometimes but not to the music y'all play here."

The pastor laughed too, "Oh, what do you like to listen to? That rap stuff?"

"Yeah, and RnB too." She said defensively.

"Okay, I can dig it. I'm sure we'll find something for you here." They stopped upon a small group of young people, varying in age, who sat and stood amongst the two back-row pews. Some were talking to each other. The younger kids ran around playing. "Hey y'all, I want you to meet Cinnamon. She and her mom are new to the church. Cinnamon, that's Karissa, Tiffany, Tammie, Malcom, and Gabe." Pastor Leonards pointed out kid after kid and Cinnamon was sure she wouldn't remember anybody's name. They all gave lazy hellos and Cinnamon waved in return. "That's Davie, Christopher, Chanel, and Reyanne running around there—Oh, and that's Generosa. Sorry, I didn't even see you sitting over there, Generosa. Why you sitting by yourself?" He spoke to one of the teens that sat at the opposite end of the pew.

She answered quietly, "I was just reading, pastor."

"Oh, okay. What'chu reading? You know the Holy Bible is the

best book. Anything else just doesn't measure up!" He said with a wink.

"I know, pastor," she rolled her eyes and smiled.

"Generosa and Gabe are Reverend and First Lady Grienbachs's kids." He explained.

"Oh," Cinnamon smiled and waved again, this time at Generosa.

"Tiffany and Karissa are on the praise dance team and Tammie sings on the choir. Cinnamon likes to listen to all that hip-hop, b-bop stuff. I was telling her maybe she might like to join the praise dance team or something. We gotta work on gettin' her in the mix!" He said excitedly as he squeezed Cinnamon's shoulder.

"Oh my God, Pastor Leonards, you so corny." Karissa laughed.

"What? I'm down! What'chu talkin' 'bout? Boom-boom pshh pshh boom-pshh," he beat boxed into the palm of his hands.

"Pastor, please stop! You embarrassing us!" Tiffany laughed and covered her face.

"See how they be try'na play me out? I got skills. Y'all just don't know." He shook his head and Cinnamon couldn't help but laugh at his attempt. "Anyway, Cinnamon, I hope you come out to our youth bible study we have on Thursdays. I teach it, and you can get better acquainted with everybody, and maybe, *just maybe*, I'll show y'all some more of my skills."

"Pastor, don't nobody wanna see that!" Tiffany twisted up her face with a playful smirk.

"See how everybody do me around here? First I don't get invited to the dinner at the Rev's house today, and now Tiffany and Karissa try'na bring me down. Well let's get you back to your mom since you *were* invited." He rolled his eyes dramatically like he really felt left out.

"She coming to *our* house?" Gabe blurted out with raised eyebrows.

"That's what they tell me!" Pastor Leonards responded. Generosa looked up from her book and exchanged worried glances with her brother.

***

John, Vivian, and Cinnamon all tried to hide their surprise at the disarray the Grienbachs residence found itself in. An aroma of garbage hit their noses as soon as First Lady Grienbachs opened the door to let them in. Two laundry baskets of clothes sat overflowing on top of another mountain of dirty clothes that lined the floor of the living room. Stacks and stacks of old newspapers sat piled on the couch, leaving room for only one person to sit. A broken lamp stood in the corner of the room. The window shades were old and dingy. One was slightly torn. The tan carpet was littered with red, brown, and black spots almost everywhere they looked with the exception of one spot that looked like it had been bleached. It was as though they forgot that they were having company. Vivian waved off a fly as they trekked through the living room into the kitchen.

The kitchen wasn't much better: small and cramped with dirty dishes piled in one of the sink basins. One of the cabinet doors hung off of the hinge, and the refrigerator looked like it had never been cleaned once the door was swung open. They crowded around the small kitchen table that sat propped up on a book on one end to keep it from wobbling.

"You'll have to excuse the mess. Things have been so busy around here that I haven't had time to tidy up." First Lady Grienbachs said, clearly embarrassed by her home.

"Oh, no need to apologize. I know how it is. Me and Cinnamon haven't even finished unpacking our little bit of stuff yet. We have bags all over the place at home." Vivian tried to make the first lady feel better. She smiled at Vivian's attempt.

"Well, I hope you all are hungry. We got fried chicken, smothered pork chops, catfish, collard greens, cornbread, cabbage, mac n' cheese, and candied yams. Oh, and some brownies and pecan pie for dessert."

"My, my, my, you certainly outdid yourself, First Lady. Everything looks so delicious!" John exclaimed eyeing the food while rubbing his stomach.

Generosa hadn't said much since they got there, but she looked up and smiled. She loved her mother's cooking, and she adored the pride she took in it. One of her favorite things to do, besides reading, was to be in the kitchen shadowing her mother when she cooked. She saw how people praised her food and wanted to be a good cook just like her.

Gabe sat next to his sister at the table, "Ma, you need help with anything?"

"Why you always try'na find a reason to be in the kitchen doing what the women supposed to be doing?" Reverend Grienbachs had emerged from upstairs.

"Sorry, Dad, I was seeing if she might need help carrying anything to the table or something—"

"She don't need no help, boy!" His voice grew loud. Then he chuckled and looked at John, "This boy always try'na find a reason to be in the kitchen with the ladies. Keep tellin' him that ain't no place for a man. Let the women do what they do, and we do what we do. Generosa, why you ain't in there helping?"

"I was, Daddy, but everything is finished now."

"Honey, Gabe, it's okay. I don't need any help. Everything is ready, really." First Lady chimed in, trying to keep the peace.

"Moni, why you ain't tell me we was having company today anyway? Look at this place. It's a mess!"

"Gerald, honey, don't you remember we invited John and Vivian over at service last Friday night?"

"Oh … well, who is this young lady?" He asked as though he was totally clueless to the entire arrangement.

"That's my baby, Cinnamon," Vivian smiled proudly.

"She can't talk? That ain't no baby there, no sir." He said while letting his eyes fall on Cinnamon's young, full breasts. Gabe and Generosa looked down at their place settings, trying not to notice their father's behavior.

The smile faded from Vivian's face as she started to feel uncomfortable. "Oh, I almost forgot! I brought some sparkling cider." She whipped out a bottle from underneath the table that was in her oversized handbag.

"How nice, thank you. Let me just find the bottle opener."

"Oh Lord, now how long is that gonna take you?" Reverend Grienbachs complained.

"You don't have to open it right now. We can drink whatever you have, and you can save that for the house or another occasion. I just didn't want to come empty handed."

"Well, you took it out, so you must want us to drink it now. Moni will find the opener." This Reverend Grienbachs was not the same man Vivian had met just a couple days prior. He was still his same inappropriate self, but now he was just nasty and rude.

"I really didn't mean to be an inconvenience." Vivian's voice fell flat as she tried to keep her cool.

"Don't worry. It's not an inconvenience at all. See! I got the opener right here!" First Lady Grienbachs smiled widely. "Now why don't you lead us all in prayer, honey, so we can dig in?" She said, enthusiastically.

After the reverend said the prayer, everyone piled their plates high. Gabe passed his sister the dish with the cornbread.

"Generosa, don't you think you better skip the cornbread? You lookin' a lil' heavy these days." Reverend Grienbachs eyed his daughter from the corner of his eye.

"*Gerald!*" First Lady hissed.

"What? She is. And you ain't too far behind, baby. You know maybe you both should hold off on the cornbread." Generosa looked down into her lap, trying to hold back tears, but it was too late. One escaped and rolled down her cheek.

"See what'chu done did. I swear…" First Lady Grienbachs's voice trailed off as she shook her head.

"For heaven's sake, if you're gonna cry about it, go on … go on and take the cornbread. Blow up to a blimp then." A small whimper escaped Generosa. She glanced up to look at Cinnamon who sat in silence.

"Aw he's just joking, Generosa. Don't you pay him any attention. Go on and eat the cornbread. Besides, ain't nothing wrong with a little extra meat on the bones." John stepped in, trying to make light of the situation.

"Na-uh I ain't joking. Look at Cinnamon and her momma. You can just tell they watch what they eat. Just look at 'em." He said, looking at Cinnamon again who gasped and crossed her arms over her chest this time.

"Now that is just enough. Can't you see you're making the poor girl cry?" Vivian couldn't sit by anymore and listen to this pig.

31

"Generosa, sweetie, I think you're beautiful. You and you're mom are both beautiful, and First Lady ain't hardly fat or anywhere near it. You got that pretty, thick hair, and your skin is just flawless. I wished my skin was clear like yours when I was your age. I had horrible acne as a teen. And your shape … girrrrl, you gon' have all them boys after you. You just wait and see. So you go ahead and eat that cornbread." She paused to shoot the reverend a quick glare before finishing, "Shoot, that's why all these young girls running around today throwing up and carrying on, thinking they gotta be skinny like them sickly looking models. Just don't make no sense at all." A small smile crept across Generosa's face due to Vivian's kind words.

"Boys? Oh no she ain't! She better not have no boys coming 'round here! She better keep them legs glued shut!" The reverend was becoming agitated.

"*Gerald! That's enough!* That ain't no conversation for the dinner table!" The first lady scolded.

"Uh uh, you done brought this woman in here talking 'bout boys chasing my lil' girl. My baby ain't gon' be no harlot! What about you, missy? Are *you* a harlot?" His eyes turned into slits as he posed his question to Cinnamon.

Her mouth dropped open, but before a word could come out, Vivian swooped in. "Now you wait just a minute! I don't know who you think you're talking to, but you don't talk to my daughter like that. You shouldn't even be talking to your own daughter like that. Are you crazy? I feel sorry for her. I feel sorry for your whole family having to deal with such a nasty man. First you fawn all over me the other night, disrespecting your wife like that and invite us all over here for dinner just to make us feel unwelcomed. You don't think I didn't notice the way you were eyeing my daughter, you dirty pervert. You better just be lucky I'm a changed woman. Otherwise I'd fly across this table and—"

"And what? You think you're gonna come up in my house and disrespect me? You got another thing coming, missy. How do you expect me to look at you and that daughter of yours when you come in here dressed like you're ready to walk the alley?"

Vivian's chair flew out from behind her as she shot up out of her seat, ready to confront the reverend. "Oh, I kno—"

John jumped up and intervened, "Okay, that's enough. I think it's time for us to go." He said while grabbing Vivian's arm.

"Yeah, you right about that, John. You better get me out of here before I hurt somebody. C'mon Cinnamon!" Cinnamon scrambled to her feet in a hurry. "First Lady, I'm really sorry it had to go this way, but thank you for the dinner."

"Please, please don't leave. Well, let me fix you all a plate at least." She said, still trying to keep the peace. The trio made their way to the door as First Lady Grienbachs followed.

"Whatchy'all just sittin' there for? I didn't buy all this food to waste. EAT!" The reverend yelled. "Ain't that what this was all about anyway? And Generosa you better eat all that cornbread 'cause we ain't wasting none of it. Ya hear?" Generosa bobbed her head up and down as she and Gabe began to quickly eat in obedience.

Outside Cinnamon and Vivian climbed into John's truck while John hung back to hear the first lady's pleas. "Let me at least fix you all a plate to take home. Please, John, I cooked all that food. You know the reverend is just going through some trials lately. His mind isn't like it used to be. You know he didn't mean any of that in there. We just have to pray for him."

"I know, First Lady. I know. Don't you worry yourself about any of it. If you're sure it's not too much trouble, you can go in and bring us out a plate if you really want to." John replied.

"Okay, just wait right there. It's no trouble at all, John. You know that. Just ask them to wait, okay?" With that, she scurried into the house. She returned minutes later with two bags filled with food.

Vivian rolled down the passenger window. "Thanks so much, First Lady. You didn't have to do that."

"Yes, I did. Really, it's no trouble at all."

"I'm really sorry about all of this. Really, I am." Vivian said, looking into her eyes with sympathy.

"I know. Say no more. I'm sorry too. He's not usually like this. Like I was telling John, we just have to pray for him. Please don't let this stop you and Cinnamon from coming to church. I'm gonna give you a call tomorrow, okay?"

"I don't know, but I'll talk to you tomorrow."

"Okay, y'all get home safe. Bye, Cinnamon. Bye, John." She waved as the truck pulled away from the curb.

CHAPTER 4

"I have to hand it to her. First Lady sure can throw down!" Vivian tossed a bare pork chop bone onto her plate before finishing up her greens.

"Mmm *hm*!" Cinnamon agreed while licking her fingers clean of chicken grease. "I'm glad she gave us enough for leftovers too. I'm about to have one of these brownies. You want one?" She asked as she unwrapped the saran and foil from one of the many styrofoam plates.

"Uh uh, I'm stuffed." Vivian leaned back in her chair and patted her belly. "Cinnamon."

"Hm?"

"You know none of that stuff the reverend said was true, right?"

"Yeah, of course I know that, Mom. But what was his problem? He got issues." Cinnamon responded, twisting up her face.

"I don't know. Something ain't right about that man. But I just wanted to make sure you know there's nothing wrong with how you look or dress. And you ain't no harlot either!"

Cinnamon let out a snicker, "I know, Mom. I feel bad for Generosa, though. Did you see her crying?"

"Yeah, poor thing. I don't know what's wrong with that first lady either. The way she lets that man talk to her and the kids like that … Cin, don't you ever let a man disrespect you like that. You hear me?"

"Yeah, Mom. I know."

"I'm just making sure. I know you've seen me go through a lot, but you know I only want better for you." Vivian said with a serious look. Something was really troubling her about Reverend Grienbachs's behavior that day. She couldn't put her finger on it, but something wasn't right; it was more than just his rudeness.

Cinnamon sighed, "Yes, Mom, yes. I know."

"So how you like them other girls that Pastor Leonards introduced you to today?" Vivian asked, switching the subject.

"I don't know. We didn't really talk or anything. Pastor Leonards is trying to get me to join the praise dance team. He said I should come to bible study on Thursday."

"Praise dance? That sounds fun."

"I guess," Cinnamon replied with no enthusiasm.

"What'chu mean *you guess*? Cin, I really want you to meet other people your age and make some new friends down here. Will you at least think about it?"

"You still want to go back to that church?" Cinnamon asked, shocked after the day's events.

"I don't know yet, but everyone else seemed okay. Pastor Leonards seemed real nice."

"Oh boy, here we go." Cinnamon rolled her eyes.

"Here we go what?"

"You know. I saw the way you were looking at him, Mom." Cinnamon said with a mouthful of brownie.

Vivian laughed, "Cin, you always think your mom is up to something. I mean yeah he's fine n' all, but all I said was he seems nice."

"You invited him over for dinner."

"I was just trying to be hospitable." Vivian defended herself.

"Yeah, sure, okay mom. What about John?"

"What *about* John?"

"Mom, you can't be seeing him and trying to see Pastor Leonards too!" Cinnamon exclaimed.

"Who said anything about seeing anybody? Me and John are friends. Nothing wrong with having friends." The phone rang, interrupting their conversation.

Cinnamon answered, then held the cordless out towards her mom. "It's for you. It's First Lady Grienbachs."

"Hello…" Vivian held the phone to her ear. She and the first lady shared a brief exchange before hanging up. "That poor woman…" That was all Vivian said as she placed the phone back on the charger.

"What did she say?" Cinnamon asked, curiously.

"Oh, she was just apologizing some more. She wants to meet up for lunch tomorrow."

"You going?"

"Yeah, I'm gonna go."

***

First Lady Grienbachs picked Vivian up the following day in her old, beat up pinto. The reverend drove a new Navigator SUV, and Vivian wondered why the first lady had to drive this. They went to a small diner in the center of town where Vivian ordered a chicken salad and the first lady had a tuna sandwich.

"This is a cute lil' spot. I hadn't even realized this was here." Vivian said in between bites.

"Yes, it's so small you can almost miss it."

"First Lady, I'm so sorry about yesterday…" Vivian started.

The first lady held her hand up. "Please just call me Moni; we're not in church, and stop apologizing. I don't blame you for any of it. That's why I wanted to have lunch with you today."

"I just don't understand what happened. Did we offend the reverend in some way?"

"Well, now that's just like asking is water wet, Sister Vivian." She chuckled. "Sometimes Gerald is …" She paused to search for the right words, "…easily agitated. He takes medication—or at least he's supposed to. Doctors are still testing out different ones trying to find the best fit for him and each one has a different effect on him. So sometimes he stops taking them. He gets down, frustrated. You know?"

"Medication?" Vivian was still puzzled.

"Vivian, I know I don't know you that well, but you seem like a trustworthy person. Not a lot of people at the church know this, but

I'm just gonna tell you because I feel like I owe you an explanation for yesterday." She was rambling.

Vivian put her hand on top of the first lady's and patted it. "It's okay. You don't have to tell me anything. I get it. He's sick."

"My husband is bi-polar."

"Oh." Vivian was at a loss for words.

"Yeah, it's been hard on all of us."

"How long have you known?" Vivian asked.

"I think it's been about four years now. At first it was just little things. All of a sudden he was interested in keeping up with the current events. He started subscribing to all these newspapers but then never read any of them. When I tried to stop the subscriptions, he went ballistic. Every week it was a different hobby. First it was the ship in the bottles, then matchbox cars, then carpentry, but his interest would fade just as quick as it came one by one. Then the mood swings started—and haven't stopped. One day he's my sweet old husband. He's just Gerald. Then the next minute he's … he's … that horrible monster you saw yesterday: mean, nasty, and over-sexualized."

"Wow. I'm so sorry. Four years and they still haven't found the right medicine for him?" Vivian asked in disbelief.

"I know. It's ridiculous. Usually signs of bi-polar disorder appear in the teen or young adult years. So his doctors are a little stumped. I know he's hurting inside. He just wants to be normal again. I try to stay prayerful and trust in God, but I am only human. Sometimes it does get trying."

"Oh, I know it has to. Well, don't worry. Your secret is safe with me." Vivian assured her.

"Thank you for being so understanding. I really do hope you and Cinnamon come back to church. Now you see why I was hesitant about inviting you over for dinner. It's not that I didn't want you there. I just never know which Gerald we're going to get." She explained.

"I don't know. After the way I talked to him—"

"Oh, don't you worry about that. Trust me, he's forgotten already." The first lady cut her off. "Why don't you come on out to bible study tomorrow tonight? I can introduce you to some of the other sisters. Gerald won't be there. I've asked Pastor Leonards to fill in. He knows about the reverend's condition, and I explained to him that he's had a rough past couple of days."

Once she heard Pastor Leonards's name, Vivian didn't need any more convincing. "Okay, I guess it would be nice to meet some of the other ladies, and I can always use a good dose of the bible."

"Good, good. Hey, are you still looking for work?"

"Yes, I never got to give the reverend my resume yesterday." Vivian remembered.

"Okay, make sure you bring it with you. Sister Kim works for an employment agency, so I'll make sure you two get acquainted."

"Thanks so much. I would really appreciate that! Shoot, Cin lucked up on finding a job before her mother even did." Vivian said.

"Oh really? Good for her. Where is she going to be working?"

"John hired her to work in his furniture store, cashiering."

"Oh," First Lady Grienbachs's voice dropped, and her smile faded quickly.

"I thought you liked John. Is something wrong?"

"Oh, it's not Brother John. It's that boy he got working in there." This was the first time Vivian witnessed the first lady's demeanor change.

"Raheem? Yes, I believe I did see him there. He was talking to Cin."

The first lady's eyes shot up in terror, "You make sure she stays away from that boy. I'm serious, Vivian. He's nothing but trouble. I don't even know why Brother John hired him. Leave it to him to be sympathetic to the entire world. I guess we all deserve second chances. He's just practicing forgiveness the way the good Lord intends, but …" Her voice trailed as though she was thinking more out loud than having a conversation. She snapped back, "Please, just make sure he stays away from Cinnamon. You tell her to be careful too. You'll tell her won't you?" She pleaded.

There was such a serious look in her eyes that worried Vivian. "Yes, I'll tell her."

The first lady sighed in relief, "Good. We're a family at Greater Saints, so we all look out for each other as such. And Cinnamon is such a beautiful young lady. We don't want anything happening to her."

Vivian smiled, "thank you."

"She seems like such a pleasant girl. You should be proud."

"Thank you. Yeah, Cin is a good girl. I can't complain. I'll just be glad when she starts school, so she can meet some more people her age. I really want her to make friends and feel comfortable here, you know?" Vivian said, before taking a sip of her cranberry juice.

"I know what you mean. I'm sure she won't have any problems making new friends. I wish I could say the same for Generosa. She doesn't have many friends at school, and she doesn't like to hang around the girls at church too much. She just keeps her head in those mystery books she likes to read and stays up under me in the kitchen."

"Aw, maybe she'll grow out of it. She's probably just shy."

"Yeah, one can only hope." First Lady Grienbachs said as she looked out the window.

"You know what we need? We should have a girls' night out!"

The first lady chuckled looking down at her plate, "Oh, I don't know about that. I haven't had a girls' night out since before I found the church and got saved."

"We don't have to do anything crazy. Maybe we can do movies or bowling and then have you over for dinner at our place after. Maybe play some Charades or Jenga—just you, me, Cin, and Generosa. It'll be fun."

She smiled at the idea. "That does sound fun, but I don't know about leaving my guys alone." She seemed hesitant.

"What is Gabe, fourteen? He's a big boy, and I'm sure the reverend can survive without you for a few hours." Vivian pressed.

"I do think Generosa might like it. I'll think it over and let you know."

"Okay fi—" Vivian stopped mid-sentence as she spotted a man exiting the diner. Her heart sped up, and she peered through the window trying to get a better look. The man got into a black BMW and pulled out of the parking lot.

"Something wrong?"

"Huh? Uh, no. I just thought I saw someone I knew for a second." Vivian squeezed her eyelids closed and tried to shake the image out of her mind. *Viv, you trippin'. Your mind is playing tricks on you, girl.* She thought, trying to calm the thumping in her chest. "Just let me know about girls' night. I really hope you do decide to join us."

CHAPTER 5

Thursday came in a hurry and Cinnamon wasn't the least bit excited about attending the teen bible study. "I just don't understand why I have to go. Shouldn't it be my choice?" She pleaded with Vivian on their way to Greater Saints First Baptist Church.

"We already talked about this, Cin. I want you to develop a relationship with God. I know I'm one to talk. I haven't been the most traditional mother, but it's time for a change—for both of us. And a good way to start is by studying the bible."

"Well, can't I just read it at home myself?" She asked.

"It doesn't really work that way, Cin. I mean, yes, you can, but to get a full understanding, you really need bible study. Besides, you need to be around some kids your age. Sister Kim and Sister Connie said their girls are going. You met Karissa and the twins, Tiffany and Tammie, right?"

"Yeah…" Cinnamon replied in a down voice.

"What's wrong? Why are you giving me such a hard time about this? I thought you liked Pastor Leonards."

"He's cool, I *guess*. But I think this is more about *you* liking him." She accused.

"What? Now don't get grown, Cinnamon." Vivian warned in a stern voice.

"Well, why did you invite him over for dinner this weekend?"

"I already told you. We were talking after bible study, and it just

40

kind of happened." Vivian couldn't understand what the big deal was. Cinnamon sighed and rolled her eyes, turning her attention out of the car window. She stared at the raindrops splashing against the glass as they rode.

Once they arrived at the church, Cinnamon huffed as she reached for the door to exit.

"Cheer up and at least give it a chance. Can you do that for me, please?" Vivian spoke gently to her daughter.

"Do I really have a choice?" She mumbled in response as she got out.

"Be back to pick you up once it's over!" Vivian cracked the passenger window and yelled out to Cinnamon's back.

There were a few other teens trickling into the church basement as Cinnamon entered. Pastor Leonards greeted her with a big smile. "Heyyyy, so glad you could make it! Everybody, I know some of you remember Cinnamon." He announced as the teens sat around in a circle staring. "Cinnamon, this is the gang." She plastered on a fake smile and waved to the group. "I see you came prepared and brought your bible. Why don't you go ahead and have a seat? We'll be getting started shortly. Just waiting on a few more folks to come."

"*Cinnamon*, what kind of name is that? Is she a stripper?" Tiffany spoke under her breath, and Karissa let out a snicker. Cinnamon didn't hear the comment, but gathered that they must be laughing at her.

She spotted Generosa who sat alone with no one on either side of her and Gabe who sat next to the twins and some other teens. She opted to sit next to Generosa who had her head down in a book.

"Hey."

Generosa's head snapped up, and she smiled once she realized who it was. "Hi, Cinnamon." There was an awkward lull that followed, but Cinnamon was quick to fill it.

"What are you reading?"

She tilted the book so Cinnamon could see the cover, "*The Disappearance*. It's by Rosa Guy."

"Oh … is it good?"

"Yeah, real good." She began to get excited, "It's about this boy who goes to live with this family after he's found innocent of

41

murder. Then the family's little girl disappears and everyone thinks he has something to do with it. It's set in New York. That's where you're from, right?"

"Yeah," Cinnamon smiled, glad to see Generosa smiling. It was a nice switch from the tears she'd witnessed the last time she saw her.

"Okay, let's get started. Everyone settle down. Who wants to do the recap of what we discussed last week?" Pastor Leonards took a seat in the circle and looked around for volunteers. No one came forward. "I don't know why we gotta go through this every week. Y'all know I'll just pick someone." Still no one offered. "Okay, Tammie! Tell us what we talked about last week."

Tammie sucked her teeth, "Dag, Pastor Leonards, I knew you was gon' pick me. *Man.*"

"Good, and since you knew that, then that should mean you have an answer for me." He smiled widely with expectancy.

"Umm, we talked about David and Ittai, and how they had a loyal friendship, and how David was friends with Ittai and wanted nothing in return. Basically that's how God wants our friendships to be today. We should be loyal and good to our friends but not because we expect something in return annnnd … that's all I remember," she said, quickly.

"Good! Good, I'm glad *somebody* was paying attention." The pastor responded. "Well, today we're gonna talk about character versus competition. We'll be reading from the book of Mark, chapter nine, verse thirty-four. Say amen when you have it." He instructed.

Cinnamon looked around and saw everyone finding the verse like they already knew where it was. She cracked open her brand new blue bible, leafing through, only to return to the front inside cover where the table of contents were. While each teen said "amen" one by one, she felt a pressure mounting.

"Cinnamon, you okay over there or you need some help finding it?" Pastor Leonards asked, noticing her struggle.

"Oh Lord, you would think she never saw a bible before." Karissa said, loud enough for the group to hear. A few snorts and snickers followed. Cinnamon looked up and shot her a glare.

"Alright, Karissa," Pastor Leonards said while raising one eyebrow in her direction.

"Here, take mine." Generosa grabbed Cinnamon's bible and swapped with hers that was already open to the scripture. "There," she pointed out the spot to begin reading. She quickly turned the pages in Cinnamon's bible to find her place again as the pastor spoke.

"Thanks, Generosa … But they held their peace…" He began to read the scripture.

Bible study was for an hour and a half but it seemed to drag for Cinnamon. She found herself fidgeting and her mind wandering. She couldn't be happier once it was finally over. She headed straight for the door after Pastor Leonards gave the closing prayer.

"Thanks for coming, Cinnamon. I'll see you this weekend!" The pastor said loud enough for everyone to hear, causing Cinnamon to stop in her tracks and spin around.

"Okay, goodnight!" She replied. Before she could get moving again, she heard another snide remark from her left.

"*See you this weekend?* Uh oh looks like pastor is getting a private show. Aww sookie now!" Karissa joked.

Cinnamon couldn't ignore her this time. "Yo, what's your problem?"

"Who is she talking to? I know she not talking to me!" Karissa looked around like she was clueless.

"Yes. I'm talking to you *and you*! Y'all the only two that have so much to say. Why don't you say it to my face?" She challenged while looking back and forth between Karissa and Tiffany.

Before they could say anything, Gabe stepped in. "Why don't y'all leave her alone?"

"Oh my God, will all of y'all just be quiet." Tammie interjected, seemingly annoyed by the whole scene. "Karissa and Tiffany, why don't y'all go somewhere?"

"*Ill*," Tiffany sucked her teeth at her sister. "We don't have to go nowhere."

Tammie made her way over to Cinnamon, taking her by the arm to gain some distance from the other girls. "Girl, don't pay them no mind. They always got something smart to say."

"Yeah, I see." Cinnamon replied.

"So you from New York?" Tammie asked.

"Yeah."

"That's cool. I've always wanted to go to New York. I'm going to F.I.T. to study fashion after I graduate." Tammie seemed genuine in her attempt to make conversation. The conversation was interrupted before she could go any further, however.

"Y'all talking 'bout us?" Karissa stood near Tammie and shifted her weight to one leg with her hand on her hip.

"Girl, ain't nobody even talking 'bout you. We talking about New York, so mind your business." Tammie rolled her eyes.

"Wellll, you know we was just joking, right?" Tiffany said with a hint of stankness in her voice. Cinnamon didn't respond right away. She just looked at the two girls.

"Yeah, girl, we didn't expect you to get all serious. You gotta be able to take a joke." Karissa chimed in.

"I *can* take a joke." She replied, still annoyed by their behavior.

"Calm down, be easy. You might as well get use to us. We like this all the time, girl." Karissa said.

"She ain't lying." Tammie mumbled while turning up her face.

Karissa was about five foot two and filled out like a grown woman. A gold nameplate necklace sat on her full double D cup chest. Her belt held on for dear life around her small waist as gravity pulled her huge, donkey-like behind downwards and her hips expanded outwards. A small mole sat near the corner of her pouty lips. A medium-brown complexion covered her from head to toe, complementing all the gold she wore nicely. In addition to the necklace, she wore two arms filled with gold bracelets, gold hoop earrings with her name on them, and two additional studs in each ear. Her hands were done in a nice French manicure. She wore her hair in a French bun with finger waves in the front. The Tommy Hilfiger T-shirt she wore was tucked into matching jeans. The outfit was finished off with matching white Tommy Hilfiger sneakers. Cinnamon took her in, thinking she would fit in just fine in New York.

The twins were a different story. Both had deep dark chocolate skin. They were tall girls, standing at about five foot nine. Slender in build, they could've easily passed for models. They were identical, but didn't dress alike. They both wore long box braid extensions like Janet Jackson. It was clear that Tiffany did her best to have that New York flavor like Karissa but she fell a little short in execution, wearing a lot of knock-off brands. Tammie seemed more conservative and more refined, wearing a set of denim overalls with a black turtleneck beneath. She wore a little bit of makeup where the other girls didn't.

"So you from New York, huh?" Tiffany asked.

"Yeah," Cinnamon was getting tired of answering that same question.

"They got a lot of cuties up there?" Karissa asked.

"I don't know. I guess."

"I know they do. My auntie's stepdaughter met her husband up there, and girl, he is fine. I saw some pictures of some of his cousins that live up there, and they fine too. They know how to dress, and they got them fly accents. I be try'na get them to take me up there with them when they go visit, but they be slow-rollin'." Karissa was going on and on.

"They got money too!" Tiffany added.

"How you know, Tiffany? You don't even know nobody in New York!" Tammie called her out.

"Shut up, Tammie." Tiffany replied.

"Well, I gotta go. My mom is probably outside waiting." Cinnamon spoke up, anxious to get away from the girls.

"Okay, Miss New York. We'll see you next week." Karissa said, sounding phony.

"Bye." Cinnamon hurried up the basement steps and out the door only to find her mother wasn't there. She pulled her windbreaker hood over her head as she waited in the drizzling rain, wishing she'd worn a heavier coat in the winter weather. Ten minutes passed, and a couple of the other teens' parents picked them up.

A black BMW slowly drove past on the opposite side of the street then reversed and came to a stop directly across the street from where Cinnamon stood. The windows were darkly tinted, so she couldn't make out who was inside but she knew it wasn't her mother's car. She didn't give it a second thought. More kids came and went but no one got in or out of the black car. Just then, a white work van slowly crept up to the curb. She grew a little nervous as the person inside leaned over from the driver's seat to roll the passenger window down.

"Cinnamon?" He called out. She hesitantly took a few steps

closer to see who it was. "It's me, Raheem, from John's Furniture Store!"

She relaxed and came closer to the van. "Oh, hey, Raheem. What are you doing here?"

"I should be asking you that. Why are you standing out here in the rain?"

"I just got out of bible study, and I'm waiting for my mom to pick me up, but I don't know what's taking her so long." She explained.

"Well, do you want a ride?"

Cinnamon wasn't sure what to do. She didn't want to have Raheem take her home and her mom already be on her way to get her. She looked around to see if there was any sign of her and there wasn't. "Um, okay, if it's not too much trouble."

"No trouble at all. Get in." As she opened the door to get in, she heard the roar of an engine go down the street and noticed the black car had pulled off. The cold and moisture from the rain made the windows and windshield foggy. Raheem had the defrost on and the cool air sent a shiver up Cinnamon's spine. "You okay? You cold? I can turn up the heat." Raheem offered.

"No, that's okay. I'm fine." There was a silence for a moment and Raheem began to fiddle with the radio. The static crackled as he tried to find a station.

"Sorry, the radio stations down here suck."

"Yeah, they do." Cinnamon agreed. Then there was more silence.

"So bible study, huh?"

"Yep, my mom made me go." She replied.

Raheem let out a chuckle. "Yeah, I remember them days."

"You used to go to bible study too?"

"Oh yeah, my momma used to make me go every week, and I hated it every week." He said.

"Well, she said she wants me to have a closer relationship with God."

"You ain't gotta go to church to have a close relationship with God."

"That's what I tried to tell her." Cinnamon agreed. "I think she just wanna get with the youth pastor. She—" Cinnamon covered her mouth quickly, realizing she said too much. She didn't want Raheem running back and telling John what she said.

Raheem glanced over at her. "Who? Pastor Leonards?" He asked.

"Yeah, how you know?"

"I used to go to Greater Saints, but that was a while ago. I see Pastor Leonards is still the hottest commodity there." He laughed while shaking his head.

"Please don't tell John I said that. I don't know if she really wants to get with him. I'm just pissed she's all of a sudden acting like a church lady, making me go to bible study and everything." Cinnamon explained.

"Don't worry. I won't say nothing." He smiled at her.

"So your mom don't make you go no more?"

"I'm a grown man. My momma can't make me do anything I don't wanna do." He boasted.

"Well grown or not, if you still living in her house—"

"I don't live in her house. I got my own lil' spot. John lets me have a room above the store." He said, proudly.

"Oh."

"I don't blame you, though. You know, for not wanting to go to church all the time. Most of those people there talk about the bible, but they don't even live by it. And don't get me started on that crazy Reverend Grienbachs." He puffed up his cheeks and let out the air.

"Oh my God, yes! Me and my mom were at his house Sunday for dinner. He made his daughter cry, and he asked me if I was a harlot!" She exclaimed with wide eyes. They both burst into laughter.

"See … nothing changes with them crazy people." Raheem said, still laughing.

They kept the conversation going during the brief ride to Cinnamon's block. Raheem pulled up behind Vivian's car and put the van in park.

"Thanks for the ride, Raheem"

"My pleasure. Can I walk you to the door?" He asked.

"Um, no, that's okay, but thank you." Cinnamon responded, looking down shyly.

"Okay, well, can I call you some time? I never did get your number that day."

Cinnamon smiled on the inside, happy that he'd asked for her number again. She was hoping he would because she wanted him to have it. "Yeah, you got something to write on?" Raheem pulled open the overstuffed glove box. As he did, something heavy fell out, hitting Cinnamon's leg on the way down.

"Oops, sorry about that." He said after picking up a big switchblade knife and tossing it back in the glove box. He pulled out a receipt and a chewed up pen for her to write with. After she scribbled her name and number down, Raheem held the small paper up to the windshield where light peered thru from outside with a wide smile on his face. He clenched the paper like he'd just won the ultimate prize. "Cool, I'll call you tomorrow?" He asked.

"Okay, that's fine. Thanks for the ride." Cinnamon hopped out and made her way up the steps as Raheem watched.

The living room was dim when Cinnamon entered, but she could see her mom sprawled out on the couch with the TV still on. One empty bottle of wine sat on the kitchen counter. Another half empty bottle was on the coffee table next to a glass that was almost empty.

"VIVIAN!" Cinnamon yelled at her mom loudly with the intent to startle her. It worked as Vivian's leg sprung out, causing her to bang her knee on the table as she sat up.

"Sh—" she clutched her teeth together, deciding not to finish the four-letter word. "Girl, what's wrong with you? Why you come in here yelling like that? You try'na give me a heart attack?" She said, groggily, as she used one hand to rub her throbbing knee and the other to rub her chest where her heart was pounding.

"You're drunk, aren't you? I swear I can't leave you alone for two minutes." Cinnamon scolded.

"I'm not ... drunk." Vivian managed to slowly get out.

"Yes, you are. You made me go to bible study. Then you left me there!" Cinnamon glared down at her mother with her arms crossed.

Vivian's eyes popped open and suddenly she was wide awake. "Oh my God! Cinni-Cin, I'm so sorry. I just decided to have a little to drink. Then I laid down to watch some TV. I must've drifted off. I'm so sorry, baby."

"You had almost two bottles!"

"I know. I know. You're right. I'm so sorry." She struggled to get up, but the pain was too much. So she reached up and grabbed Cinnamon's arm. "Come here. Please don't be mad at me, Cin. Come here, I'm sorry. Really I am." She pulled harder and Cinnamon stumbled over the table, falling onto the couch next to Vivian. She crossed her arms tighter and glared at her mother through the corner of her eye. Vivian pressed her cheek up against Cinnamon's and put both arms around her daughter, hugging tightly.

Cinnamon hated to see her mother like this. Since she was eight-years-old, she'd found herself taking care of her drunk mother when things got too rough for Vivian. It usually happened after a breakup with a man. She would go into deep depressions for weeks at a time and do nothing but drink all day. Cinnamon wasn't expecting it this particular evening. She wondered what had triggered her mother's drinking this time.

"Please forgive me, Cin. I just fell asleep this time. I promise I'm fine. It won't happen again. Okay?" She pleaded with her daughter. Cinnamon just sighed in response. "How was bible study?"

"It was fine," she grunted. "I don't like them girls, though, Mommy."

Vivian gave a concerned and surprised look, "What girls? Aww, what happened, baby?" She asked as she smoothed Cinnamon's hair back into the ponytail she wore.

"Them girls, Karissa, Tiffany, and Tammie—well, Tammie seems okay, but I don't like them other two. They made fun of me 'cause I couldn't find the bible verse, and they just kept gettin' smart with me for no reason."

"Oh, you know they probably just jealous. Cin, you know you da bomb, and girls are gonna be jealous of you for no reason. I hope you didn't let them get to you. I know my Cin is tougher than that." Vivian said.

"Pshh, Mom, please! After I called them out, you know they ain't want it, but still…" Her voice trailed off with a hint of sadness in it.

"Just give it time, Cin. You know how y'all girls can be. They probably was just testing you 'cause you the new girl in town. Now they see you ain't no punk, so they probably won't bother you no more. How did you get home?" She asked, changing the subject.

"Raheem gave me a ride." Cinnamon couldn't hide her excitement at that point.

"*Raheem?*"

"Yeah, you know the boy from John's store? He was passing by, and he saw me standing outside waiting in the rain for *you*." She explained.

"Ohhhh no, no, no. I don't want you taking no rides from him anymore, Cin."

"*What? Why not?*" Cinnamon asked defensively.

"Uh uh, First Lady Grienbachs told me he's bad news. I don't want you hanging around him. And she said I should tell you to be careful."

"*Careful?* For what? What did he do?" She asked.

"I don't know, but First Lady seemed really concerned about you and him."

"Wait, what do you mean *me and him?* What did you tell her?"

"I just mentioned to her that you would be working at the store and that I'd seen you two talking. That's all." Vivian responded.

"What did she say?"

"I told you. She just said he's bad news, and that you should stay away from him. He's not safe." Vivian explained.

"That's it? So because First Lady Grienbachs says I shouldn't be around him, you automatically agree? You saw how crazy her and her family was. You're just gonna take her word without even knowing what she's talking about?" Cinnamon challenged.

"She explained that to me. The reverend is ... sick. It's hard on them, but this isn't about them. It's about you, my daughter. And if someone tells me it's not safe for you to be hanging out with this boy, then I don't want you hanging out with him."

"Well that's gonna be kind of hard. Did you forget John hired me to work in the store? What do you want me to do? Quit before I even start?" Cinnamon asked, sarcastically.

"No, you don't have to quit. You go to work and do your job, but after that, that's it. I don't want you running around with him outside of work."

"And if you decide to get drunk and leave me stranded again?" Cinnamon rolled her eyes and looked at Vivian with her mouth twisted up.

"I already told you what happened, and I'm sorry, for the last time. This is serious, though. You know we already have to be careful. We're not out of the woods just yet, and we don't need any additional threats to our safety. You know what I'm talking about?" She asked her daughter with a serious look on her face.

"Yeah, Mom, I know." Cinnamon's voiced dropped, and her face turned serious too. "Is that what this is all about?" Cinnamon waved towards the wine on the table. "You still worried?"

"Yeah, Cin, I am. I could've sworn I saw a man that looked just like him the other day." Vivian's voice shook as she spoke with fear.

"Mommy, you know that's not possible. He's dead." Cinnamon put her arm around her mother's back and rubbed.

"I don't know, Cin. It looked a lot like him, but I only got a quick glimpse."

"Mom, look at me." Cinnamon instructed. "He's dead ... Besides, even if he wasn't how would he know where to find us?" She asked, trying to comfort her mother while trying to comfort herself as well.

CHAPTER 6

After dinner with Pastor Leonards, Cinnamon decided to excuse herself to her room. She didn't feel like watching her mother throw herself at this man. Vivian couldn't be happier at her daughter taking her cue. She was ready to pull out her bag of tricks to reel in the pastor. *This will be a piece of cake*, she thought. This evening she wore a long sleeve tan midriff that hung off her shoulders, allowing her breasts to be noticed and her navel to peek thru. The long-flowing skirt she wore could be seen through, and she counted on that, wearing only a thong underneath.

After fixing them some dessert, peach cobbler with a scoop of vanilla ice cream, she moved to the seat closest to Pastor Leonards. As the pastor went on to talk about all of the upcoming youth events, Vivian did her best to draw the pastor's attention to her mouth, taking her time to envelop each spoonful slowly and licking the spoon after each portion. When that didn't seem to work, she purposely let a little bit of melted ice cream dribble onto her cleavage.

"Oh, look at me. I'm just a mess." She licked some of the melted ice cream from her finger.

The pastor chuckled, "Let me get you a napkin." Vivian sat helpless with spoon in one hand and sticky melted ice cream on the fingers of her other hand. She waited for the pastor to wipe up the ice cream. Instead he held the napkin out to her, "here you go."

"Oh, thank you." She responded and the pastor went back to

talking about the upcoming events.

Vivian let him talk for a little while longer, pretending to be interested. Then she couldn't take it anymore. "Pastor Leonards, would you like to move to the living room? I just rented a couple of new movies. You can take your pick."

"Oh, you know dinner was great. You definitely know your way around the kitchen, but I should probably get going soon."

Vivian frowned and made her best sad face. "Now you can't leave just yet." Before she could say anything else, the phone rang. "Hello? … Who is this? … Oh, just a minute." She put her hand over the cordless and flashed a smile towards Pastor Leonards. "CINNAMON!" She yelled.

"YEAH?"

"PICK UP THE PHONE! IT'S FOR YOU!" Once she heard Cinnamon click on the other end, she didn't give Raheem a chance to say anything. "Cinnamon, you know we need to talk about this later." She said, sternly. Then she hung up. "Now back to you, Mr. Antsy-pants…"

"I really should be going soon. I need to study and prepare for next week's bible study, amongst other things."

"All work and no play. Now that's no fun. Come on, let's go sit in the living room. It'll be more comfortable. Just for a little while. Then you can go. I promise. I wouldn't want to hold you hostage here against your will." She said the last part with just enough attitude to make Pastor Leonards feel guilty.

"Okay, but only for a little while." He tried to be polite.

Vivian plopped down and patted the seat right next to her. Once Pastor Leonards was seated, she placed her hand on his thigh and said, "Now, Leon—oh, is it okay that I call you Leon?"

"Sure."

"So Leon, tell me more about this fundraiser." Vivian continued with her charade.

"Right! So for the MLK fair, we're going to set it up like we normally do inside the high school gym. Only half of the proceeds from the different vendors will go towards the Find Our Missing Fund that we set up for Sister Daisy's daughter. It's a big yearly event. All the other churches in Gracious Meadows and folks from the neighborhood come, so we should raise a decent amount of money." He explained.

"I don't think I've met Sister Daisy yet."

"No, probably not. She hasn't been to church in a few weeks, not since Larissa went missing. Larissa is the fifth girl to go missing from Gracious Meadows within the last three months. A lot of the other families have set up rewards for information leading to the discovery of their teens. Unfortunately, Sister Daisy really can't afford to offer a reward. So we're pitching in to help raise the money."

"You know I did run into another lady the other day handing out flyers for her missing daughter too. Wow! Five girls?" Vivian asked.

"Yup, all teens and the cops still aren't any closer to finding them or the person responsible for their disappearance." He seemed really concerned.

"Gosh that makes me so scared for my baby to be out alone at all without me. You just never know these days." Vivian ran her hand back and forth across her chest.

"Well, I don't think you have anything to worry about. Cinnamon seems like she can hold her own." He chuckled.

"Oh yeah, that's for sure." Vivian chuckled in return. Then she placed her hand on top of Pastor Leonards's. "Well, Leon, you know you have my support. Anything you need me to do, just ask." The look she gave suggested she wasn't talking about the fundraiser anymore.

The pastor placed his other hand on top of hers and squeezed. "Thank you, Sister Vivian."

"Would you please stop calling me that. I told you, just call me Viv." He smiled and raised his eyebrows like he was unsure of something but said nothing. She picked his hand up and caressed it between hers. "Wow, look at these big strong hands, and so smooth. And these arms … Do you work out?"

Pastor Leonards took a deep breath before answering like he was nervous. "Yeah, a little. Nothing major, though."

"I can tell." Vivian said as she slowly brought his hand down onto her thigh and slid it up towards her crotch. Pastor Leonards gulped before being saved by the bell, *literally*. The annoyance showed on Vivian's face. "Ugh who could that be?" She said as she looked at her wristwatch. It was close to eight-thirty.

"I'll get it!" Pastor Leonards jumped up before she could

protest.

The front door creaked open and Vivian could hear Pastor Leonards, "Brother John, good to see you. How you doing?" She scrunched her face up wondering what he was doing there.

He stepped into the apartment holding a bouquet of flowers, "I hope I'm not interrupting anything."

"Oh no, not at all, Brother John. I was just about to leave." Pastor Leonards spoke fast.

"Hey, John. What are you doing here?" Vivian said, as she wished he was the one about to leave.

"I came to bring you these." He said with an embarrassed smile. Once again his ego was hurt seeing Pastor Leonards there, but he tried to hide it with a smile.

"You should've called first." Vivian said, flatly.

"Oh, uh, I'm sorry, Viv. I was trying to surprise you." He scratched the back of his head nervously.

"Isn't that nice? Well, Vivian, thanks so much for dinner. Brother John, always good to see you. Y'all take care." The pastor did not miss his chance to escape. Vivian barely got to say goodbye before she heard the door close.

"Should I just put them on the table?" John asked.

"Yeah, sure John. Thanks, they look really lovely." Vivian tried to force herself to soften even though she felt like whacking John upside his head for imposing on her evening.

"You look nice." He said, eyeing her hungrily.

"Thanks," *I didn't wear this for you*, she thought.

"Well, maybe I should just go. Look, I'm sorry for just showing up. I'll be sure to call next time." He said as he turned to leave.

"Oh, I'm sorry, John. Where are my manners?" Vivian reluctantly got up off of the couch. "Come on in. Sit down."

"You sure?" He asked, feeling the sense that he was obviously unwelcomed this evening.

"Yeah, yeah of course. Can I fix you a plate?" Vivian put on her most gracious fake smile.

"That sure would be nice. Thank you."

Vivian sat at the kitchen table with her elbow on the table and her chin in her palm. John ate fast and sloppily, making a mess on the table and leaving crumbs around his mouth. The more he spoke with his mouth full, the more turned off Vivian became. She couldn't wait for him to finish, so she could put him out. He was a *just in case* man and right now she didn't need him for anything.

"So uh, Viv, there's another reason I stopped by tonight," he started. Vivian just looked at him, as she waited for him to continue. "So you know the church is having the MLK fair next week over at the high school?"

"Oh yeah, Pastor Leonards and I were just talking about that."

John clenched his jaw at the mention of the pastor's name. "Yeah, well, I was wondering if you wanted to go together?"

"Oh, I don't know, John. From what I understand, it's not really a date type thing, and I might just go with Cinnamon anyway."

"Oh," John looked down at his plate and swallowed. He was disappointed.

"But I'll think about it and let you know! Either way, I'm sure we'll see you there." Vivian, feeling bad, tried to sound cheerful.

"Yeah. Yeah, that's cool." John tried to quickly hide his disappointment.

"You all done there? I'll take that." Vivian grabbed his plate and walked it over to the sink where she began to rinse it off.

He followed, stopping behind her to gently glide his arms around her waist. "Let me help you with that." He tried to sound sexy.

Vivian quickly dropped the plate in the sink and shut the water off. Then she spun around. "That's okay, John. I'll take care of it later." She pulled his hands from around her waist and yawned, trying to give him signals to leave.

"You wanna sit in the living room and talk for a minute or maybe watch a movie?"

Vivian stretched and did a fake yawn this time. "No, I'm sorry. I'm just so exhausted, John. I think I'm just gonna get ready and call it a night." She grabbed his coat from the back of the chair and started inching her way towards the front door. "Thanks so much again for the flowers. They're beautiful."

John unwillingly took the hint and shrugged his shoulders, "Okay, I understand. Thanks for dinner. I'll give you a call later."

He leaned in for a kiss and Vivian quickly turned her head, so he could catch her cheek. "Okay, goodnight, John." He put on his coat, turned up the collar and headed out into the cold. She watched him get into his work van, then closed the door. Relieved he was finally out, she leaned against the door and sighed heavily.

She made her way down the hall and knocked on Cinnamon's door. "Cinnamon? You still on the phone?"

"No, come in!" She lay on her stomach on her bed, looking at a magazine and listening to a Foxy Brown CD on her radio. She'd decorated the small space with posters and cutouts from magazines of her favorite singers and rappers.

As a slew of obscenities poured out of the speakers, Vivian twisted up her face. "Cin, why do you listen to this stuff?"

"Oh, Mom, cut it out. Just a couple of months ago this was your song, and you know it!" Cinnamon rolled her eyes. She called her mom out, and Vivian couldn't even deny it.

"Who dat, Foxy?" She asked as she sat down on the foot of the bed.

"Yeah."

"Yeah, I guess I can't front. That *is* my girl ... now how nasty can ya get, all the way from da hood to ya neck of the woods ..." She sang along. "So, missy, why is Raheem calling my house after I told you I didn't want you hanging around him?" She asked, getting to the point.

"That was after I had already given him the number, Mom. Besides, you said not to hang around him. You ain't say nothing about talking to him."

"Don't get smart. You know what I meant. I already told you what the first lady said."

"I know, Mommy, but don't you trust me? The first lady didn't even tell you why she said that." Cinnamon said.

"Yeah, I know, but it's not you I don't trust, Cin. You know that."

"He really does seem nice, Mom. Plus, you're the one who said I need to make friends! What's the difference between you and John or you and Pastor Leonards being friends and me and Raheem being friends? Pray tell." She turned her head to face her mother, widened her eyes and batted her eyelashes.

Vivian smirked and yawned. "Ugh, I'm too tired to argue with you tonight, Cin. Just be careful, please. Pastor Leonards said girls are popping up missing left and right. I can't have nothing happening to my baby." She playfully smacked Cinnamon on her butt.

"Oh boy, so now you think Raheem is a serial killer or something? Really, Mom?" She looked at her mom with her eyebrows burrowed and her mouth twisted up to the side.

Vivian laughed, "Oh hush, Cinnamon. You know what I mean!"

"Yes, Mom, I know what you mean, and I promise to be careful. If I find out Raheem is around here snatching up girls, you'll be the first to know."

***

BANG! BANG! BANG! DING DONG! DING DONG! "I'M COMING! HOLD YOUR HORSES!" Cinnamon yelled down the hall towards the front door, annoyed at whoever was banging and ringing the doorbell like that so early in the morning. She wished Vivian had heard it first and got up, but she was knocked out in her own room. Wearing Tweety Bird pajama bottoms and only a tank top, she shivered and rubbed her arms as the cold air rushed in when she opened the door.

"Hello, are your parents home?" One of the officers asked.

Cinnamon's eyes widened immediately and her heart rate sped up, "hold on." She closed the door, leaving them to wait on the stoop. Then she rushed to the back of the apartment, bursting in her mother's room. "Mom! Mom! Wake up!" She whispered loudly.

"Wh-what, Cinnamon? What do you want?" She answered, annoyed.

"The cops are here!"

"What?" Vivian wanted to make sure she heard right.

"There's two of 'em at the front door. They wanna speak to you." Cinnamon's eyes were bulging with panic. Now Vivian's were too as she shot up out of the bed. She began pacing back and forth in her tank top and panties.

"What did they say? What do they want?"

"They just said they wanna speak to my parents."

"What did you tell them? You didn't tell them anything did you, Cin?" She asked in a worried whisper.

Cinnamon sucked her teeth, "Of course not, Mom. I just told them to wait and I closed the door. Oh my God. How did they find us? We're going to jail!"

"Calm down! Nobody's going to jail. Cin, look at me! You hear me? I would never let you go to jail. Now just calm down and tell me exactly what they said." Vivian grabbed her by the shoulders and instructed.

"I opened the door, and they said '*hello, are your parents home?*'"

Now Vivian sucked her teeth, "That's it?" Cinnamon nodded. "So they didn't ask for me by name?" Cinnamon shook her head. "Okay, hand me my robe."

The policemen started ringing the bell again as Vivian made her way to the door. She tied the belt around her robe and opened the door with Cinnamon standing in the back nearby.

"Hi, sorry to bother you so early, ma'am." The officer said.

"That's okay. How can I help you?" Vivian remained calm.

"We're investigating the disappearance of this girl, canvassing the neighborhood to talk to all the residents. Does she look familiar?" He asked while the other officer just stood by looking up and down the street.

"Ohhh, no, sorry I don't recognize her, but I've heard a lot about these girls that are missing over the past few days."

"This one was just seen last night, about two blocks from here." He explained.

"Oh my God!" Vivian put her hand on her chest.

"Is it okay if we show your daughter the picture? Maybe she might know her."

"Sure. Cinnamon, have you ever seen this girl?" Cinnamon stepped forward to look at the photo then shook her head.

"Do either of you remember seeing any suspicious activity on your street last night or in the past couple of days? Anyone standing around that doesn't belong or any strange vehicles?" The other officer spoke now.

"No," Cinnamon said.

"No, but we just moved here, so we're not that familiar with all of our neighbors just yet." Vivian explained.

"Okay, thank you for your time. If you do see anything or anyone that looks suspicious, please report it to the police. You ladies have a good day." The first officer said, before they both left. After the officers were out of sight and the door was closed, the two shared a tight embrace and a sigh of relief.

CHAPTER 7

"Mom, we're going to be right here in the same place you are. What can possibly happen?" Cinnamon pleaded with her mother as they approached Meadows High School. She waited until the last minute to tell her that she and Raheem made plans to meet up at the fair to hang out.

"I thought I already told you that I didn't want you hanging out with him, Cin?"

"I thought you also said you trusted me, Mom." She retorted. "We're going to be *right* here."

"Well, why didn't you tell me before we got here? Now I gotta be by myself." Vivian pouted like a big kid.

"Because I knew you wouldn't let me. The whole church is gonna be here. How are you gonna be by yourself?"

"Fine, Cin. Go ahead. Just leave me hanging like that." Vivian tried to make her feel guilty. It didn't work.

"Great! Thanks, Mommy!" Cinnamon planted a kiss on Vivian's cheek then hurried off to the entrance where she planned to meet Raheem.

"I want you to meet me back by the front no later than ten o' clock!" She yelled after her.

"Okay!" Cinnamon replied with a smile plastered on her face.

Folks weren't lying when they said the whole town came out to the MLK fair. All the dividers were pushed back, opening the gym to make it look three times bigger than it already was. Big Dr. Martin Luther King Jr. posters and banners could be seen throughout. There was a stage set up where different plays, songs, monologues, and readings were done in tribute to Dr. King throughout the night. The rows of vendors seemed never ending, and one whole side was dedicated to food stands. There was even a section in the back that had games. That's where Pastor Leonards had a dunk tank set up to collect even more donations for the Find The Missing Fund. Of course, this is where Vivian found herself.

She grinned in awe as she watched the different children from the church line up for their chance to dunk the pastor. He seemed to enjoy it, cheerful as always. It was Gabe's turn, and he grinned too, ready for his chance to dunk the pastor he looked up to so much. He threw the ball hard, hitting the target on his first try. The pastor dropped in, making a big splash. On his way out is when he noticed Vivian. He flashed her a smile and waved. Gabe took notice and turned to follow the pastor's gaze.

"Wow, that was really good, Gabe!" Vivian laughed.

"Thank you, Sister Vivian." Gabe tossed the ball up and caught it in his hand. "Do you want a try?"

"Oh, I don't know. I don't have any kind of aim."

"Here, give it a try. I get three turns anyway if you miss." He coaxed.

"You're getting in on the action now too, huh? I see how it is." The pastor joked.

"Pastor Leonards, you're going down ...   again!" Gabe shouted.

"Here goes nothing," Vivian said, before giving her best throw. She missed and Gabe laughed.

"Here, let me show you how it's done." He said, after being handed another ball.

"That's not fair! You already dunked me!" The pastor shouted.

"I get three turns. Get ready to go under!" After sinking him again, the pastor got out and called a time-out. "Where you going?" Gabe asked.

"I'm taking a little break before you drown me, Jackie Robinson." The pastor laughed and patted Gabe on the head as he made his way to Vivian. One of the deacons climbed up on the seat to take his place.

He wore a scuba suit that made him look a little silly and out of place, but Vivian still found him irresistible with all the water dripping down his face and body. That charming smile graced his face as he and Vivian began to walk and talk. They made their way over towards the food stands to get hot dogs. As they talked, Vivian could feel someone watching her. She glanced over and a few feet away spotted Sister Connie staring at them. She sat at a table with Sister Kim and First Lady Grienbachs. They were doing missionary work handing out pamphlets and spreading the gospel to people at the fair. Sister Connie tried to look away quickly like she didn't see Vivian and the pastor, but Vivian decided to walk over and say hello. She nudged the pastor to follow her lead.

"Hi, ladies," she spoke.

"Oh, hi, Sister Vivian. It's so good to see you." First Lady Grienbachs gave her usual, genuine smile and hug. Connie spoke dryly.

"Sister Vivian, I was hoping I'd run into you here. If not, I was going to call you tomorrow. I gave your resume to one of my recruiters, and he thinks he has something for you. They're looking for someone to start right away too, so the sooner you can come in for testing, the sooner we can get you working." Sister Kim said.

"Really? Oh my God, that's great. Thank you so much, Sister Kim!" Vivian, in her excitement, leaned over and hugged Sister Kim unexpectedly. "I'm bringing Cin here to enroll in school tomorrow, but I can come if he's available in the afternoon."

"That should be just fine."

"Look at that. God is answering prayers every time we turn around!" Pastor Leonards said, cheerfully.

"Yeah, because it must be awfully depressing being a single woman, a single mother, *and* broke and unemployed too." Connie said, with a smirk and catty tone.

"Well, now, none of that matters when you have the Lord on your side." The first lady chimed in.

"Amen to that!" Pastor Leonards said in agreement.

Vivian picked up on her tone and saw her eyeing Pastor Leonards in jealousy. It was written all over her face, and Vivian was use to dealing with women like Connie. She grabbed the towel from the pastor's hand and began to subtly, but seductively, dab his brow.

"We should get you back over to the dunk tank, Pastor Leonards. Look at you, you're dripping wet all over." The pastor shifted in his stance and chuckled nervously. Connie couldn't take it. She didn't like Vivian coming into her church and stealing all the attention; first John and now Pastor Leonards. She jumped up suddenly, startling both Sister Kim and the first lady.

"Oh, Pastor Leonards! You can't leave yet without telling us how the fundraiser is coming along." She hooked her arm thru his.

"Well, the night isn't over just yet, ladies. I won't know how well we did until the fair is over and we do the ticket count. You know the kids couldn't wait to dunk me, so I know we're racking up a good amount at the dunk tank."

Connie laughed and playfully tapped his chest. "Oh my goodness, don't let them kids drown you now, pastor. We can't afford to lose you now, can we?"

"No we can't!" Vivian looped her arm thru his free arm. "First Lady, Gabe has quite an arm on him, took Leon down twice! You should've seen his face!" She laughed.

"*Leon?*" Connie questioned as she jerked her neck back. "Sister Vivian, I know you're new to the church but we try to show respect by referring to the pastor as *pastor*, honey."

"Oh, it's okay, Sister Connie. I told her it was okay to call me that." He defended. Connie grunted and exchanged glances of disapproval with Sister Kim. There was a brief silence and Vivian wore a smug look of victory on her face. "I should be getting back. Poor Deacon Roberts is over there taking the heat while I'm gone."

"Let me walk you back over." Vivian suggested.

"No, no that's okay. I know y'all probably got some lady-talk to catch up on." The pastor replied. He unhooked his arms from both women and scurried away before either had a chance to rebuttal.

Connie sat back down and Vivian turned her attention to First Lady Griendbachs. "Gabe is such a gentleman. He let me have one of his turns at the dunk tank. Where is that lovely Generosa and the reverend?"

The first lady smiled, "The reverend wasn't feeling too well, so

Generosa stayed home to look after him."

"I swear that girl is just like you, First Lady. Always trying to take care of everyone." Sister Kim said.

"Aww, well, I hope he feels better." Vivian responded.

Unbeknownst to her, Sister Connie hadn't been the only pair of eyes watching Vivian that evening. The bleachers were pushed back, and John stood on the side of them, out of view, fuming as the ladies continued their conversation. He watched in jealousy the way the two ladies had fawned all over Pastor Leonards. He clenched the brown teddy bear he'd won earlier that evening tightly in his hand before dropping it to the floor. He was planning to give it to Vivian once he ran into her at the fair. A vein popped out of his forehead as he stormed from the gym.

Meanwhile, Raheem and Cinnamon walked hand in hand through the rows of vendors. They laughed and talked while munching on a soft pretzel they shared. After the steady conversations they'd been having over the phone, Cinnamon was warming up to Raheem quickly. They stopped at a booth that sold handmade jewelry. Cinnamon eyed a beaded bracelet.

"You like it?" Raheem asked.

"Yeah, it's really pretty. It'll go perfect with a pair of earrings I already have."

"How much for the bracelet?" Raheem asked the lady selling the jewelry.

"They're ten dollars each or two for fifteen." She replied.

"We'll take that one, and go ahead and pick another one out you like." He instructed.

"Oh, Raheem, you don't have to buy anything for me. I was just looking." Cinnamon said, sweetly.

"I know I don't *have* to but you like it, and I want you to have it. So go ahead." Cinnamon smiled and pointed to another bracelet. She turned around while Raheem paid and waited for her bag. Just as she did, Karissa and Tiffany walked by.

Karissa stopped in her tracks, "Look, Tiff, it's Miss New York. Hey girl, what'chu doing here?" She said as if they were good old friends.

"Hey," Cinnamon replied without so much as a smile.

"Hey, Cinnamon. I like that top, girl. You buying some jewelry?" Tiffany asked.

"Yeah…" Before she had a chance to say anything else Raheem spun around with her bag in hand.

"Here," he said, as he handed it to Cinnamon.

Tiffany's mouth dropped open. "You here with *him*?"

"Um, yeah. Raheem this is Tiffany and Ka—"

"Oh, he knows exactly who I am!" Karissa cut her off. In a matter of seconds, her whole demeanor changed. "Why would you even come here? I should call the police! You know this violates your orders!" She was clearly heated and Cinnamon was confused.

"Look, Karissa, I don't want no problems. I'm just here to have a good time like everybody else." Raheem said, calmly. Cinnamon studied his face, and he almost looked frightened.

"Come on, Karissa. Let's go find your mother." Tiffany grabbed her by the arm, pulling her away. "I hope you know who you dealing with!" She cautioned Cinnamon.

"Look, I gotta get out of here." Raheem looked and sounded nervous as he spoke.

"What was that about? What did she mean *'violates your orders?'*" Cinnamon asked.

"Look, don't worry about it. It's nothing, but I should go."

"Wait! Where are you going? My mom said I don't have to meet her until ten." Cinnamon said. In perfect timing, Raheem's beeper went off. "What is that?"

He lifted his shirt and yanked it from his waist. "It's my beeper. It's John. He needs me. I'm really sorry. I have to cut this short. I'll make it up to you, though. Promise!" With that, he placed a quick peck on Cinnamon's cheek and took off, glancing in all directions like someone was after him.

Cinnamon, dumbfounded and unsure which direction to go, moved her feet slowly making her way towards the stage where some children were putting on a performance. There weren't any empty chairs, so she stood behind the last row of chairs and watched.

"Martin Luther had a dream. His dream was meant for you and me…" some children recited in unison as others signed what they said.

All of a sudden, two smoke bombs went off, and the gym began to get cloudy. Everyone looked around in all different directions, wondering what was going on. Parents began to grab their children. Soon the smoke was so thick that no one knew what was going on. Vendors began to pack up. Cinnamon, not able to see much, turned to go find her mother. She took a few steps, and someone suddenly grabbed her from behind, lifting her from the floor by her waist. They cupped a hand over her mouth as she struggled. No one seemed to notice since they were all in a frenzy and couldn't see through the thick haze.

She kicked and tried to scream muffled screams as she was dragged towards the door. Just as they made it to the door, shots rang out near the other end of the gym. POP! POP! POP! POP! Startled by the shots, her abductor froze. She seized this opportunity and bit down hard on his hand, causing him to let go. She began to flail her arms and legs about and screamed as loud as she could, "SOMEBODY HELP! HELP! MOMMY!" Then she shot one elbow back that landed in his rib. The instant pain left him with no choice but to release his other hand that held her. She turned quickly and kneed him in the groin before running.

Vivian, knelt down by Sister Kim's side, could barely hear anything through all the commotion. One of the bullets had Sister Kim leaking from her shoulder. The shots were fired so close to the ladies, it had Vivian's ears ringing. All four ladies had tried to run when they saw the arm through the smoke pointed right in their direction. Sister Connie took off and didn't look back. When Sister Kim fell, Vivian and the first lady stayed behind with her.

The air was so thick with smoke and Vivian felt conflicted. She wanted to make sure Sister Kim was okay, but she needed to find her child. "Oh my God, we gotta find the kids!"

"Please, please don't leave me here. He might come back!" Sister Kim begged.

"Here tie this around her arm." Vivian instructed First Lady Grienbachs. She handed her the pastor's towel that she still had. "Come on, your legs are fine. We're not gonna leave you." She said, before they hoisted her up. "Let's get her outside, and I'll come back and look for the kids."

The three ladies walked quickly towards the door. Once they

were outside, Vivian wasted no time as she spun around to go back in. "Wait, it's not safe for you to go in there by yourself. I'm sure the cops are on the way. Let them go in and find them." First Lady Grienbachs said.

"*What?* I'm not about to wait for no cops. My child is in there, and *I'm* going to find her right now!" Vivian snapped and didn't waste another second arguing about it.

As she ran back into the school, a man carrying two small children came rushing out. "You going the wrong way!" She ignored him and kept going. Some of the smoke started to filter out since the gym doors and the outside doors were opened.

Once inside, she ran up to a young girl and spun her around, "Cinnamon?" The girl was crying, obviously scared to move an inch. It wasn't Cinnamon. "Honey, you gotta get out of here. Go that way. There's the door." Vivian instructed and gave the girl a push. She continued her search yelling, "CINNAMON! CINNAMON WHERE ARE YOU?"

Cinnamon ran through the rows of tables, bumping into them and bumping into other people who still hadn't found their way to the door. She jumped each time someone touched her, scared the man was back to take her. She sniffled as tears streamed down her cheeks, "MOMMY? VIVIAN! VIVIAN MICHELLE MACKEY!" She called out.

Vivian could hear her full government name being yelled out. "CIN, IS THAT YOU, BABE? WHERE ARE YOU?" She followed her calls.

"Mommy!" Cinnamon found her first through the settling smoke and grabbed her arm.

"Oh my God, Cinnamon!" Vivian examined her daughter, touching all over her face. "Are you okay? Are you hurt?"

"Mommy," she sobbed. "Somebody tried to take me. He grabbed me and put his hand over my mouth, and he tried to drag me outside. It was him, Mommy. It was the kidnapper. Then somebody started shooting, and I thought you was dead, Mommy. I thought they killed you." She buried her head into Vivian's chest, crying heavily as she held on to her mother tightly.

Bewildered by her story, she grabbed her shoulders and asked,

"Who? Who tried to take you, Cinnamon?"

"I don't knowwww," she droned.

"Okay, baby. It's okay. I'm here now. I'm not dead. You're safe, okay?"

Cinnamon sniffled and shook her head. "I just wanna get out of here. Can we go home?"

"Yeah, have you seen Gabe?" Cinnamon shook her head. "Okay, let's go. C'mon."

Once they got outside, the first lady ran up to them and hugged Vivian. "Oh thank God! Thank you Jesus! I was so worried! Is she alright?"

"Yeah, she's fine. We couldn't find Gabe, though." Vivian said.

"Oh no, he's fine. Pastor Leonards made sure he got out okay. He just took him home for me while I waited out here for you."

"Thank goodness." Vivian grabbed her chest and exhaled. "Where's Sister Kim?"

"The paramedics took her. She'll be fine, though. It looks like the bullet just grazed her." As the first lady spoke they all heard tires screech from the parking lot. Vivian looked to see that same black BMW she'd seen at the diner speeding away. Her fears turned into paranoia, facing the possibility that those bullets were meant for her.

CHAPTER 8

The events at the fair had everyone's feathers ruffled and Gracious Meadows was a ghost town. In addition to the shooting, another young girl was abducted that night. She was last seen after the shooting, walking home from the fair with some friends. Given the story that Cinnamon shared with her mother about someone trying to snatch her, Vivian kept a tight leash. The school was shut down for the rest of the week, so Cinnamon would have to wait for enrollment. In the meantime, Vivian didn't let her go anywhere without her. This drove Cinnamon crazy. She even went as far as to buy them both beepers so they could reach each other at any time.

"Mommy, come on. It's been days since the shooting. Raheem only wants to take me to the movies. I promise to come right back." She begged.

"Uh uh, not taking any chances. I still don't like you hanging with that boy. For all you know, he could've been the one trying to snatch you up out of that gym." Vivian stood at the kitchen sink washing dishes. Cinnamon sat at the table and placed her forehead on it. She let out a frustrated burst of air. "Cinnamon, maybe you don't realize the seriousness of this. Someone pointed a gun at us and tried to kill me!"

"You don't know for sure he was trying to kill *you*. He could've been trying to shoot either one of y'all. It could've been some crazy person doing a random shooting."

70

Vivian turned and looked at her daughter with an expression that said *yeah right*. "Not to mention, somebody tried to kidnap you, Cin! *Kidnap!*" She repeated for emphasis. Cinnamon sat up and crossed her arms. "Look, I know you're probably getting cabin fever sittin' up in the house. I'll tell you what. I'll call the first lady and see if her and Generosa want to come with us to the movies. I did promise her a girls' night out."

"Whatever," Cinnamon, disappointed, shrugged and went to her room.

Vivian hated telling her no, but she didn't have time to discuss it right now. Sister Kim recovered from her grazed arm quickly and kept her word about setting up an appointment for Vivian at the employment agency. Even in her professional look, she was still sexy, wearing a black Donna Karen suit. She wondered if her patent leather pumps were too much with the skirt but decided to go with it. Her hair was neatly swooped back into a bun.

She made a quick call to First Lady Grienbachs before leaving. After much convincing, the first lady agreed to have girls' night. During their brief discussion they also decided, given the recent events, that maybe it would be safer to just do a girls' night in—no movie theatre. First Lady Grienbachs also suggested Vivian invite Sister Kim, Sister Connie, and their girls. "The more the merrier!" She told her. So it was settled. Everyone would be over later that evening.

"I'm going, Cin. Make sure the living room and bathroom are presentable. We're having company tonight!" She yelled down the hall as she put on her coat. There was no response. "Cinnamon!"

"I heard you." She answered with an attitude.

"Beep me if you need me and don't let anybody in here. I don't care who it is." She instructed sternly.

"Okay," Cinnamon mumbled in response.

***

"First Lady, I'm surprised you made it out tonight. You never leave those boys alone." Sister Kim spoke as she spooned more dip onto her plate.

Vivian went all out in the short time she had when she returned from her appointment with the recruiter. She made a spinach dip, guacamole, and salsa for the platter of carrots, chips, and celery. She also made some buffalo wings and regular fried wings as well as burgers. Her fruit punch was perfection. It went well with the sweet potato pie she made and the brownies First Lady Grienbachs brought over. Sister Connie brought potato salad and Sister Kim, soda.

"Oh I know it, and believe me, they didn't want to see us leave." The first lady chuckled as she crunched a carrot in her cheek. "Gerald carried on like a big baby, asking who was gonna take care of him. Since Gabe is going with Pastor Leonards to the Young Men's revival over at Mount Zion, he's by himself. I told him Gabe would only be gone a couple hours. He's gotten so use to either me or Generosa being there. I almost think he's scared to be home alone!" She joked. The ladies laughed.

The night was going well. They laughed and ate. They played Jenga, Charades, and Taboo. The teams were the daughters against the mothers and the girls found themselves getting along a lot better than they had previously. Throughout the night, Karissa pushed to see Cinnamon's room. Once everyone was tired of playing games, she finally gave in.

"Where y'all going?" Vivian asked as all the girls rose, except for Generosa.

"I'm just going to show them my room." Cinnamon responded.

"You girls don't stay in there too long. Tiff and Tammie, we gotta get going soon." Sister Kim instructed.

All the girls replied in unison, "okay."

"Generosa, you not coming?" Cinnamon noticed she was hanging back.

"I'm still hungry. I'm just gonna go in the kitchen and have another burger—if that's okay with you, Sister Vivian?" She asked, shyly.

"Girl, eat! Help yourself. I hope y'all take some leftovers home 'cause me and Cinnamon can't finish all that ourselves anyway." Vivian spoke to the group of women. Generosa went to the kitchen as the girls headed down the hallway.

"Oh snap! This is kinda hot!" Karissa said, wide-eyed as she looked all around the room at Cinnamon's posters. Tammie plopped down on the bed and Tiffany sat in a chair. Cinnamon turned on the radio and Wu Tang Clan started pumping out. She turned it down so the adults wouldn't hear it.

"Your mom lets you listen to this?" Tammie asked in disbelief.

"Yeah! Yours doesn't?" Cinnamon replied.

"Heck no! She would never let us listen to this or hang up any posters like these in our room." Tiffany cut in.

"Why not?" Cinnamon asked.

"I don't know. She calls it *secular* music or something like that. We can listen to Kirk Franklin, though!" She boasted proudly.

"Who's that?" Cinnamon asked, innocently.

"You don't know who Kirk Franklin is?" Karissa jerked her head around and asked like she was a dummy. "Oh my God," she mumbled and rolled her eyes, turning her head back around to look at posters. The twins snickered.

"Well, my mom let's me listen to whatever I want." Cinnamon said, proudly.

"So does mine, but I still know who Kirk Franklin is!" Karissa didn't want to be outdone.

"No she don't! Why you lying, Karissa?" Tammie spoke up.

"What'chu talkin' 'bout? I listen to all that stuff; Wu Tang, Biggie, Tupac, Nas—all of them!"

"Yeah, but your momma don't know that!" Tammie challenged.

"She don't need to know. I mind my business, and she minds hers."

"Girl, you fifteen. You ain't got no business!" Tammie replied and Tiffany and Cinnamon laughed.

"Whatever."

"Karissa's mom isn't allowed in her room. She has to knock and wait 'til Karissa tells her to come in every time." Tiffany explained. "She has her own private phone line, and she gets to lock her door when she leaves."

"What?" Cinnamon couldn't believe it.

"That's right, and she know better too!" Karissa confirmed.

"Well me and my mom talk to each other about everything so I don't have to hide anything from her." Cinnamon said.

"Dag, I wish our mom was like that. Your mom seems mad cool." Tammie expressed. Cinnamon didn't want to break her tough exterior just yet, but she was smiling on the inside at her comment.

"So Cinnamon, you going to Meadows High, right?" Tiffany asked.

"Yeah, I was supposed to get enrolled this week, but now I gotta wait 'til next week."

"Dang. You lucky. We all go to St. Mary's. It's a private school. I wish I went to the high." Karissa confessed.

"I know. They got all the cuties on the football and basketball teams over there." Tiffany said.

"It's nothing but cornballs at our school, except for Georgie, Brian, Ty and 'em! Ooh! We should hook her up with Ty!"

"Ugh! Don't do that to her. The only thing he wants is what's between your legs, girl!" Tammie gave her two cents.

"So what, he got mad money!" Karissa debated.

"Yup," Tiffany cosigned.

"That's all y'all care about is looks and money. I'm pretty sure Cinnamon wants to be with someone who wants more than just her body." Tammie rolled her eyes.

"Tammie, you always acting all stuck up. That's why nobody be try'na holler at'chu with that flat butt." Karissa shot. Tiffany started laughing.

"Tiffany, I don't know what you laughing at. In case you didn't know, you're my twin and your butt is just as flat as mine." Tammie said, with her face twisted up. Tiffany sucked her teeth, knowing it was true.

"She is kinda right, Tiff, your butt could use some weight on it too." Karissa stood sideways in front of Cinnamon's full-length mirror. "See all this I got back here?" She playfully smacked her butt to make it jiggle. "You know how I got all this, don't'cha?"

"We know. We know. You told us a million times, doing it doggy style." Tammie rolled her eyes again.

"I'm telling you. He ain't doing it right if your butt ain't gettin' bigger." A wide grin spread across Karissa's face. Cinnamon blushed and looked down. "Cinnamon know what I'm talking about. She got them wide hips and a fatty. Don't you?"

Cinnamon quietly replied, "Um, I have heard that rumor before, but I really wouldn't know."

"What'chu mean you wouldn't know? You never let a dude hit it from the back?" Karissa asked as she eyed Cinnamon's physique up and down in confusion.

"Um …" Cinnamon laughed nervously. "I've never let a man hit *anything* before."

"You're a *virgin*?" Tammie asked as though she had the plague.

"Yeah."

"Get outta here! I don't believe that for a second!" Tiffany replied.

"You don't have to believe it but it's true." Cinnamon replied in defense. "All of y'all have done it before?" She asked, curiously.

Out of all of her friends and cousins her age back home, Cinnamon only knew of one personally that had lost their virginity already, and it hadn't been by choice. Her cousin had been raped as a little girl by one of her mother's boyfriends. The horrific story her cousin confided in her only made Cinnamon want to hold on to her virginity even longer.

All three girls nodded their heads emphatically. "Uhhhh ya!" Karissa responded out loud for all three. "Shoot, I bet even Generosa has gotten a little nookie on the low as wide as she is!" The girls all snickered, but Cinnamon didn't find her comment funny.

"But you're all … *church girls* …" Cinnamon seemed confused.

"Oh, you ain't know?" Karissa raised her hands, snapping her fingers to the beat and swaying her hips. "They say church girls be the freakiest ones." She laughed as she stuck out her long tongue.

"Heyyyy," Tiffany sprung to her feet, dancing and copying Karissa by sticking her tongue out too. "What are you waiting for?" She asked.

"I don't know," Cinnamon shrugged and mumbled, feeling a little embarrassed. "I'm waiting for someone special and the right moment. I don't want my first time to just be with any ol' body."

"Aww, I know how you feel, girl. I used to feel the same exact way, but then I got tired of waiting and just went ahead and got it over with. Yup, right in the back of Tarique's father's truck." Tammie shared.

"Tired of waiting? But aren't you only sixteen?" Cinnamon questioned.

"Yeah, girl. See, right now you're just fifteen. Just wait until next year. You'll see. You'll get tired of waiting too. Trust me." Cinnamon looked at all three girls like they were crazy.

The phone rang and Vivian yelled down the hall to tell Cinnamon it was for her.

"Hello?… Oh hey, Raheem …" Tiffany and Karissa looked at each other as Karissa's demeanor turned cold.

Tammie burrowed her eyebrows, noticing the girls knew something she didn't. Then she whispered and mouthed to them, "*Raheem?*"

Tiffany sighed heavily, "I tried to tell her the other day." Tammie's eyes grew wide as they waited for her to end the call. After a few seconds, Cinnamon told him she had company and would have to call him back.

"So I see you're still talking to Raheem …" Tiffany said, flatly.

"Yeah … *and?*" Cinnamon really wished they hadn't been there when she answered the phone.

"Cinnamon, you don't know him and what he's capable of. You really shouldn't be messing with him. For real." Tammie's voice turned serious.

"Why not? Why does everyone keep telling me to stay away from him, but nobody is willing to tell me why!" Cinnamon was tired of all the warnings with no back story to go with them.

The girls just grew quiet, not knowing what to say. Karissa seemed to be getting angrier by the second until she just stormed out of the room without uttering a word. The other three girls followed behind her.

"What's going on, girls? Everything okay?" Sister Kim asked, noticing their tense facial expressions. Everyone was quiet.

"What's going on, Cinnamon?" Vivian asked.

"I don't know."

"Karissa, baby, what's wrong? You look upset." Sister Connie sounded concerned as she eyed her daughter's face.

Tiffany shifted back and forth before deciding to be the brave one to answer. "Um … I guess Cinnamon has been kind of messing with Raheem."

"*Raheem?*" Sister Connie blasted in disbelief.

"Messing with? What she mean *messing with*? Cin, you ain't having sex yet are you?" Now Vivian sounded concerned.

"No, Mom!" Cinnamon answered, annoyed and embarrassed her mom would ask her that in front of a room full of people.

"You sure? 'Cause I already to—"

"That boy is the devil! He's evil! You hear me, little girl? You better stay away from him!" Sister Connie cut Vivian off in a rage.

"Oh my God! If one more person tells me to stay away from Raheem!" Cinnamon was annoyed beyond her limit and losing patience. "*Why? Why* should I stay away from him? *Why* is he evil? Everybody seems to know something but nobody's telling me and my mom!"

"Okay, you wanna know, Missy?" Sister Connie's voice took on a sinister vibe. "Your lil' prince charming, Raheem … is a rapist! He's a predator and a sexual deviant who likes to take advantage of people."

"Wh-what?" Cinnamon felt crushed as tears began to well up in her eyes. Why was this woman making these awful accusations? Why was she being so mean? "That's not true," she managed to eek out.

"Don't believe me? Just check his record! I don't have any reason to lie to you. You think you're so special? You just better be careful, sweetheart." Sister Connie spat.

"Alright, alright. I think that's enough." First Lady Grienbachs tried to diffuse the situation. "Sister Vivian, I tried to tell you."

"I-I know, and I told Cin what you said, but you know teenagers…" Vivian was holding her chest, still digesting Connie's words. She didn't like the way she was talking to her daughter, but she needed to know too.

"I think it's time for us to leave. Thanks for having us over. Karissa, get your coat." Sister Connie said, flatly, with an ice cold expression.

"Yeah, I think we should be going too, girls." Sister Kim said, and the twins headed for their coats as well.

Generosa sat at the kitchen table alone, eating a brownie. She had been reading another one of her books and only stopped momentarily to listen in on the commotion. She didn't need instructions from her mother. She got up and followed suit, grabbing her coat as everyone cleared out.

After everyone was gone, Cinnamon stood, frozen in the same spot. Unable to speak, her fists were clenched as tears rolled down her eyes.

"Oh, I'm so sorry, honey." Vivian hugged her daughter.

"It's not true, Mommy. I just know it can't be true. I know he's not like that." She wept.

CHAPTER 9

January approached its end and that week was a big week for both of the Mackey women. Vivian would start her new job at Medical Supplies 4 U where she'd work as a file clerk and do some data entry. This was a new scene for her, but she was adjusting well and caught on quickly. She loved to get dressed up in her business casual wear. It just gave her another reason to shop. Her coworkers all seemed pleasant and helpful.

Cinnamon started school at Meadows High. She ended up having two classes with Generosa. On her first day, she was a little nervous about where she would sit for lunch. She thought she would have to find a table all on her own and impose since she didn't have any friends yet. Her heart beat harder than usual from the apprehension. After getting her food, she just stood and looked around, trying to decide where she should sit. She scanned the whole room and had to take a double take to notice Generosa, who sat way in the back corner of the cafeteria. There were a few other people at her table, but, as usual, she sat alone reading a book. Cinnamon was relieved to see two empty chairs at the table.

"Hey, is it cool if I sit here?"

Generosa looked up and smiled once she saw that it was Cinnamon. "Yeah, of course. Hi, Cinnamon." She actually looked excited to have the company. This must've been the table for the loners because the other students that sat there didn't seem to even notice or care about the new girl at the table. Everyone seemed to be in their own world, reading or writing in notebooks. There wasn't much interaction amongst one another taking place. Looking around her table, she felt unprepared for lunch. Looking around at other tables, she realized this was the geek squad. It was better than being alone.

"Wow, you sure do like to read a lot, huh?"

Generosa tilted her head and looked down. "Yeah".

"Nothing wrong with that! I need to start reading more too." Cinnamon tried to let her know she hadn't asked because she thought it was a bad thing. "What are you reading today?" Generosa perked up, once again excited to talk about her books. Cinnamon allowed her to ramble on, pretending to be interested to make her feel good. "Sounds good. I might have to read that some time."

"You can borrow it when I'm done." Generosa replied with excitement.

"Thanks," Cinnamon smiled. "So what do you like to do besides read?"

Generosa shrugged, seemingly stumped by the simple question. "I don't know. I like going to church and helping with the little ones. I volunteer for the Sunday daycare we have at church."

"Oh yeah? I didn't even know there was a daycare."

"Yup! They have it throughout the week too. Sister Connie and my mom run it, but I'm not allowed to volunteer during the week." She said, sadly.

"Why not?"

"Mom says somebody needs to be home for Dad in case anything happens." She took a huge bite out of her ham sandwich as though she felt defeated. That's when Cinnamon noticed she had quite a spread in front of her: the sandwich, two bags of salt n' vinegar chips, one pack of chocolate chip cookies, a yogurt, a fruit cup, and two cartons of ice tea.

"What about Gabe?"

"He helps sometimes, but he works with Pastor Leonards sometimes after school. Plus, I'm the oldest so…"

"Well maybe that will change once your father gets better."

She raised her eyebrows like she wasn't banking on it. "Yeah…"

"I'm starting work today after school myself." Cinnamon

boasted proudly.

"That's great. Where are you working?"

"At John's Furniture Store."

"Oh," a hush quickly fell over them.

"I know. I know. I know. I shouldn't be hanging around Raheem." Cinnamon rolled her eyes and sounded exasperated, tired of everyone saying that. "But I'm not working there because of him. John offered me the job before we even started to see each other. Besides, I haven't talked to him since ... that night." She said, referring to the girls' night.

"I didn't say anything," Generosa replied with wide eyes.

"I know. I just figured you were thinking it since everyone always is." Cinnamon paused for a moment in thought. "Did he really rape Karissa?"

"*Karissa?* No, not Karissa. Sister Connie."

"*Sister Connie?*" Cinnamon wasn't expecting that. Her face scrunched up in confusion. "All this time I thought it was Karissa. Are you sure?" She asked suspiciously, thinking the loner might have her facts mixed up.

"Yeah, that's what they say." Generosa answered matter-of-factly.

Wrapping her mind around this new tidbit of information, Cinnamon still just couldn't picture Raheem hurting anyone, let alone Sister Connie. "Do you really think he did it?"

Generosa shrugged, "I don't know, but he sure went to jail for doing it."

"Really?"

"Yup," Generosa answered between crunches as she munched on her chips. "Two and a half years."

Cinnamon felt as though someone took her air away. She had been avoiding Raheem's calls since the girls' night all the while wondering if she was doing the right thing. *'Predator'*, *'sexual deviant'*, Sister Connie's words rang over and over in Cinnamon's ears. Close to tears, she needed a distraction. She decided to change the subject.

"So back to you ... besides reading and church daycare, what else do you do? Do you have a boyfriend?" She already knew the answer but anything to redirect her train of thoughts.

Generosa's fair skin blushed and she chuckled nervously, "No way!"

"No way? Why not?" Cinnamon teased her.

"My mom and dad would not let me have a boyfriend. Are you kidding me?"

"Fine, well, what if they didn't know? Is there anyone that you like? You know, anybody you crushing on?" She probed. Generosa's cheeks felt heated, and she smiled looking down at her tray. Then she fumbled around with the cookie package, struggling to open it.

Seeing the overwhelming nervousness, Cinnamon placed her hand over Generosa's to calm her and stop her from fiddling with the cookies. "Ha! Uuuuhhh huuuhhhhh! I knew it! Ooh I'm telling!" She grinned.

"Who you gon' tell? I never said 'yes,' and I never said who." Generosa playfully shot back.

"Okay, I'm only joking. Now tell me! Tell me! Tell me!" Cinnamon whispered excitedly.

"You know Anthony? In our second period History class?" She whispered.

"No, I don't know who's who yet. Describe him to me."

"Okay, he sits in the last row near the window. He's kind of brown skin, wears glasses, has red hair?" Cinnamon made a face and shook her head, still unsure of who she was talking about. "Okay, don't turn and look right now…" Generosa started before turning to look herself. "Look two tables over to my left, then one table back. He's sitting near the middle of that table in the black shirt."

Cinnamon discreetly counted the tables and found Anthony. "Oh him. *That's* who you like?" He didn't look like much from what she could see.

"Yeah, you don't think he's cute?"

"He's okay, I guess." She lied.

"Well, he's real smart. He has the second highest GPA in our class right now. He held the door for me once going into class. He's nice like that. And … I like his glasses. Oh, and his red hair! It makes him stand out from the other boys."

Cinnamon smiled, enjoying this moment as Generosa opened up to her. "Do you know if he has a girlfriend?"

"I don't know. I bet he probably does." She said in a down voice.

"Well, we'll just have to find out. Won't we?" Cinnamon said, before finishing her chicken patty.

***

Cinnamon caught on to her role at John's store quickly. For most of her first day, she shadowed John out on the floor, watching him interact with the customers. Towards the end, he trained her on the register, showed her how to ring people up and how to fill out the different forms for layaway and those buying on credit. Raheem was in and out with the other older man, Rick, making deliveries. Cinnamon avoided eye contact with him as much as possible, but that wouldn't work forever. Raheem was determined, and when John left the two alone to close the store it was his perfect opportunity.

"Hey," he said as he approached Cinnamon who stood behind the front counter, counting down until closing time.

"Hey."

"So you know you obviously can't keep avoiding me forever. We work together now, so you gonna tell me what's up or what?" He asked.

"What do you mean?" Cinnamon played stupid.

"C'mon, Cinnamon. You know what I'm talkin' 'bout. Everything was all cool between us—at least I thought—then out of nowhere you just start avoiding me. Is this about what Tiffany and Karissa said at the fair?"

"No—yes ... well sort of."

"Which is it?" He asked.

"Look, everybody keeps telling me that I shouldn't be seeing you. They said you've been to jail and…" Cinnamon searched for the right words.

"*And?*"

"And that you raped Sister Connie!"

Raheem's jaw clenched and his nostrils flared as his breath rushed out of them. "And you believe them just like that? Without even asking me about it?"

"Well, Generosa sa—"

"*Generosa?*" He sucked his teeth after cutting her off, tilting his head up as he rolled his eyes. "*That* poor girl. She don't know up from down or left from right. I can't believe you listening to her."

"Well, not just her! Tiffany, Tammie, and even Sister Connie said it straight from her mouth. Why would she lie?"

"'Cause that's what they do over there at that church. They all liars!" Raheem was struggling to keep his cool.

Cinnamon looked down at the floor and mumbled, "My mom said I'm not allowed to talk to you anymore."

"Cinnamon," he started. "Cinnamon, please look at me. I did not rape that woman. That's not what happened. Her and her daughter both lied to the judge, and I had to do almost three years because of them."

The pain in his voice tore at Cinnamon's heart. "Karissa?"

He cringed at the sound of her name. "Yeah, *Karissa*. I'm telling you, none of those people are who they seem to be over there." He paused before continuing. "Do I look like a rapist to you?" Cinnamon shook her head. "Do you think I raped her?"

Cinnamon shrugged, "I don't know, Raheem."

He sighed a heavy, aggravated sigh then checked his watch. He walked out the front door and pulled the gate halfway down. Stepping back inside, he finished pulling it down and locked it from the inside. Cinnamon grew nervous. She checked the time and saw that it was time for closing. It was time for her to leave but the look on Raheem's face told her she wasn't leaving just yet.

"Raheem, I gotta go home. My mom will be worried if I don't come straight home." She said.

"Please, just give me ten minutes. I want to show you something." Cinnamon shifted around nervously. "Look, I'll drive you home. I promise. I just want you to hear my side of the story. Please?"

"I don't know, Raheem." Cinnamon gulped.

"Please, just trust me. Just this one time. Let me show you what I got to show you and tell you what I got to tell you. Then if you decide you never want to talk to me again, I'll leave you alone. Forever. I promise." Cinnamon breathed in deeply, still unsure if she should go anywhere with him. "I'll drive you straight home right after. That way you won't be late and get in trouble."

She gave in, "Okay—but only for a second!"

"That's all I ask." Raheem held his hand out to escort Cinnamon toward the back stairs of the building.

It was dark as they climbed the stairs and there was a stale smell in the hall. It gave Cinnamon an eerie feeling and she couldn't stand the silence. "So John lets you close the store?" She asked.

"Every night!"

"Wow, he must trust you a lot."

"Yeah, I guess you can say that. Plus, since I live up here it's just easier that way."

They arrived at the top of the landing in front of a black door. Raheem unclipped his keys from the back of his pants and unlocked both locks on the door. Small would be an understatement to describe his living quarters. The room was just big enough for his double bed. Right next to it sat a crate with a TV and VCR on it. In the corner was a mini fridge with a microwave on top of it. The bathroom was out in the hallway. Two big posters hung on opposite walls. One was of Bob Marley and the other was Malcom X.

"Sit down," he insisted. "Do you want a soda?" He swung open the door of the mini fridge and took out an orange soda for himself, popping the can open. Cinnamon shook her head and stuffed her hands into her jacket pockets. She began bouncing her leg up and down. "You nervous about something?" He smiled and asked.

"No," she lied.

He sat on the bed next to her so that his leg touched hers and Cinnamon felt an electric current run up her spine. "I want to show you something … about them church girlfriends of yours."

"They're not my friends." Cinnamon shot.

"They must be since you willing to just believe them with no hesitations." Raheem said, sarcastically, as he reached over Cinnamon's legs to dig in another crate that sat next to the TV. It was filled with videos on one side and tape cassettes on the other. He found the video he was looking for and popped it into the VCR, then turned on the TV.

Cinnamon gasped in embarrassment as a big butt in a red thong popped up on the screen. "What is this?" She asked.

"Just wait and watch." Raheem glanced over at her with a straight face of anticipation on it.

"You've seen Girls Gone Crazy Spring Break Miami and Girls Gone Crazy Teen Exclusive … Now wait 'til you see this!" The voice on the video said. As he paused, two brown nipples attached to a pair of double D breasts sprung into the screen and Cinnamon gasped again. This time she had to cover her mouth. "It's *Church* Girls Gone Crazy!" The animated voice announced in the background. The camera zoomed out and there was Karissa wearing a wild smile, juggling her breasts up and down into the screen.

"Oh my God," A stifled laugh of disbelief escaped Cinnamon's mouth as she grabbed her chest.

"Yeah, exactly…" Raheem cosigned. "I'm try'na tell you them girls is wild … *and* crazy."

Cinnamon couldn't take her eyes from the screen now as Karissa French kissed some other teen girl she didn't recognize. "How did you find this?"

"I didn't really. Well, you know … I'm a guy, so I have a few tapes that my boy shares with me sometimes. This one was in the mix. I saw it and couldn't believe it—then again, I could." He said, raising his eyebrows. "All they do over there at Greater Saints is lie and pretend. They act all sanctified and filled with the holy ghost, but it's all just an act. Soon as they leave those church doors, it's another story. And you better believe the apple don't fall far from the tree." He hit the power button on the TV.

"You mean Sister Connie…"

"Yeah," he said, quietly, as he looked down in his lap. "Two and a half years. Two and a half years I can't get back all because of that woman and her lying daughter." His demeanor wanted to be angry, but sadness is all that Cinnamon saw in his face. "And now … now I'm labeled for life." His voice cracked.

"So you're saying you didn't do it?"

"That's exactly what I'm saying." He looked at Cinnamon through the corner of his slit eyes. The anger was returning as his nostrils flared and his jaw tightened. "I knew I shouldn't have went over there that day. I knew it. Something told me not to go, but…"

"But what? What happened?" Cinnamon searched his eyes for

answers.

"See Karissa used to have a lil' thing for me," he started.

"Like a crush?"

"Yeah. She used to pass me notes in church and stuff. But I was only fifteen. I wasn't thinking about having no girlfriend back then. And she was only twelve. I just looked at her like a little girl at the time. I thought I was just a phase that she'd easily get over. So I let her down easy. Told her she was cute or whatever, but I wasn't allowed to have girlfriends." Cinnamon chuckled at the idea. "Hey, it was true at the time. My momma wasn't going for that stuff." He said with a smirk, his mood lightening but only for a moment. "But her mom … her mom was a different story. She was a woman, a grown, older woman. I didn't know anything about women yet and the sneaky things they do."

"Hey!" Cinnamon protested.

"Look, I'm just being honest. Okay, maybe not *all* women."

"Thank you."

"Sister Connie used to always ask me to do all kinds of stuff for her. *Raheem, can you come cut my grass this weekend? Raheem, can you come shovel my walkway? Raheem, can you clean the gutters for me?*" He mocked. "She'd always invite me in for a drink afterwards and, of course, I wouldn't object to that. I'd just finished working hard. Plus, she'd always make me come in to get paid anyway." He put his elbows on his knees and rested his face in his palms. "I felt kind of bad for them, you know? Sister Connie's husband just up and left them without a word when Karissa was only three or four. Not to mention, my mom was always volunteering my services around to the other women at the church. That was when she was still going there, you know?" He looked half sad, half happy talking about his mother.

"Anyway, it started out with little things. Sister Connie would wear little tight clothes every time I came to do something. She'd bend over in short shorts when I came in the house. Sometimes she'd wear a white T-shirt with no bra underneath. I was only fifteen, but shoot, I was still human." He raised his eyebrows. "I would always try to act like I didn't notice what she was doing and just try to get out of there as fast as I could. Then, one day I went over to rake the lawn for her, and she invited me in after as always. I didn't even want to sit down so I just stood in the kitchen drinking my lemonade and waiting for her to come back with my money. Karissa was out playing, so it was just the two of us. That's when she made her move. I still can't forget. She came in the kitchen with the money wearing nothing but her bra and panties."

Raheem's face changed into a daze as he recounted the story. "She walks up to me and tries to grab the glass of lemonade from my hand, but it slips and falls to the floor, breaking. I go to try to clean it up. 'Sorry' I say and she puts her finger over my mouth. 'Shhh' she says. Then she just starts kissing me. At first, I'm frozen. I don't know what to do. I try to push her away, but she won't stop. She grabs my shirt and pushes me against the wall, away from all the glass. Now she's kissing me all over, making her way further and further down until..." Raheem's voice drifted off for a moment. He took a sip of his soda before continuing. "I couldn't help it. It felt so good with her ... you know ... *down there*. So I let her. Then she stops and pulls me down to the floor with her. On top of her. *'You know you're such a handsome boy, Raheem'* she says. *'I want you inside of me'* she says. *'Don't you want to feel a real woman, Raheem?'* she says. Just as I'm about to put it in, I hear this scream from behind me."

"Karissa," Cinnamon says, already knowing.

He sighed, "Yeah ... Karissa. Next thing I know, Sister Connie starts slapping me and yelling *'Get off me! Get off me! Get him off me!'* She says *'Karissa, he's trying to rape me! Get him off me!'* I jump up quick, and I'll never forget the look on Karissa's face. Tears streamed down her cheeks, and she says, *'how could you?'* But it's not a look of fear—like fear of a man who is raping her mother. It's a look of hurt. I didn't know what else to do, so I just ran." He took another sigh and looked at Cinnamon.

"Wow ... I don't even know what to say."

"There is nothing to say. The next thing I know, the police are knocking on the door. They dragged me out right in front of my mother. She was crying and begging them to let her baby go. My dad was still at work, so there was no one there to console her. I hated seeing her like that." Cinnamon thought she saw tears welling up in his eyes so she put her hand on top of his, stroking it softly. "Sister Connie told the police I raped her. When they got to her house and saw the broken glass and Karissa backed up her mother's story, it was their word against mine. I knew Karissa was mad and hurt, but I didn't think she was mad enough to lie on me, send me away to jail. I still think her mother paid her to lie."

"I can't believe it. I can't believe two people would do such a thing."

"Yeah, well, believe it because they did. They ruined my life. I would've been facing twelve years if I went to trial; so I just took the plea bargain. But that's not the worst of it. What hurts most is that when my mom and dad found out about the charges, they believed them. They really believe I did it. My mom had to stop going to church because of the way everyone was treating her. They stopped talking to me. They never came to visit the whole time I was locked away." The crack in his voice sounded like he wanted to cry but dared not.

"I'm so sorry you had to go through that. That must've been awful." Cinnamon sympathized.

"Well it's in the past now—even though no one in Gracious Meadows will let me forget. They all think I'm guilty too—except for John. He's the only one who believes in me. I owe him everything."

"I believe in you, Raheem." Cinnamon said, quietly.

Raheem smiled a painful smile as he gazed into Cinnamon's eyes. "That's why I wanted to tell you my side. The true story." He stroked her cheek lightly and she looked away nervously. "Cinnamon, you know you really are the most beautiful girl I've ever seen before."

She smiled shyly, "Thank you."

"I really mean it. I want you in my life to stay. You're not like the other girls around here. I can tell." She smiled again. They sat in silence as Raheem studied her face before leaning in close. He pressed his lips against hers. She pulled back, nervously at first, but he tried again. Kissing her bottom lip softly, he lifted her chin and ran his thumb over it. This time she returned the gesture, lightly planting a peck on his top lip. He slipped his tongue smoothly in between her lips, entering her mouth. She followed suit. That's when her beeper sounded.

"Oh shoot! That's my mom! I gotta get home!" She said, as she jumped up and smoothed out her clothes.

"Do you want to call her to let her know you're on your way first?"

"No, no. Just take me home, please. She's gonna be pissed."

"Okay, just calm down." Raheem grabbed her shoulders and kissed her once more on the mouth before opening the door.

CHAPTER 10

So many days had passed she'd lost track. Her body hung there with her wrists bound together stretched above her head. Weak and sore, she clung to life with no end in sight of the torture. One eye was so badly bruised it was swollen shut. She struggled to look through the blur in the other one, but it was so puffy it hurt even to blink. A whimper escaped as she heard footsteps come down the stairs. *He's back*, she thought. Then she heard two sets of footsteps and thought, *oh maybe it's the police. Maybe they've finally found me and I can go home.* It wasn't until she heard his familiar voice that she knew she was wrong.

"Ugh! You smell, you know that?" He spit on her cheek and her single whimper turned into cries as snot slowly rolled from her nose to the top of her lip. "It's time to clean this place up."

Her blood formed a pool beneath her where she dangled just barely on her tiptoes. She could tell there were two figures in the room even though she couldn't make out the faces. She cried out to the one who hadn't yet spoken. "Please. Please help me." Her voice was dry and hoarse, barely a whisper. That's when she felt the sting of the iron rod cause a sharp pain in her rib.

"Shut up! I didn't tell you you can talk! And quit that sniffling." Her head bobbed up and down as she tried to gain control of her crying. Her side throbbed and so did the rest of her body. All feeling was lost in her right breast where the nipple had been removed. The cool air grazed her scalp, causing a stinging sensation amongst the many cuts from where he shaved her head. Her back stung the most, both from the repetitive whippings she endured over the days and the alcohol that had been cruelly poured on the open wounds.

As she sensed the end of her life approaching, all she could think about was the night of the fair. *I knew I shouldn't have went. I knew I shouldn't have walked home alone after the shooting. Why did I accept his offer for a ride? But I know him. He was always nice to me. Why did I get in the van? Why?*

"Get her down. This one's of no more use. It's time to get rid of her." He said, coldly.

"How do you wanna do it?"

He nodded towards the suitcase that sat in the corner. "We'll put her in there. We're running out of room, but there's still a little space where the others are. I'll grab the saw so we can get started."

***

First Lady Grienbachs was hesitant, but how could she say no? Reverend Grienbachs seemed to be having a good day. He must've taken his meds the past few days because he was well enough to give the sermon earlier that morning. Now the church, as well as others in the Gracious Meadows neighborhood, agreed to meet at their home to have an emergency meeting. Teen girls were disappearing at an alarming rate and since the police seemed no closer to catching the culprits responsible, everyone felt it best to take matters in their own hands by taking initiative. They met to form a neighborhood watch.

Everyone crammed into their littered living room. Cinnamon sat on the arm of the couch next to her mother. Vivian felt awkward being there given the last time she was there, but Reverend Grienbachs greeted her with a big hug and smile when she came in. It was as if nothing ever happened between the two. First Lady Grienbachs passed around a tray of desserts for everyone.

"They say Sister Daisy's daughter and that child from the fair both were last seen getting into a white van." Sister Kim said.

"Yeah, well, that's half of the town." Pastor Leonards said. "Shoot, me and Reverend both got white vans in addition to our other vehicles."

"Me too!" one of the other neighbors expressed.

Cinnamon immediately thought of Raheem. John let him drive one of his three white work vans all the time.

"Well, I say we all need to arm ourselves. If this predator, whoever he is, knows there's a chance he'll catch a bullet the next time he tries to take one of our girls, I bet he'll think twice!" Another neighbor, an angry father, shouted. A few other neighbors agreed, giving nods and grunts of approval.

"Now. Now. I don't think addressing violence with more violence is the answer here, folks." Pastor Leonards said.

"What *is* the answer then? 'Cause this maniac obviously has no intention of stopping, and I have my three girls to think about!" Another angry neighbor said. "Pastor Leonards, with all due respect, you don't have any children to worry about."

"Hey, now that's not fair. I look at all the children of Gracious Meadows as my own. You know that. I'm affected by this too." He argued.

"Okay, let's not go turning on each other," Reverend Grienbachs's voice boomed over everyone else's. "That's exactly what he probably wants. Pastor Leonards is one of us. He's on our side, and we all need to band together right now."

"The reverend is right, y'all. We should be talking solutions and organizing who will take rounds doing the watch." John chimed in.

Cinnamon kicked her foot up and down out of boredom. The meeting dragged out way longer than she'd hoped. But as far as she saw, the later the better. For the past few days, she'd been waiting until Vivian fell asleep to sneak on the phone with Raheem. This night would be no different as she thought about what he was doing at that moment. It took her a moment to realize that Generosa had been trying to catch her eye from where she stood near the doorway that led to the kitchen. Once she did, she rolled her eyes and stuck out her tongue mimicking Cinnamon's same boredom. Then she nodded her head towards the kitchen, signaling Cinnamon to follow behind her to get away from the adults as they rambled on.

"Hey, it looked like you could use the escape." Generosa smiled.

"Yeah, I was about to fall asleep and fall right off that couch in a minute." Cinnamon joked.

"I know right."

"Where were you today? I looked for you in the children's daycare."

"I wasn't feeling all that well today." Generosa answered as her eyes shifted downward.

"Oh, well, you look like you're feeling better now."

"Yeah, I am. I'm fine now. Guess it was just a little bug or something." Generosa replied.

"So guess what?" Cinnamon lowered her voice.

"What?"

"On Friday when we were in History class, I noticed Anthony looking at you." Cinnamon said with a sly smile.

"What? No way! You need to get your eyes checked." Generosa looked away bashfully, dismissing the idea with the wave of her hand, but she couldn't hold back her grin.

"No, I'm for real. He was checkin' for you, girl."

"Really? Like how was he lookin'?" Generosa asked.

Cinnamon went on to explain and the girls continued talking about this and that while the adults continued to argue while making the neighborhood watch plans. After two cups of Kool-Aid, Cinnamon started to squirm in her seat.

"Can I use your bathroom?" she asked.

"Yeah, it's downstairs on the left. Let me turn the light on for you." Generosa replied as Cinnamon followed her to the basement stairs. The one lit bulb shined like a single tiny star amongst a great dark galaxy. It gave a spooky feeling and Cinnamon couldn't help but look back up towards the stairs to make sure the door stayed open. The steps creaked, startling her, as she made her way down one by one. As soon as she hit the bottom stair, the strong smell of ammonia rushed her senses. She let out a choked cough and used her knuckle to dab the corner of her eye. It was so overwhelming she'd begun to tear.

Once in the small space of the bathroom, the smell was even stronger. She moved fast, using the last four squares of toilet paper that had been left on the roll. A limp stream of cold water trickled out of the rust-stained sink. She looked around for something to dry her hands but there was nothing. She shook them then wiped them on the front of her jeans. She twisted the knob and opened the door. Just as she was about to step out, something caught her eye. Something tiny and black wiggled on the floor. She bent down under the sink and twisted her face once she realized it was larvae. Another one fell to the floor, causing her to flinch. Her eyes ran up the side of the wall to discover where they'd fallen from. There was a small door about two feet high and one foot wide just next to the sink near the floor. It was painted white just like the rest of the wall and easy to miss. She pulled on the small knob to find dozens of larvae wiggling around the corners and on the surface of a piece of wood. Car air fresheners dangled over it. The wood had been nailed in place, blocking the darkness that stood behind it.

Grossed out with her skin crawling from the sight of the larvae, Cinnamon quickly slammed the small door shut and stood up, blood rushing to her head.

"What are you looking for?" Gabe calmly stood in the doorway.

Cinnamon jumped and grabbed her chest, her heart racing. "Gabe, you scared me. I didn't even hear you come down." She released a long stretch of breath. Gabe stood, stone-faced, waiting for an answer to his question. "Uh I-I was looking for some paper towels." Cinnamon stammered.

"There are none. Besides, your hands look dry from where I'm standing." He said, his voice monotone, and his expression unwavering.

Cinnamon held up her hands and looked at them. "Yep, you're right. I guess they dried already that fast." She chuckled nervously.

"You shouldn't be down here. You should go upstairs. Everyone's getting ready to leave." Cinnamon heard his words and wanted nothing more than to leave at that moment, but Gabe just stood there blocking the doorway.

"Yeah," she finally answered, pushing past him. "See you later." Gabe just turned and gave a cold stare as she made her way back up the stairs. With her heart racing and having been crept out by Gabe and thoughts of whatever was causing larvae to multiply behind the small door, she ran up the basement steps in a hurry. The clamor of the metal dessert tray hitting the kitchen floor was loud.

"Oh, First Lady Grienbachs, I'm so sorry!" Cinnamon said, out of breath as she bent down to pick up the tray. The first lady beat her to it.

"Don't worry, I got it. What were you doing down there anyway?" She shot Generosa a suspicious glance.

"Looking for paper towels," Gabe's head popped up from behind Cinnamon as he emerged from the dark basement.

"Well, actually, I used the bathroom first. Then I was trying to find something to dry my hands."

"Oh ... Generosa, why didn't you let Cinnamon use the bathroom upstairs? No tellin' when that one was last cleaned. You know better." First Lady Grienbachs's expression looked slightly annoyed.

Generosa wrung her hands, "I—"

"That's okay. It was just fine." Cinnamon cut in.

The first lady didn't respond. She looked at Gabe who said nothing either, searching his face for a clue. No words were exchanged, only silent expressions as though they spoke through telepathy. Whatever was going on, his look seemed to put the first lady back at ease before he left the kitchen.

"Cinnamon, won't you take some cookies home with you?" She said with a calm smile.

"Oh, no, thank you."

"Wait, don't say no too fast! Now you know we might want something to snack on later in the week, Cin." Vivian entered the kitchen, oblivious to the awkward tension just moments earlier.

"Let me get you a baggie." First Lady Grienbachs opened a drawer as she continued talking. "Please take as much as you want. It's a sin to waste. Although, I'm pretty sure they won't go to waste the way Generosa has been eating everything in sight lately." Generosa looked at Cinnamon then away, sadly.

"Bye," she mumbled as she rose from her seat, grabbed her book from the table, and exited the kitchen.

"You okay, honey?" Vivian asked, noticing her face as she passed.

"Oh, she's alright. Aren't you, Generosa?" First Lady Grienbachs answered for her.

"Yes, ma'am. I'm just going to go upstairs to finishing reading my book."

"Well alright. I hope it cheers you up." Vivian poked out her lip and pinched her eyebrows together, making a sad face.

"See you tomorrow, Generosa!" Cinnamon called out to her.

Once the first lady finished bagging up a variety of cookies for them, Cinnamon and Vivian made their way back through the living room to say their goodbyes to the few people that were still there.

"Now I know you wasn't gonna leave without giving me my hug goodbye!" Reverend Grienbachs held out his arms and licked the lips that held his grin.

"Uh, no, Reverend. Of course not." Vivian felt and sounded unsure as she made her way into his embrace. This was the reverend she'd met the first time, eyeing her like a piece of meat. Squeezing her awkwardly one inch too close and one second too long.

"Come on over here, baby. Don't be shy now. I know you ain't think you was leaving without showing the rev some love too!" He shifted his weight on one leg and held his arms out again. Cinnamon looked over at her mother nervously for an intervention, but Vivian couldn't think of anything fast enough. Cinnamon leaned in, maintaining the space between their bodies, tapped him on the back a few times, and quickly broke the embrace, scurrying away.

Once outside, Vivian spotted Sister Connie talking to Pastor Leonards. That didn't stop Vivian from walking over with the intention to interrupt and gain the pastor's attention. As she approached, though, Sister Connie folded her arms and gave her one disgraced look from head to toe. She grunted something quickly to Pastor Leonards and spun on her heels, walking away towards her car.

"Goodnight, Sister Connie!" Vivian yelled, putting on her phoniest voice.

"Night."

"Sister Vivian, so good to see you again." Pastor Leonards gave his same award-winning smile.

"Leon, please, how many times do I have to tell you to just call me Viv?" She batted her lashes.

"I know. I know. I know. Sorry, I forgot." Pastor Leonards's cheeks began to warm as he fiddled with his shirt collar inside of his coat.

"Well. You can make it up to me, you know. Why don't you stop by tonight?" She slowly ran her finger down his arm and licked her lips seductively, stopping only to bite the bottom lip.

Swallowing before he answered, the pastor smiled widely. "You know I'd love to, but unfortunately, I can't. I promised Gabe I'd let him interview me for a school project tonight. They have to do some kind of presentation on a person they see as a positive role model in the community, and he chose me. Can you believe that?"

"Yes, yes I can believe that. You do so much for the kids around here. I really admire that, Leon."

"Thank you. I just try to go in the direction the lord leads me and hope I help a child in the process. That's all I can do."

"Well, you are doing an awesome job." Vivian poked him in the side.

"Thank you, Sis—I mean Viv."

"Ahhh, I see you're catching on." She teased.

"Wouldn't want to make the same mistake twice." He scratched behind his ear.

"Well, you go on in and help Gabe. Maybe some other time we can get together."

"Yes, I'd like that. Maybe later this week. I'll call you."

"Alright, then. Goodnight, Leon." Vivian bounced up on her tiptoes and planted an unexpected kiss on the pastor's cheek. Cinnamon, who watched the whole exchange from nearby, rolled her eyes in embarrassment.

"Your mom is something else." John appeared from the house and stood next to Cinnamon near the car. Catching the same view, his veins pumped with jealously.

"Tell me about it." Cinnamon replied.

"So, you ready for work tomorrow?" He asked, changing the subject.

"Yup, I'll be there right after school."

"How is everything working out? Do you like it so far? Raheem isn't bothering you too much, is he?" He joked.

"No, not at all." Cinnamon couldn't hold back her smile while talking about Raheem. "He's real nice, and everything is going good."

"Good. I'm glad to hear that. If you ever have any problems make sure you let me know right away." He instructed.

"Okay."

"John, heyyy," Vivian's phony voice found its way back on.

"Vivian, how are you? Looking lovely as always."

"Thank you," her smile beamed.

"We haven't had a chance to catch up in a while."

"I know. I'm so sorry, John. You know, I just been so busy with starting the new job and everything."

"Oh yeah, I heard about that. Congratulations." The flatness in his voice gave the impression he didn't really mean it. "So what are you up to tonight? Maybe I can come over. Cook you and Cinnamon dinner?" Cinnamon's eyebrows shot up. She didn't want to be included in this awkward love triangle. Besides, all she could think about was sneaking on the phone to talk to Raheem. This wasn't part of the plan.

"Oh, John, you know that sounds real nice, but it's a school night for Cin. Plus I have to get up early for work. I'll have to take a rain check." She did her best to sound genuinely apologetic.

"Okay, no worries. I understand." John bit the inside of his cheek and bounced on the balls of his feet with his hands in his pocket, making a serious effort not to sound or look too disappointed. "Maybe another time then?"

"Yes. Yes, definitely. We'll get together real soon." Vivian wrapped her arms around John, hugging him quickly. "See you later, John." She said, as she made her way around the car to the driver door.

"Okay, goodnight ladies. Drive safe."

CHAPTER 11

With the neighborhood watch under way, the next few weeks seemed to return to normal. Vivian thrived at her new job and Cinnamon continued to work at John's store after school while keeping her relationship with Raheem a secret. She and Generosa were also becoming close. As much as she disliked going to bible study, Vivian still made her go. Although she and Tammie were friendly, there was still something about Tiffany and Karissa that rubbed Cinnamon the wrong way. So she was happy to have Generosa there to make things more bearable.

Elated bible study had finally reached its end, Cinnamon put on her jacket in a hurry, anxious to leave so she could sneak on the phone with Raheem like she'd been doing every night.

"You leaving?" Generosa asked.

"Yeah, I'll see you tomorrow in class."

"Wait, I gotta tell you something." Generosa said in an excited, hushed whisper.

Cinnamon slowed up, "What's up?"

"Why did you give Anthony my number?" She asked, accusingly.

"So he could call you, *duh*!" Cinnamon had spent the past few weeks playing match maker between Generosa and their red-headed classmate, Anthony. She got the ball rolling by passing notes between the two, and even helped to write some of the notes for Generosa. She noticed a giddy glow increasing in Generosa with every exchange, and she was proud of herself for helping to make things happen. He was interested, so Cinnamon thought it was time to kick it up a notch and get the two to actually talk to each other.

"Cinnamon, I can't have calls from boys!" She exclaimed.

"*Really?*"

"Really. I'm not allowed to have boyfriends, so what would make you think I could talk on the phone to boys either? Did you forget I *am* the reverend's daughter?" She asked with her eyes wide.

"Oh, my bad. I didn't know. I'll fix it." Generosa lifted her eyebrow to complete her look of doubt. "I promise." Cinnamon added. "Anthony asked for your number, and I thought you would want to talk to him. Sorry, I hope I didn't get you into too much trouble."

"No, thankfully my mom answered. She just told him I couldn't have calls from boys, and I told her I didn't know how he'd gotten my number … Now had my dad answered, that would've been another story. I probably would be on punishment right now." Generosa sighed gloomily. "I kinda do wish I could talk to him, though. But I wouldn't even know what to say anyway."

"Welllll … there might be a way you guys can talk." Cinnamon thought aloud.

"How?"

"Well, you know me and Raheem talk on the phone every night after my mom goes to sleep, right?"

"Yeah."

"You can do the same thing. Just wait until your parents are asleep. Then call Anthony."

"I don't know. I'm scared I might get caught. Besides, I don't even know what to say to him."

"We could always use three-way. That way your parents won't get suspicious because I'll call first and then we can call Anthony. Then you'll have me on the phone to fill in when you run out of stuff to talk about." Cinnamon suggested.

Generosa's eyes lit up with an evil glint, "Okay, yeah! Let's do that!"

"Alright, I'll explain everything to Anthony tomorrow."

"Thanks," Generosa engulfed Cinnamon in a tight hug with her belly pressed up against her.

Cinnamon, surprised by the sudden burst of affection, chuckled. "You're welcome."

"Awww, aren't y'all cute." Karissa said, mockingly. Generosa quickly broke the embrace and scurried off. "Cinnamon, we gotta talk to you."

"Talk to me about what?" she responded defensively.

That's when Tammy and Tiffany appeared, standing on either side of Karissa. "We want you to take us to New York—this weekend." Tammy spoke lowly so others wouldn't hear.

"*Take you to New York?*" Cinnamon questioned, confused by the request.

"Yeah, we can all take the bus up there, and we want you to show us around. Show us all the hot spots." Karissa instructed.

"And introduce us to some cuties too!" Tiffany said, with an excited grin.

"Um, no, I don't think so." Cinnamon responded flatly.

"Told y'all she would say no." Tiffany's demeanor instantly changed to an attitude, crossing her arms like a bratty child.

"Come on. Don't say no, Cinnamon. Please please pleeeeeeease. You have to." Tammy pleaded.

"No … I don't. Why y'all want me to go anyway?"

"Because you're from there! You know all the places to go, what to wear, what *not* to wear…" Karissa's voice trailed off. "Come on. Do it for Tammy." Now Cinnamon brought both of her eyebrows in and down to the center of her forehead, causing a wrinkle in between, and squinted.

"Yeah! Do it for me! I want to go to F.I.T. while we're up there, so I can check out the school." Tammy reasoned.

"Tammy, why don't you just have your mom take you? She'll take you if she knows it's for school." Cinnamon suggested.

"Girl, are you crazy? No, she won't. She doesn't even know I'm going there. I mentioned it to her once last year, and she said the idea was absolutely off the table. She wants me local so she can keep tabs on me, but little does she know. Soon as I graduate, I'm outta here!" Tammy's voice got real serious.

"I don't know. I don't think my mom is gonna want me going

back up there." Cinnamon sounded unsure because now she was having a change of heart and actually considered the idea—not for the girls, but because she would be able to see her family and friends she so yearned to visit.

"That's why we not telling them we're going." Karissa explained.

"I don't know," Cinnamon repeated.

"What? You scared? I thought people from Brooklyn was supposed to be all tough or whatever." Tiffany challenged.

"*No*," Cinnamon shot back with attitude. The events of her last days in Brooklyn played in her mind. She didn't want to tell the girls that she and her mom had a pact never to return to New York, or at least not until things cooled down and were safe for them again. "I just don't want to get caught by my mom. She'll be real mad if she finds out I went back to New York without her."

"That's why she's not going to find out." Karissa put her arm around Cinnamon.

She went on to share the plan she and the girls had already concocted prior to her cooperation. Both Sister Kim and Sister Connie were going out of town together Saturday for a missionary conference, not to return until early Sunday morning. Deacon MoMoney would be gone most of the day Saturday as well, leaving the twins unattended. The plan was to tell Vivian that they were meeting up to go to the movies and then spending the night at Karissa's Saturday night. Of course they intended to leave out the detail about Sister Connie going out of town. So long as they all made it back to their homes by Sunday morning, all would go as planned.

***

As always, Generosa was left behind, excluded from the girls' day trip. Even if she had been invited, there was no getting out of the Grienbachs's sight. Cinnamon would have to deal with the girls all on her own. To her it was worth it if she was able to visit with old friends and family.

Everything started out as planned. Cinnamon had no problems getting out of the house. Vivian was happy to see her finally getting along with the girls from church. Besides, she'd finally given in to John and would accompany him for most of the day for a lavish date he'd planned for the two. She did, however, question Cinnamon about her leaving the house so early before noon.

"Who goes to the movies this early on a Saturday? When I was your age, all the kids waited for the late night show." She'd said. Cinnamon went on to explain to her that first the girls planned to go shopping and grab something to eat. She left her convinced that they were making a whole day out of hanging out.

The three girls waited anxiously for her arrival to Karissa's house. Less than ten seconds later, a cab appeared to whisk them off to the bus station where they were to catch the Greyhound straight to New York's Port Authority. Cinnamon was grateful she thought to bring her walkman. It would prove necessary as the girls chattered endlessly in their excitement. It was evident that the excursion was probably the biggest adventure they'd ever been on. Mary J. Blige's *You Bring Me Joy* blasted through the headphones, drowning out the restless talk that surrounded her as Cinnamon tilted her head against the glass, looking out the window. Butterflies filled her stomach with anticipation of surprising her friends in Brooklyn, or were the butterflies from the guilt she felt for going against her mother's will? Either way, it was too late. They were on their way.

Cinnamon felt revived, like life had somehow reentered her body in a whole new way when they pulled into Port Authority and stepped off the large bus. She inhaled the stale air that reeked of cigarettes and fresh urine and gave a big stretch as she waited for the others to exit behind her. A smile spread across her face. *Home sweet home*, she thought. Tammie was the last to step off the bus and before both of her feet could hit the ground good, Cinnamon took off, leading the way. She fell right in stride with the busy hustle and bustle of the city's energy.

They made their way up some stairs and down a long corridor towards one of the street exits. Cinnamon moved fast, weaving in and out of other pedestrians like a pro, as the others found themselves practically jogging to match her pace. It was no wonder she hadn't even noticed the soiled man that sat on the dirty tile in a doorway.

It appeared that he was once a Caucasian man, but the layers of dirt caked on his skin now made him look to be almost Arab. A wild beard framed his jaw and the matted coils atop his head were a singed-colored orange and brown. It was still cold and he wore flip-flops, exposing blackened soles and long dirty toenails. He held a cardboard sign with illegible scribble on it and dangled a large styrofoam cup up into the air, shaking the change inside of it.

"Spare some change?" He said, out loud to no one in particular.

Tammie slowed down, rummaging through her purse. "Cinnamon, hold up!"

Cinnamon took a double take over her shoulder, before quickly growing annoyed once she saw why they'd stopped. A scowl took over her face as she grabbed Tammie by the arm. "Girl, if you don't come on. You feed one bum, you better be prepared to feed 'em all. Let's go." She chastised, shaking her head in disapproval as she pulled Tammie along. "Acting just like a tourist…" Before Tammie had a chance to protest, Cinnamon had regained her stride.

Once they hit the street, she decided F.I.T. should be their first stop. She began to make her way down 8th Ave. After walking just one block Tiffany asked, "We walking there?"

"Yeah," Cinnamon responded as though she should've already known the answer.

"Well how far is it?" Tiffany looked cold, wearing only a light jacket with no hat or gloves.

"Like eleven or twelve blocks from here."

"*Eleven or twelve blocks?!*" Tiffany and Tammie both exclaimed in unison.

"Yeah."

"Cinnamon that's a long walk! Can't we take one of them yellow cabs or something?" Karissa asked.

Cinnamon laughed, "We'll pay more money just for sitting in traffic if we do that. Eleven blocks really isn't that bad. I told y'all to wear comfortable shoes. Not my fault *somebody* wanted to be cute instead." She shot her eyes down to Tiffany's feet. She wore brown suede heels that clearly already bothered her feet. Evident in the way she shifted her weight back and forth.

She rolled her eyes and sucked her teeth in response. "Whatever, I'm not about to walk no eleven or twelve blocks. Tammie you gon' have to see F.I.T. another time."

"Oh no I'm not! Ain't nobody tell y'all not to listen and wear them ridiculous heels." She referenced Tiffany and Karissa, who wore black patent leather pumps. If her feet were bothering her, she pretended well.

"Can't we take a bus, then, or something?" Karissa asked.

Cinnamon tooted her mouth to the side and eyed the girls with clear annoyance, huffing before she answered, "Come on, we can hop on the train right quick. It'll get us there faster." She led the way across the street once the light changed and down the stairs of a subway entrance.

Once down in the dark, dank area, she made her way to the booth to buy tokens. As they waited in the short line Tiffany asked, "Can't we just hop over that thing?" She motioned towards the turnstile.

"Are you serious?" Cinnamon asked.

"Oh yeah, we saw that in that movie that time." Karissa added, smiling at Tiffany.

"*In a movie?* Y'all can't be serious. You know y'all really need to get out more often." Cinnamon shook her head and turned back around in the line.

"What?" Karissa asked, unsure of what the big deal was.

"You two go right ahead. Hop it, but don't call me to come get you out of jail when you get caught. It's the middle of the day and maybe you haven't noticed that guard right over there." Cinnamon pointed to a man standing towards the end of the platform.

"Oh," both girls said, feeling dumb.

"Y'all so stupid. Tiffany, sometimes I really wonder how you're my twin. I swear." Tammie added to their humiliation.

"Shut up, Tammie," Tiffany mumbled in response.

Once the girls made it to the other side of the turnstile, the subway pulled up right away. There was a mad rush to get on as everyone packed in like sardines. Cinnamon spotted the only seat and grabbed it immediately, as she enjoyed the amusement of watching the other three pressed up against strangers as they struggled to keep their balance once the train took off. Poor Tiffany struggled to hang on to her small portion of the shared pole, bumping into people and stepping on a lady's foot as the jerking motion of the subway car had its way with her, tossing her back and forth like a ragdoll.

F.I.T. seemed so grand to Tammie as they approached the outside of the building. "Here it is! I'm finally here!" She said, excitedly, as she looked up at the flags blowing in the wind. There was a glimmer in her eye, but the experience was short lived once they made it through the entrance. The girls hadn't taken into account that they would need school ID's or a scheduled tour to access the rest of the school. The disappointment took the form of tears in Tammie's eyes, being so close to her dreams and not being able to touch them.

"I'm sorry, Tammie." Cinnamon could see the disappointment. "Well at least you were able to get some more information and the admissions applications. Plus, the guard did say we can go across the street to check out the school's museum. That's something at least."

"Yeah," Tammie sighed as she avoided speaking through the knot that formed in her throat. She knew if she said anything more, the tears would unwillingly follow. Tiffany and Karissa were quiet as they made their way across the street to the museum.

Although there were other people present, the museum was silent. Several students stood before different exhibits with their large pads out as the faint sound of pencils scratched across the paper. There were a lot of couture and Avant guard displayed. There was one piece in particular, a puke green gown. The fabric was textured, giving it a bumpy look. One of the shoulders was abstractly misshapen as though the person wearing it might be carrying a large bowling ball. Karissa and Tiffany looked at each other and simultaneously began to snicker.

"Tiff, I'ma get you this for your birthday." Karissa whispered and the girls laughed harder, causing the other visitors to glare with cold stares.

"Will you shut up?" Tammie hissed. "Can't take y'all nowhere." She was in awe as she saw her possible future in these designs.

The girls quieted themselves for a few moments longer until they became antsy. After going through the whole exhibit, they couldn't understand what they were still doing there. "Ugh can we go now?" Tiffany whined.

"I'm still looking. Gosh, you know you are so immature and inconsiderate." Tammie snarled.

"What else is there to see, Tammie? We already been through the whole thing." Tiffany pushed.

"You and Karissa can go wait outside. This is my trip too. It's not all about y'all try'na chase some boys. Dag, you don't see Cinnamon complaining."

Cinnamon stood nearby admiring a blazer that stood behind a glass case. She didn't see all that Tammie saw in the pieces, but she could tell being there was very important to her; so she didn't mind extending her patience. Part of her knew they probably should make the move to their next destination if they were to keep to their schedule and make it back on time. The other part wanted to somehow make up for Tammie's disappointment in not being able to tour the school like she'd planned.

Tired of the bickering and the unwanted attention they were attracting, Cinnamon stepped in to diffuse the situation. "Fifteen more minutes won't kill anybody. Karissa and Tiffany, if you're that bored just go wait outside. But we really shouldn't stay much longer than fifteen minutes if we're gonna make it back on time." She said, gently to Tammie.

Tammie sighed, "I know … I'm ready. Let's go." She said, sadly, while clutching the admissions applications in her fist.

The next stop would be Brownsville. Cinnamon could hardly contain herself as they rode the subway towards her old stomping grounds. She must've checked her beeper for the time five times, worried that the cousins she longed to see might not be home on a Saturday. She reminisced, staring down at the subway car floor of how she used to spend her Saturdays running the streets with her favorite cousins, Roxxy and Trae. Before the train could come to a complete stop, she'd popped up out of her seat to make her way towards the doors.

"C'mon," She instructed coolly. The others, who were fortunate to score seats this time, took their time getting up; Karissa and Tiffany reluctant to feel the pressure back on their aching feet.

Cinnamon could feel the butterflies in her stomach as she looked around cautiously before crossing the street to head to the tall, raggedy building that sat back one block just off of Eastern Parkway. A couple of young guys stood out front smoking.

"How y'all doin'?" The short one called out as they passed by. *Always the short ones try'na holler,* Cinnamon thought as she ignored his catcall. Karissa flashed a smile before she and Tiffany exchanged looks and shared a giggle. They hadn't even taken close inventory. They were just happy to have the attention of these New Yorkers.

"I see you smiling, sweetheart. Why don't'chu come on over here so I can get to know you better?" He baited.

"*Dang!*" The second one exclaimed as his eyes fell on Karissa's backside assets.

"Chill, B. That's 'bout to be all me right there. You can have one of the skinny ones." The short one said, staking his claim on Karissa.

"Nah, I want the one in the front. The one with the attitude. She actin' all stank now, but you know once I blow that back out, she gon' be blowin' my pager up all day!" He said, as he swung his hips forward and grabbed his crotch. "Let Qua take the skinny one. He like them stick figure broads." They all shared a laugh before Qua added his two cents.

"Don't mind if I do! *And they twins too?* Psshhh they can both get it … *at* the same time! 'Nah mean?" He lifted his fist in the air before bringing it down to pound the other two's fists as they shared more laughter. Tiffany and Karissa were amused, glancing back once more and giggling before heading through the entrance.

Cinnamon, not amused at all, led the way to the elevators. Tammie was either unamused as well, or just not even aware of what was going on, showing no emotion either way as she followed behind Cinnamon. The mint green tile that covered the lobby floor wore a film of dirt and mud across it, leaving not one tile untouched. *Ping!* The elevator doors slid open and two junkies, possibly a couple, came scurrying out on a mission, their eyes glazed over. Their backs hunched over as they spoke fast gibberish amongst themselves on their way out the door.

As soon as the girls stepped in, the aroma bum rushed them; overwhelming their senses to the point that they all had the same knee-jerk reaction, cupping their hands over their noses and mouths.

"Oh my God, what is that?" Karissa spoke through her cupped palm.

"Probably piss," Cinnamon answered nonchalantly. Although this wasn't where she and her mother ever lived, she was use to coming to this building on the regular basis to visit her family. The smell for her, while gagging, was also nostalgic. It felt like she'd been away for a lifetime instead of just a couple of months.

"*Piss?*" Tiffany suddenly sprung from the wall she'd been leaning on, looking around the small space for any signs of confirmation.

Cinnamon chuckled, "You wanted to see New York. Well, you're seeing it!"

They all took huge breaths of air once they vacated the elevator, but the hallway stench wasn't much better. It smelled stale of cigarettes and sweat. Cinnamon walked fast down the hall until she came to a corner apartment. She knocked on the door and waited. She could hear music blaring from inside. She gave another three knocks, this time more of a banging. Then the music cut down suddenly.

"Who is it?" Someone yelled from the other side.

"It's Cinnamon!"

"*Who?*" The person sounded unsure.

"Cinn-a-mon!" She yelled phonetically. Next the locks and chains could be heard being removed from the door.

"Oh snap! It's Cinnamon!" Her cousin, Petey, yelled towards the back of the apartment. He looked around at the other girls hesitantly before pulling her in for a hug. "Knockin' on the door like you the police! What'chu doing here, girl?"

Petey was older at twenty-six. Governing a life of crime, he was always fresh out of prison and always looked it with his swollen tatted arms. His big, broad stature muffled Cinnamon's response through his bear hug. "I'm here to see y'all!"

"What the f—you brought backup or something?" He joked, still trying to figure out who the other three strangers were that stood before him.

Cinnamon laughed, "No, these are my fri—these are some girls from the church we go to down in Delaware. That's Karissa and that's Tiffany and Tammie. We took the bus up. They never been to New York before so…"

"Oh, I see. I see."

"So you gon' let me in or what? Where's Roxxy and Trae?"

"Oh my bad, cousin. Of course, come on in. Y'all can have a seat on the couch." He said towards the girls. "Roxxy and Trae went over to Ke-Ke's. I'll call 'em for you if you want. You know they gon' be mad if they find out you was here, and they ain't get to see you."

"I know. I figured they'd probably be out running the streets, but I took a chance anyway."

"Yeah, you know ain't nothing changed there. Let me go call 'em." He said as he turned and headed for the kitchen. On his way he yelled, "Ma! Come're! Come see who came to visit us!"

The other three girls sat closely together in silence on the plastic covered couch. Their eyes darted in all directions as they silently judged the humble living area. Tiffany spotted a roach speeding up the wall and nudged Tammie's rib in a panic. They looked at each other with wide eyes, trying to decide what to do next.

"Cinnamon!" Tammie whispered. Cinnamon's eyebrows bore down in concern at the alarm in Tammie's voice. Tammie pointed to the roach and Cinnamon's face relaxed when she saw. She swiftly used the tip of her sneaker to pull off the heel of her other sneaker. Then she headed to the wall. *SPLAT!*

"That ain't nothing but a lil' ol' ro—"

"What is all that noise? Who is banging on my walls like—OH MY GOD!" Cinnamon's Aunt Valerie cut her off in her own surprise. "I know that is not my favorite niece!" She exclaimed.

"Hey Auntie," Cinnamon replied with a smile as she wiggled her foot back into her shoe.

"Girl get over here and give me a hug!" Cinnamon did as told. "Where's your momma?"

"Oh—uh, she's not here." Cinnamon hadn't thought this part of the plan through.

"Cinnamon, now you know you can't keep nothing from me. I been able to tell when you was hiding something ever since you was a lil' girl, the way your eyes start getting all big and wild. So just save me the song n' dance." She lifted one stern eyebrow.

"Well … my mom doesn't know I'm up here." She answered quickly. Aunt Valerie opened her mouth to share her disapproval, but before she could, Cinnamon began her plea. "Please don't tell her,

Auntie Val. Pleeeease."

"Now you know you my favorite niece, but you also know I ain't about to lie to my only sister. What'chu mean she don't know you up here? Cin, you know it's not safe for you to be here."

Cinnamon took one glance at the girls, who obviously wanted to know more about the reasons why. Then she gently grabbed her aunt's arm, guiding her out of earshot of them and dropping her tone to a whisper. "I know, Auntie, but it isn't lying if she don't know."

"Don't you even try that with me. You know the reason your momma don't want you up here is for your own safety." She scolded.

"I know, but I just missed y'all so much. I just wanted to see you ... and my cousins. It's not the same not having y'all around." Cinnamon tried to work some tears into her eyes to win her case.

Aunt Valerie turned her mouth to the side, not wanting to give in. "Aww, I know, honey. We miss you too, but you gotta be careful. Anybody find out you up here and—"

"They won't, Auntie. I promise. Please just don't tell my mom. We going back tonight anyway." She begged.

After a pause, Aunt Valerie crossed her arms, won over by her favorite niece's puppy dog face. "Fine, I won't tell her—unless she asks. I ain't lying to her if she directly asks me, but otherwise I won't let her know you were here."

"Oh, thank you thank you thank you, Auntie." Cinnamon squeezed her arms around her aunt's waist, planting kisses all over her face.

"Yeah yeah yeah, but just know if you get caught, that's your butt." She warned. "Now who is them stuffy looking girls you got planted on my couch like they ready to sprout roots?" She asked peering over Cinnamon's shoulders.

"Oh—oh I'm sorry, Auntie. That's Tammie, Tiffany, and Karissa. They go to the church we've been going to down in Gracious Meadows. This is my Aunt Val." The girls gave fake smiles and said their hellos.

"Roxxy and Trae gon' be so mad they missed you, Cin."

"Oh, Petey already told me they over at Ke-Ke's. He's calling them for me right now." She explained.

"Oh ... So tell me what's been going on. Fill me in on

Gracious Meadows. How's your momma doing? How y'all liking it down there? Y'all want something to eat? I think I got some leftover spare ribs and collards in there if you want me to heat it—"

"AAAAAAHHHHHH!!!!" Aunt Valerie's hospitality was cut short by Karissa's shrill scream. They turned to see her jump up with heels digging into the couch's plastic.

"Wh-what is it, chile?" Aunt Valerie asked.

"Oh my God, I think I just saw a rat! THERE IT IS!" She hollered. The two other girls saw it fly past this time and followed suit, digging their feet into the couch.

Aunt Valerie clutched her chest and let out a sigh of relief just as Petey ran into the room. "A rat? Girl that ain't nothing but a lil' ol' mouse. *It's* probably more afraid of *you* than you are of *it* with all that hollering!" She, Petey, and Cinnamon began to laugh hysterically as the three girls stayed crouched up in the couch wearing looks of horror. "Now, I know you're not used to the city and you're scared of the lil' thing, but y'all gon' have to get your feet off my couch, though." She said more seriously.

The girls retreated eventually but only after Petey went on a wild goose chase through the apartment to hunt the critter down and kill it, trapping it with a broom then stomping it with his construction boot. The girls sat nervously on the edge of the couch for the rest of the visit, refusing to partake in the delicious leftovers their hostess had offered. Cinnamon didn't let that stop her as she sat at the kitchen table chowing down.

"Ciniiiiii!" Roxxy ran into the kitchen, pouncing from behind, as she hugged her cousin with arms around the neck nearly choking her. She was so excited.

Cinnamon, mid-chew, dropped her fork and returned the hug the best she could from the way she was seated. "Roxxxxyyyy!" She slid her chair out and stood up excitedly just as cousin number two entered. "Traaaaaae! Oh my God, I missed y'all so much!"

Tracey and Roxxy were only eighteen months apart at fifteen and sixteen, respectively. The trio were a tight knit group, spending almost all their free time together from birth up until Cinnamon and Vivian left the state. The girls were more like sisters than cousins. The resemblance in their skin tones and features would also have any person believe they were sisters.

The girls started rambling non-stop and Cinnamon almost forgot all about Karissa, Tiffany, and Tammie sitting in the living room. It wasn't until the cousins invited her back to their bedroom that she remembered. All six girls crowded into the small room that was similarly decorated to Cinnamon's. The three didn't say much as they focused their attention to all the different posters that hung on the walls.

"I can't believe you're here. Girl, you missed so much! Let me tell you..." Roxxy started. "Chaos got shot over on Avenue A at Smitty's house party a couple weeks ago. Tasha found out that Martin was cheating on her with her little sister, Tianti. You know that lil' girl is only thirteen years old? Doing the nasty with her grown lil' self. Ashanti finally got them braces taken off, and girrrl ... all you see is gums now." She started to laugh. "She looked better before, in my opinion. Let me see ... what else you miss? Dag, it seems like you been gone so long. Trae what else happened?"

Tracey hesitated before responding while she thought. "Oh! Guess who's pregnant?"

"Oh yeah! Guess who's pregnant!" Roxxy repeated.

"Who?" Cinnamon asked.

"Girl, guess. You already know who." Tracey insisted.

"Don't tell me ... Meeka?"

"Yup! I told you before you left she looked pregnant to me. Remember? I should've put money on it ... Word!" Tracey said, confidently.

"Dannnng, you sure did say that. I can't believe it." Cinnamon said.

"Pshh! I don't know why not! You know she was letting mad dudes run trains on her like every other week. She don't even know who the father is." Roxxy added.

"Dang, that's messed up." Cinnamon said, shaking her head.

"I know right..." There was a pause of silence as the girls reflected on the news rundown. Then Roxxy continued, "So what's up with your friends? Y'all so quiet."

They weren't in Kansas anymore, and the trio seemed somewhat intimidated by Roxxy and Trae and their whole surroundings. No one rushed to give an answer, so Cinnamon did. "I don't know why they acting so quiet now. They ain't never this quiet at church." She challenged. "They never been to Brooklyn before—They never been to New York before, period. They saw a mouse and some roaches earlier. I think it got 'em a little shook." She joked.

"No, we just want to go out. Maybe talk to those guys that's out front." Tiffany said, defensively.

"*Guys*? What guys she talking 'bout, Cin?" Tracey asked.

"Oh, she talking 'bout Quan and some other dudes he was out there with." Cinnamon answered.

"You *know* them?" Karissa sounded almost star struck. Tracey and Roxxy looked at one another and burst into laughter.

"Look ma-ma, if y'all wanna meet some cuties we'll introduce you to some, but you don't want to talk to a bum like Quan. That's not a good look for you. Shoot, that's not a good look for *me* if y'all gon' be seen kickin' it with us."

"For real, though," Tracey cosigned.

"Cin, when you going back? Lil' Vicious gon' be at Empire tonight. Me, Trae, Ke-Ke, Tori 'n 'em is going. Everybody gon' be there. You down?" Roxxy asked.

"I don't know. We really gotta get back by a certain time."

"Oh, come on Cinnamon. We haven't really done anything fun since we been up here. We'll make it back in time. What's Empire?" Karissa asked.

"That's the skating rink. C'mon, Cin. We haven't kicked it in so long. We miss you, cuz." Tracey pleaded.

It didn't take much convincing, "Fine, but we have to be back to Port Authority by one o' clock, no later."

"Aight, bet!" Roxxy replied excitedly.

"Um, there's just one thing." Karissa spoke up.

"What's that?" Tracey asked.

"We not really dressed for the skating rink. We thought we would be able to work a little shopping in the trip."

"Ooh, yeah! I wanna go shopping!" This was the most Tammie had said since they'd left F.I.T.

"I don't know. That's cutting it close." Cinnamon said.

"We got time. It's still early. We can just go right to the

Boulevard. Plus, I could use some fresh Uptowns myself." Roxxy said.

"Okay, fine. If you really think we have enough time for all that." Cinnamon answered.

***

The loud "Ooh's" and "Ahh's" pouring from the Gracious Meadows crew was almost embarrassing. Once on the Boulevard, they wanted to go in every store and buy everything. Though they soon learned their money wouldn't stretch as far in this neck of the woods. They spent their money quickly but they insisted on torturing themselves by continuing to window shop. Roxxy and Tracey didn't seem to mind. Roxxy had already purchased the sneakers she came for. Yet the sisters continued to still exit each store with an additional article of clothing. Tiffany watched closely and quickly took notice that no money had been exchanged. She and Karissa knew all about shoplifting. They were pros around the Gracious Meadows Mall. She pulled her to the side and let her in on the game plan.

Cinnamon's beeper went off and when she checked it, a smile spread across her face. "Who's that?" Roxxy asked, noticing the smile.

"Nobody," Cinnamon said, coyly.

"Nobody, huh? Nobody got you all cheesing like that too?"

"Shut up; it's my boyfriend."

"*Boyfriend?* You done went down there and got a man and ain't tell nobody? Ooh you wrong, cousin."

"Shh," Cinnamon shot her eyes over to the other girls then back to her cousin.

"Oh, okay. I got'chu. Well you know you still gon' have to tell me all about it before you leave."

"I know. I know, but look. Since y'all still looking, I'ma go outside and call him."

"Aight, lovebird. Go call your man, girl." Roxxy teased.

Cinnamon had to walk down a couple of stores before she came to a payphone. She picked up the receiver and wiped it off with her sleeve before making the call.

"Cinnamon?" Raheem answered.

"Yeah, what's up?"

116

"You still in New York?"

"Yeah. Why, you miss me already?"

"You know I do, baby."

"I miss you too, but I'll see you tomorrow, right?"

"Of course. So what are you doing?" He asked.

"We're just doing some shopping right now. I'm waiting for them to get done. Karissa, Tiffany, and Tammie trying to buy the whole store with no money." She laughed.

"Wow. I still don't know why you hanging with them girls, especially after everything I told you about Karissa."

"I know, babe, but this was the only way I could get to see my cousins. I missed them so much."

"I still don't understand why your mom just couldn't take you."

"I already told you. She doesn't want to come back up here." That's all she told Raheem. She never went into detail as to why they not so much *shouldn't*, but *couldn't*, go back to New York.

"Well, just be careful up there with them girls. You know they're bad news."

"I knooooooow. Tammie isn't that bad, though. She came up here to check out a school."

"Yeah, well, birds of a feather—"

"RUUUUUUNNNNN!!!" Cinnamon's conversation was abruptly cut short when the girls came storming up the block like a wild herd. Roxxy yanked her by the arm as she screamed out the command. There wasn't time to protest.

"Hello? Hello? Cinnamon, you okay? Hello?" Raheem's voice could be heard blaring through the receiver while it swung back and forth.

CHAPTER 12

Back in Gracious Meadows John put all his best moves on Vivian. Though she'd only agreed to the day's events out of feelings of obligation. Tired of coming up with excuses not to go out with him, she figured one date wouldn't hurt. He was a nice guy, and he'd been so helpful to her and Cinnamon when they first got into town. They had only been on that first initial date before Pastor Leonards stole her attention. By now, she was growing weary of competing with Sister Connie for his attention when John was ready and willing, in fact, insisting she could have all of his.

They spent practically the entire day together. First they went to a small art studio in town where John arranged for a private pottery-making lesson for the two of them. Vivian actually enjoyed it up until the moment John attempted to reenact the scene out of the movie *Ghost*. She made it no secret that she was immediately turned off. Still, that didn't keep John from trying over the course of the day.

An expensive bottle of champagne was toasted over an early dinner. It was a most romantic setting at a five-star authentic French restaurant that sat on the water. The sunset view was something from a post card. Still, Vivian wasn't impressed. She couldn't see herself being serious with John. He just didn't have what she was looking for—whatever it was she was looking for.

Their last stop was a cozy lounge that boasted an extensive drink menu and live music. They moved in sync on the dance floor as the band covered the Top 40. John only had one drink. Vivian had three different cocktails, clearly forgetting she was in the company of a church-going man. She was ready to cut loose, but not as loose as John hoped.

As the band slowed it down, the pair slow danced to the musicians' rendition of 112's *"Cupid."* Vivian could feel a bulge rising as John pulled her hips in firmly to his. He planted a single kiss on her neck, but it was the feel of his palms slowly gliding down to Vivian's rotund backside that made her suddenly pull away.

"E-everything okay?" He asked in heat.

"I'm ready for you to take me home, John."

"Okay, no problem." An embarrassed look quickly swept over his face as his Adam's apple bounced up then back down.

They waited in silence for valet to pull his truck around. Once the drive began, more silence. *I blew it!* He thought, sadly. "Look, Viv, I'm sorry. I didn't mean to overstep my boundaries back there. It's just that I like you so much, and I'm really attracted to you." Vivian didn't say anything, so he continued. "Plus I don't normally drink and tonight with the champagne and then the cocktail … I guess I just read you wrong. I misjudged. I'm sorry."

Vivian kept her attention out the window. "Let's just forget it."

"I hope you're not too upset with me. Everything was going so well. Maybe we should've skipped the lounge, I guess."

"John, really, just forget it. You know we're friends, right?"

"Yeah," he replied, sadly.

"I'm really grateful to you for helping Cin and me out. I am." She paused before continuing to choose her words carefully. "But I'm not attracted to you in that way. I just want us to be friends. I'm sorry if I gave you the wrong impression."

Wrong impression? Of course you gave me the wrong impression! All that bending over and flirting, stopping by my store to bring me lunch. What the heck did you expect me to think? John clenched his jaw tight to keep from saying what he was thinking out loud. He gripped the steering wheel tightly, fighting back the anger and humiliation.

"John?"

"Oh—oh yeah," he tried to sound nonchalant. "Of course, I know that. Friends … Just friends."

"Good—Hey! I didn't know there was service at church tonight!" As they approached Greater Saints First Baptist Church along their route to Vivian's place, the building's lights caught her eye.

John squinted, "Hm, I didn't know either. There's not supposed to be anything going on tonight."

"Wait! Slow down. That's Pastor Leonard's truck!" Vivian got excited and John rolled his eyes. "Let's go in and see what's going on tonight." She suggested.

John took a deep breath and tried to hide his annoyance as he parked and turned off the engine. His head tilted to the side as if it were too heavy or he was too weary to hold it up. *That's all you care about is Pastor Leonards. Pastor Leonards didn't take you out, did he? Pastor Leonards didn't give you flowers, did he?* He mocked in a taunting voice inside his head as they headed to the entrance. Vivian smoothed back her hair and reapplied lip-gloss as she walked quickly in excitement.

John tried the front door, but it was locked. "Oh, well, maybe the Reverend is just doing some cleaning or studying."

"But I'm pretty sure that's Leon's truck right there. They're having something in there tonight, maybe a prayer meeting. What about the side door?" She suggested as she led the way around to the side of the building. It was dark on that side except for the little bit of light that peeked out from the basement window.

Oh, he's Leon now. John's hands were both balled into fists as his eyes burned holes of hatred into the back of Vivian's head. He looked over his shoulder towards the street to see if anyone was around. The anger was rising quickly. After all he'd done that day, all she could think about was Pastor Leonards. And here he was playing the sucker, following *her* lead. Who did she think she was? Slowly, he removed one of this clenched fists from a pocket and slowly brought it up as the venom pumped angry fire through his veins when Vivian suddenly spun around.

"You hear that?" She whispered.

John quickly scratched his head. "What?"

"Shh!" They both paused to listen in. "That. Hear it?" Music came from the basement. She pushed the side door open and John followed in behind her. They stood at the top of the basement steps where several voices could be heard. John's anger quickly subsided to confusion as they listened in before making their way down the steps. Pastor Leonards's laugh echoed up the steps and sudden outbursts of hoops and hollers ignited over the sound of Genuwine's *"Pony"* streaming from a boom box.

As soon as Vivian's feet were firmly planted on the basement floor, she recognized another voice as she turned the corner with John right on her heels. With jaws dropped and eyes popped, the sight displayed before them left them both speechless.

***

Panting out of breath, some doubled over, some sprawled across the subway seats, the girls didn't stop running until they were safely back on the train. Roxxy was visibly upset. Her chest pumped up and down heavily as she glared at Tiffany. She couldn't contain herself as she jumped up out of her seat and thrust her palms into Tiffany's chest.

"What's wrong wit'chu? You try'na get us all locked up?"

"I know you better get out of my face!" Tiffany shot back, catching her balance as she did. It was a wonder she and Karissa were able to keep up, running with those heels on, but they made it.

"Make me get out your face! Dummy!"

"Who you calling a dummy?" Now Tiffany was in Roxxy's face.

"*You*! Dummy!" Roxxy shoved her again, hard this time. Tiffany flew backward into a crowd of people who muttered and frowned in response.

Tammie had no choice but to defend her sister. "I know you got one more time to put your hands on my sister!" Now she was in Roxxy's face, no sign of fear present.

"Or what? You better back up 'cause I promise you don't want it with me!" Now Tracey joined the mix and it was two on one.

"Stop, y'all. Stop!" Cinnamon got between them. "Tammie, just go sit over there." Tammie stood, grounded and stone-faced. "Go 'head. *Please!*" It wasn't until Karissa intervened, grabbing Tammie to escort her to the other end of the car.

"What the heck happened?" Cinnamon asked with her face twisted.

"Dumb and Dumber over there got caught boostin' and almost

got us caught *with* them!" Tracey explained as she pointed out Tiffany and Karissa. "This idiot tried to walk out the store wearing a leather jacket and a pair of Jordans stuffed under her shirt. She didn't even bother to switch the tags on the jacket. Seriously, how stupid can you be?" She looked at Tiffany as if expecting a real answer. By this time the whole subway car looked at Tiffany who just rolled her eyes.

"And then the other one decides to lift two pairs of jeans with the safety alarm still on 'em!" Roxxy released a snicker of insanity. "We try to walk out and the alarm goes off. I'm looking at Trae like *'what's up?'* and she looking at me all confused like I messed up the operation. Security grabs the dingbat, and we both had to jump him to get him off her. That's when we all just ran."

"I didn't know the safety alarm was on 'em." Karissa finally spoke up. "Sorry," she said, sheepishly.

"I don't know what y'all do down there in the boondocks, but me and my sis got our thing on lock! Now we can't even go back there. You should've just told us what you had your eye on. We would've scooped it for you." Roxxy spoke like it was nothing. For them, it wasn't. They'd been boosting for as long as Cinnamon could remember. Cinnamon's Aunt Valerie is the one who showed them how to do it.

"Well, we steal from the mall all the time and never had any problems before." Tiffany's neck jerked back and forth as she spoke.

"Well, this ain't Great Meadows or wherever the heck y'all from!" Tracey jerked her neck in the same fashion.

"Wait a minute … y'all *steal?*" Cinnamon looked at the Gracious Meadows trio.

"Uh, *yeah!* Don't you?" Tiffany replied.

"Girl, please, this is Miss Goody Two Shoes you talking to right here. Cin knows the tricks of the trade but she don't get down like that." Roxxy explained.

"That's right! Never have, never will." Now Cinnamon jerked her neck and rolled her eyes in pride at all the girls. "I don't believe in taking what's not mine unless it's absolutely necessary. Unless it's for survival. And whatever happened to thou shalt not steal?" Again she looked to the Gracious Meadows girls for an answer. She already knew her family were crooks and criminals. She expected different from the church girls.

"Girl, please. I repent for my sins every night before I got to sleep." Karissa boasted. "Besides, God understands a sista can't pass up on the five-finger discount."

"Hello! I know that's right!" Now Roxxy broke into a smile and all the girls laughed except for Cinnamon and Tammie, who neither confirmed nor denied her participation in the sinful activity.

Once the girls made it back to the Brooklyn apartment, a primp and prep session started. The girls chattered excitedly as they picked out outfits to be worn that night from their selection of stolen goods.

"Now this is why y'all should've told us what you wanted in the store. Karissa, hand me them jeans you took so I can take the devices off." Tracey instructed as she whipped out a handheld sensor tag detacher.

Tiffany's eyes widened like she'd spotted gold. "Where'd you get that?"

"Pshh! This old thing? You don't have one? See y'all amateurs. Every good booster has to have a detacher in her snatch n' grab kit."

"What's a snatch n' grab kit?" Karissa, Tiffany, and Tammie all asked in unison.

"You need this, a medium sized pocketbook—you don't want a big ol' duffle bag that'll draw attention but you want one just big enough to stuff a couple small items in, a baggy, oversized sweat suit— one that you can fit at least 2-3 layers under, and a couple of big-face counterfeit bills. That's in case one of the workers starts eyeing you or even calls your bluff. You take one of the items to the counter and make a big deal of waving around the big-face bills to show that you don't need to steal anything. And dark shades and a hat just in case they catch you on camera later on."

"Dang, how do you know all this?" Karissa asked in amazement as she fingered a pair of stolen earrings in the palm of her hand.

"We learned from the best. Mommy!" Roxxy called down the hall to their mother's room.

Aunt Valerie came floating into the room on her own personal cloud, her eyes low and bloodshot as she puffed on a blunt. "What's up?"

"We was telling them about our snatch n' grab kit. You know they almost got us caught today? Security was chasing us down the street!" Roxxy laughed.

"What'chu mean you almost got caught? That ain't funny, Roxxy!" Aunt Valerie looked worried. "Told you already, you get caught there's no money to bail your lil' tails out!" She lifted a brow and pointed the blunt that was pinched between two fingers towards her girls.

"Calm down, Mommy. Obviously we didn't get caught. We learned from the best. Remember?" Tracey flashed a smile and Aunt Valerie returned it.

"Yup, you sure did. I been boosting since I was younger than y'all. Cin knows. Her momma used to be right with me."

"*Aunt Val,*" Cinnamon hissed in a hushing whisper.

"What? They don't know your momma got sticky fingers? Let me find out she done went down there and changed."

"She *has,*" Cinnamon said with a hint of attitude. She didn't like airing the Mackey laundry in front of these girls. They didn't need to know anything about her or her mother's past as far as she was concerned.

"Yeah, right. I know my sister, but if you say so ... I'm sorry, didn't mean to spill the beans. This some strong stuff right here. You know I ain't thinking straight, baby." Smoke leapt out of her mouth as she spoke.

"Mommy, let me hit that." Roxxy extended her hand with her fingers pinched.

"Here, take it. I'm ready to cool out. Y'all going to the rink tonight?"

"Yeah," Roxxy answered as she inhaled.

"Alright, see y'all later." Aunt Valerie said, as she sashayed out of the room with her robe flowing behind her.

"Your mom smokes weed *and* lets you smoke it too?" Tammie asked in disbelief.

"Yeah, of course." Tracy replied matter-of-factly as she took the blunt from her sister's fingers for her turn. It didn't take long for the small room to get cloudy.

Cinnamon coughed, "Ugh, that stinks. I don't know how you

smoke that stuff."

"You want a pull?" Tracey held it out towards her cousin. Cinnamon waved her hand and shook her head. "You?" She gestured towards Tiffany.

"Yeah!" She said, excitedly. She took the blunt in her fingers like she'd been smoking for years. Not too soon after her initial inhale, smoke came zooming right back out of her virgin lungs as she coughed heavily, barking as her eyes watered. Roxxy and Tracey both laughed, as their eyes turned to light pink.

"You never smoked before, huh?" Roxxy asked. Tiffany shook her head and pounded her chest as she continued to cough. "You gotta take it in slowly and easily, not too fast or it'll burn. Then hold your breath a second and let it back out slowly." Tiffany gave it another try and found herself coughing again; though not as much this time. Next Karissa, and even a curious Tammie, took their turns, having the same knee jerk reaction. The room was full of smoke and coughing virgin lungs. Cinnamon, catching contact, began to laugh at the scene.

By the time the blunt had been passed around a couple more times, the group was mellow, dressed to impress, and ready to head out. They met up with Ke-Ke and a few more of Cinnamon's old friends from the neighborhood. The pack was thick as they took their time strutting to the subway and someone else lit another blunt that was passed around. Cinnamon still refused, but the other three girls continued to indulge as they enjoyed their little field trip.

The line ran long alongside of the building. Teen girls from all over Brooklyn were anxious to see the reggae artist, especially the Jamaicans from Flatbush. They proudly wore their flags in different ways, displaying their patriotism. The cold weather didn't stop them from wearing their pum-pum shorts either.

"Oh my gosh. Look at this line. We'll never get in." Tammie quietly said to her sister.

"Don't worry. We ain't even about to stand in this ridiculous line. Trae, go see if Bobby is working tonight." Roxxy instructed her sister.

Bobby was one of the security guards that worked the door. He'd dated Aunt Valerie for a while, and even though they'd long since broken up due to his cheating, he still held a torch for her. He'd do anything to get her back and stay in her good graces, including getting her daughter and her large group of friends into the skating rink.

The speakers blared Chaka Demus & Pliers as soon as the girls walked in. The place was packed, on and off the floor. Teenagers were flying past in a whirlwind. The lights were low, making it hard to see. Even though she wasn't high like the rest of the group, Cinnamon felt herself relaxing quickly. She felt a sense of nostalgia at home in her old stomping grounds. It wasn't long before her beeper started to vibrate. It was Raheem again. After the fast break from the Boulevard she'd completely forgotten to call him back so he'd know she was okay.

"Hey, I'm gonna go use the payphone right quick. Get me a size eight!" She yelled over the music into Roxxy's ear, who nodded in return. She left the group there, then headed to a dark corner where a phone booth stood.

"Cinnamon!" Raheem answered in a panic.

"Hey, Raheem. Sorry, I forgot to call you back." She shouted into the phone over the music.

"Where are you? What is all that noise? Are you okay?" He fired off the questions.

"I'm okay. I'm okay. I'm with my cousins and the girls at the skating rink."

"The skating rink? Cinnamon, I thought something happened. Why'd you just hang up like that before? I been worrying like crazy!" He sounded annoyed.

"I know. My bad, baby. I had to run. Security was chasing us and there wasn't time to talk. I'm sorry. But everything is fine now."

"Security? Why was security chasing you?" He demanded to know.

"I can't get into it right now. I'll tell you when I get back. I don't have a lot of minutes on the phone, you know."

"Fine. As long as you're sure you're okay. When are you coming back? You guys are gonna get caught." He cautioned.

"No, we're not. My mom thinks we're all spending the night at Karissa's and her mom is out of town at a conference. It'll all be fine. Stop worrying."

"Alright, Cinnamon, but don't say I didn't warn you about them girls."

"Okay, father." She mocked jokingly.

"Well, have fun skating—but not *too* much fun."

"Okay, bye."

"Later."

By the time Cinnamon returned, all the girls were already out on the floor skating. A group of boys surrounded them, flirting. You could tell from a far that Tiffany and Karissa were eating it up. Roxxy waited nearby for Cinnamon with her skates in hand.

"Girl, why your friends act like they ain't never been nowhere?" She asked.

"Number one, they are not my friends. They're just people I know from church. And number two, because they haven't." She joked and the two shared a laugh.

Once they made it out on the floor to join the herd of girls, the party was in full swing. The DJ played all the best dancehall in honor of their featured artist for that evening. By the time Lil Vicious hit the floor for his performance, there was standing room only. The die-hard Jamaican fans bum rushed the area, swarming like bees to honey. He performed his hit, *"Freaks"*, and the crowd went wild. People had removed their skates and were winding and gyrating all over each other. Girls were bent over. Some were on the floor doing crazy headstands. The hormonal teen boys took full advantage of the scene, grinding against the under-aged and underdressed girls at every opportunity.

Tammie, Tiffany, and Karissa's eyes looked like they would pop out of their heads. They clearly had never witnessed such a scene, but they found it all exciting and amusing. A few of the guys from earlier found their way behind them, joining in on the grind session. Tammie stepped to the side, unsure of herself and the music itself. Tiffany and Karissa took it as their moment to shine, giving their best attempts at winding. Ke-Ke nudged Cinnamon and directed her attention at the girls. She couldn't help but laugh, but she was happy the girls were getting what they wanted—male attention.

Once Lil Vicious's performance came to an end, a few of the girls found themselves paired off with their new male interests, including Roxxy, Karissa and Tiffany. They went to sit on some benches and get better acquainted. Tracey, Ke-Ke, Tammie, and

Cinnamon returned to the floor to skate. The girls were having a good time, laughing it up, and weaving in and out of traffic. At one point a boy bumped hard into Cinnamon, almost making her fall. He gave a quick evil glance before turning around and flying off into the crowd. Cinnamon thought she recognized him, but wasn't sure since she'd only caught a profile of a glimpse. Shrugging him off as an ill-mannered rude boy, she continued skating.

Cinnamon looked over to still see the girls sitting on the bench. Tiffany, enjoying a slurpee, grinned as she talked to a boy with gold teeth. His friend had his arm swung around Karissa. Their friends stood and sat nearby talking amongst themselves and trying to talk to every girl that walked by. Roxxy stood leaning over the rink wall as she and her male companion watched the skaters fly by. It wasn't until about her eighth time around, when Tammie tugged on her elbow, that Cinnamon noticed that the scene had changed.

"You see Tiff?" Tammie asked, yelling over the music.

Once they made it back around to where the girls had been, Cinnamon could see Karissa and Roxxy but Tiffany wasn't there. "No, where she go?"

"I don't know. That's why I'm asking."

"Trae, you see Tiffany over there? We don't see her?" Now the three girls were linked elbow-to-elbow, slowing down their pace as they came around to approach the spot again.

"No, don't see her. There's Roxxy, though."

"I'm getting off to go find her." Tammie notified them.

"Hold up, let's just tell Ke-Ke n'em and we'll come with you." Tracey suggested.

After notifying the rest of the gang of their departure from the floor, the trio exchanged their shoes and made their way over to Karissa and Roxxy. Karissa, preoccupied with the tongue that was down her throat, barely noticed them.

"Dang, Karissa. You ain't waste no time! Where's my sister?" Tammie interrupted.

"She went to the bathroom." Something about Karissa was different. Most of the girls were coming down from their weed high, but there was something about the way the words slowly rolled from her mouth and the glassy look of her eyes. The guy she was with openly had his hand up her shirt and hadn't bothered to remove it, continuing to caress her breast in front of everyone. She didn't seem bothered either.

"Karissa!" Tammie lightly pushed her friend's shoulder. "What's wrong with you, girl? You letting that boy feel you all up in public!"

"Oh, calm down, Tammie. Why you always overreacting?" The words continued to drip from Karissa's mouth like thick caramel.

"Yeah, chill out, shorty. Your sister is with my mans. Don't worry. She in good hands." He had the same glassy look as he chuckled.

"Oh shoot, Cin, they done took one of them E pills." Tracey informed them, studying the pair closely. Her face and voice hinted that there was cause to worry.

"E pill? What's an E pill?" Tammie demanded.

"Yeah, what is that? I never heard of that before." Cinnamon looked just as confused.

"Ecstasy. They call it a hug drug or something. Basically it makes you wanna feel everybody up and have sex with anything moving—or *not* moving, whatever." Tracey quickly educated them.

Roxxy saw the concern on their faces and walked over, leaving her gentleman friend behind. "What's up?"

"These fools done gave this girl Ecstasy. Look at her." Tracey pointed at Karissa, who had returned to her tongue wrestling session as if the rest of the world around her was non-existent.

"I'm going to find my sister." Tammie said.

"Come on. I'll go with you. I gotta use the bathroom anyway." Tracey said, before the pair walked off.

"Karissa," Cinnamon tried to get her attention.

"Mmmm," she moaned in response and continued her mission.

"*Karissa!*" Cinnamon threw a little more authority in her voice for the second try to no avail.

"Cin, watch out." Roxxy commanded as she stepped around her cousin and grabbed Karissa by the arm. "Excuse me, we need to borrow this one for a minute." She notified the boy as she forced Karissa up onto her feet.

"Wh-what's wrong? Cinnamon, what's wrong? Tiffany said

she's coming right back. She just went to take a leak. Geesh!" Karissa reached out to Roxxy with a smile and stroked her hair. "You have really pretty hair. You know that? It's so ... so ... *hairy.*" She giggled.

"Oh Lord, I knew this was a mistake. How am I gonna take her back home like this?" Cinnamon began to worry.

"Relax, cuz, it'll wear off by tomorrow. Just get her home and into be—"

POP! ... POP! POP! ... POP! Before Roxxy could finish her sentence bullets began flying past them and bounced off the table right in front of them.

"Oh sweat! RUN!" Roxxy shouted and grabbed both girls by the hand as the shots continued.

POP! POP! POP! Screams and shouts could be heard along with the music now as the packed rink quickly turned to chaos. Everywhere you looked, bodies were ducking and running. Some dropped to the floor and froze behind objects of obstruction. Some tripped over ankles in front or next to them and were trampled by the frightened mob of teenagers. Roxxy held on tight to Cinnamon and Karissa's wrists as they ran, and the shots seemed to follow them.

She only let go when one landed in her shoulder. "OOOH!" She groaned loudly as she grabbed her arm.

"Oh my God! Roxxy!" Cinnamon stopped for a brief moment, but not a second too long because the shots continued coming right at her.

"KEEP RUNNING!" Roxxy yelled and followed her own advice, keeping up closely behind them, still squeezing her shoulder while she tried to block out the pain.

Cinnamon did as told. POP! POP! The shots continued, but she and Karissa didn't stop until they were outside with the rest of the patrons. It wasn't until then that she realized Roxxy was no longer behind them.

"Roxxy! Roxxy!" Cinnamon called out as she searched the crowd frantically. Karissa stood frozen as people bumped and shoved past her while she remained in her state of intoxication. "Stay here. Don't move." She grabbed Karissa by both of her shoulders and spoke into the eyes of an empty shell.

Realizing Roxxy was nowhere to be found outside, Cinnamon

tried to push her way against the traffic to get back in. It was a struggle. By the time she made it back in, she wasn't given much time to look for Roxxy before her arm was being yanked by Tammie.

"Oh my God! Cinnamon, it's Tiffany! She's hurt bad. Hurry up!" Tammie had tears smeared across her cheeks and she hurried Cinnamon along to the men's bathroom. There, they found Tracey cradling the half-conscious head of Tiffany in her lap. She'd been beaten badly, her face bruised and swollen. One shoe was on, the other strewn inside one of the stalls. Her jeans had been pulled down with one pant leg completely off and her panties torn almost to shreds. She wore no shirt and no bra. The bathroom was crowded with onlookers, some that were already in there and the other half who'd run in for cover from the shooting.

CHAPTER 13

"*Vivian! Brother John!*" Pastor Leonards was clearly taken by total surprise when he leapt up off of the chair he'd been sitting in. He quickly grabbed his jeans from the floor, covering his half naked body.

Gabe, who'd been giving some sort of strip show/lap dance, spun around quickly, frozen like a deer in headlights. Dressed in all black leather, he wore cowboy boots with spurs on the back of the heels, chaps with his small cheeks displayed where the fabric was missing, a vest with matching shingles dangling along the sides, and a cowboy hat. The pair wasn't alone. Sister Kim's husband, Deacon MoMoney, lay sprawled out completely nude on an air mattress with another young boy's head positioned between his legs. The boy, also from the church, wore a bright neon pink speedo and white tube socks.

"Gabe!" Vivian was shocked and disgusted at the same time. John scoffed and turned away, squeezing his eyes shut as though just the very sight would blind him eternally.

"It-it's not what it looks like! It's not what you think!" Pastor Leonards exclaimed.

"It's *exactly* what it looks like from what I can see. What is wrong with you? These are *children*." Vivian scolded.

"It's okay, Sister Vivian. They didn't force us … We wanted it." Gabe timidly defended.

Vivian almost lost her dinner. "No, this is *not* okay, Gabe. You don't know what you're saying or what you're doing. Pastor Leonards,

Deacon MoMoney, y'all need to be ashamed. Straight to hell is where you're going! Gabe, go put some clothes on! We're taking you home— and you too, whatever your name is." She instructed both boys.

"No, please! Please don't tell my mom and dad about this, Sister Vivian. Please, you don't know what they'll do to me." Gabe pleaded.

"Can't be no worse than what the pastor is doing to yo—" She was cut off by the sound of her beeper. She dismissed it, momentarily wondering who the unfamiliar number was. "Gabe, get your stuff. This isn't up for discussion." She said, sternly.

"No, I don't have to listen to you." He shot back.

Before Vivian had the chance to respond, John stepped in, opening his eyes while cringing. "Boy, this ain't up for discussion! You better be lucky I don't come over there and go upside your head! I'm positive your daddy wouldn't mind at all. You heard Sister Vivian, get your stuff!"

"Now just hold on a minute, Brother John," Pastor Leonards held a hand up in protest.

"Ain't nobody ask you nothing, Leon. You better just shut your mouth before I come over there and shut it for you. You lucky I have respect for the house of the Lord. Otherwise, you and the deacon would've been had my foot up your behinds two minutes ago. Messing with these little boys … Sick perverts! That's what you are!" With that, Pastor Leonards swallowed hard in embarrassment and backed off.

Vivian's beeper went off a second time. Once again, she dismissed it, preoccupied with the matter at hand. Once back inside of John's van, everyone was silent except for Vivian.

"I can't believe them. Pastor Leonards, especially." She said out loud in disgust as she looked out the window with a strain on her face. "How did I not see this?" She spoke to herself. "Gabe, how long has this been going on?"

"I dunno," he mumbled.

"Oh, *you don't know.*" She mocked with dissatisfaction. "John, maybe we should go to the police and just call their parents to meet us there."

John coolly dismissed the idea. "Let's just get them home to their parents. Let them decide how they want to proceed. I think that's best."

"Yeah, I guess you're right ... I just can't believe this."

Vivian's beeper went off three more times by the time they arrived at the Grienbachs's residence. As the four of them stood on the porch waiting, Gabe shuffled back and forth nervously. Clearly frightened of the repercussions that were to come, he saw his opportunity and dashed from the porch in an attempt to escape his fate.

"Wh-what—" John didn't bother to finish his thought as he took off down the street after him. Gabe didn't make it far before John caught him by the back of his collar and wrestled him down to the lawn of a neighboring home.

"Get off of me, Brother John! Get off! Let me go!" Gabe screamed and tussled wildly, trying to free himself.

"Now, just relax. Just calm down! Boy, what's the matter with you?" John said, breathlessly.

"You don't know. You don't understand! He'll kill me when he finds out! He'll kill me!"

By now, First Lady Grienbachs joined the other two on the porch as she looked out into the dark to see her son in John's grip. "Sister Vivian? Is everything alright? What's going on here?"

"Sorry to stop by so late, but I think we'd all better go inside." She said with her arm around the other boy. She didn't want to take a chance of losing him too. "John! Everything okay?" She called over to the wrestling pair.

"Yeah! Yeah, don't worry! I got 'em!" He called back as he let up off of Gabe, helping him to his feet while still keeping a good grip. "Now just settle down. Nobody's gonna kill you, boy! Let's just go on in and sit down and talk about this. That Pastor Leonards is the one at fault here. You hear me?" He shook Gabe by the arm as he reluctantly walked with his captor. The words floated off into nowhere as Gabe looked down at the sidewalk in despair.

Once inside the cluttered house, First Lady Grienbachs ushered them all to a seat on the couch. "Harold, Gabe, you boys wanna tell me what this is all about? Gabe, were you over there fighting Brother John?"

"No, I wasn't fighting Brother John, Mom. I just—"

"First Lady, is the reverend here? I think he better be here for this." John cut in. Gabe immediately clenched up.

"Well, yeah, he's upstairs watching TV. Generosa, go get your dad." She instructed Generosa who'd nosily planted herself on the base of the stairs once she heard all the commotion.

It was clear that Reverend Grienbachs wasn't thrilled about being disturbed from his program. "What's all this noise down here? What's going on?" His voice boomed as he trotted down the steps, each foot met with a creak beneath the stairs. He wore a white tank top that pronounced his enlarged belly with a pair of loose khakis.

"Hi, Reverend Grienbachs. Sorry to bother you." Vivian started.

"Sister Vivian. Oh, Brother John! Good to see you! How are you?" His mood seemed to momentarily cheer once he noticed John was there.

"Reverend! Always good to see you. Sorry it has to be under unfortunate circumstances this time." He stood to shake the reverend's hand.

"Unfortunate circumstances? What kind of unfortunate circumstances?"

Gabe seemed to shrink three sizes right before everyone's eyes as he avoided eye contact with his father, slouching down into his spot on the couch.

"And don't I know you? Brother Washington's boy, ain't'cha?" He asked the other boy.

"Yes, sir."

"Honey, you remember Harold. Don't you?" First Lady Grienbachs said with a worried smile.

"Harold! Oh yeah! Right. Right. Of course I remember, Moni. That's why I just said that, woman." He said sternly. "So what's all this about?"

Vivian and John glanced at each other, deciding telepathically who should start. "Well, uh, Reverend, there's no easy way to say this." John began. "Vivian and I were out together this evening, and we happened to ride past the church and noticed the lights were on and—"

"Y'all two still courtin'? Aww, ain't that so precious." The reverend mocked.

John smiled, embarrassed by the reverend's teasing and Vivian's earlier declaration that they were definitely not courting. "Well, you know, we're just good friends hanging out on a Saturday night." Vivian looked at him with wide eyes, wanting him to get to the reason they were there. "But anyway, like I said, we rode past the church. Saw the lights on—"

"Lights on? Ain't nothin' going on over there tonight. Is there, Moni?" The reverend cut John off again in confusion.

"No, there's nothing on my calendar for tonight."

"Right. Exactly. That's why we stopped. You know, to make sure everything was on the up and up and ..." John paused, unsure how to continue.

Vivian's beeper went off again, and she silenced it. She sat up on the edge of her seat. "Well, Reverend, we went on in down to the basement. And that's when we found Gabe and ... Harold?" She looked towards the boy with a question mark to confirm she had the right name.

As though she knew where the conversation was headed, First Lady Grienbachs's face turned to worry as she looked at her son. Reverend Grienbachs's face turned ice cold as he glared at him too. "Well, what do you have to say for yourselves? What were you doing down there, Gabe? You know you're not supposed to be in there playing around." He scolded.

Gabe opened his mouth to say something, but Vivian continued, "They were down there with Pastor Leonards and Deacon MoMoney."

Now the reverend's face looked confused and surprised. "Pastor Leonards? He didn't tell me he had anything planned for tonight. Hmm."

"Well, when we found them all down there, they were engaging in some very inappropriate behavior." Vivian chose her words carefully.

"Inappropriate behavior? What that mean?" The reverend demanded.

"*Sexual* behavior?" Vivian said it as a suggestion.

"SEXUAL BEHAVIOR!" The reverend blurted out and

Generosa gasped quietly from her seat on the steps. Now he looked like a raging bull waiting to be let from its pen.

"Na-uh, Dad! I wasn't doing anything." Gabe whined in a girl-like voice.

"Well, Harold and the deacon were engaging in sexual activity. Gabe was …" She trailed off.

"Was what?" The reverend demanded again.

"He was … *dancing* … in a sexy costume in a sexual way for Pastor Leonards. And Pastor Leonards had no pants or underwear on."

The reverend froze. Vivian tried to make out which way his mood might be headed. She couldn't tell if he was shocked, embarrassed, hurt, angry, or what. It was as though the reverend had checked out of his own body completely as he stood stone faced. Vivian's beeper went off again and that called him back to the scene at hand.

"Can't you shut that thing off!" He blurted at Vivian loudly. Everyone in the room jumped. Gabe was a nervous wreck trying to predict his father's next move. Tears began to run down his face.

"I-I'm sorry. It's been going off all night. Can I use your phone please?"

"Sure," First Lady Grienbachs said as she motioned towards the kitchen for Vivian to use that phone.

"Thank you."

As she picked up the phone, she could hear the reverend come to life. "So you wanna be a lil' dancer, huh? That's what you like? You like shaking your tail for other men?" His eyes were slits as he spoke.

"No," Gabe's voice droned in fear.

"No? Well you must do. You were down there shaking your little tail feather in our church basement. Weren't you?" Gabe sniffled in return. "Well? Weren't you?"

In the kitchen, Vivian dialed the New York number that had been blowing up her beeper all evening. The phone rang quite a few times before Cinnamon's voiced could be heard through sobs on the other end.

"Mommy? Is this you?"

"Cinnamon? Yeah, it's me. Are you crying? Where are you calling me from?" Vivian had a million questions.

"Mooommmmy! I'm so sorry I didn't listen. I'm so sorry, Mommy. Can you please come get meeee?" Cinnamon didn't sound like the fifteen-year-old that had left her house that morning. To Vivian, she sounded more like her five-year-old from years ago.

"What's wrong, Cinnamon? What's going on? I can barely understand you. Where are you?"

Cinnamon cried into the phone more before she got her words together. "They shot Roxxy, Mommy. Roxxy's dead!" Now she sobbed uncontrollably.

"*Roxxy?* Girl, what are you talking about? You're gonna have to calm down. I can't understand you if you keep crying, Cinnamon. Now where are you?" She repeated.

"Ki-Kings County Hospitalllll. Can you please come get us?"

"*KINGS COUNTY HOSPITAL?*" Vivian's voice came out louder than she'd expected. That caused John to spring up to her aid in the kitchen. "Cinnamon, you're in New York?"

"Yeeessss. I'm so sorry, Mommy. I'm sorry. Please come get us. Please!"

"*Us?* Who the heck is *us*, Cinnamon?"

"Meeee, Karissaaa, Tiffany, and Tammie. They hurt Tiffany real bad too, Mommy. I'm soooo sorry. This is all my fault." Her face was wet on the other end of the phone.

"Karissa, Tiff—Oh my God, Cinnamon. What were y'all thinking? I can't believe you go behind my back and sneak up there, knowing we can't be seen up there. And you got them girls up there with you? What were you trying to do?"

John mouthed the words, "What is it?" Vivian shrugged with her face distorted and hands frozen in the air.

"I knooowwww. Please, please just come get us. *PLEASE!*" Cinnamon's voiced squeaked at the end of her last plea. All types of emotions whirled inside of Vivian at once. It tore her apart to hear how terrified her only baby was, and she was miles away, unable to do anything to protect her. The other part of her was confused and angry that she had even gone up there.

"Okay, I'm coming right now. Stay right by that phone and don't you move. You hear me, Cinnamon? Don't even move to go pee! Are there police up there?"

"Yes."

"Well, you stick close, but if they start asking questions, you don't say a word about anything at all. *Nothing*, Cinnamon. You understand me?"

"Yeeessss."

"And you tell them other girls the same thing. Y'all say *nothing!*"

"Okaaayyy, we won't, Mommy."

"Okay, I love you. I'm leaving right now." She hung up and breathed deeply. Her adrenaline kicked in and her heart pounded.

"What's wrong, Viv? What's going on?" John was genuinely concerned by her change in demeanor.

"Cinnamon went up to New York without my permission. She's in trouble. I have to go get her. I gotta get my baby right now!" She started to fume and weep from the anguish of being so far away.

John wrapped his arms around her and rubbed her back. "It's okay. I'll take you up there right now. Don't worry. Everything's gonna be fine. Okay?" Vivian broke the embrace, her face red and flustered as she shook her head. She wiped the tears from her eyes before reentering the living room.

"I'm so sorry, Reverend, First Lady Grienbachs. That was Cinnamon trying to reach me. She's in trouble in New York. I gotta go get her."

"*New York?*" First Lady Grienbachs sounded surprised.

"Yeah, that's exactly what I said. I specifically told her that she is not to go up there. Apparently, her and a couple of the other girls from the church decided to mosey on up there anyway." Generosa gasped again. This time everyone turned their attention towards her.

"Generosa, you didn't know anything about this. Did you?" The first lady questioned with a raised eyebrow. She didn't answer right away, but the guilty look on her face gave her away.

"Generosa, honey, please. If you know anything about them going up there, please tell me. Trust me, you can't get them in anymore trouble than they're already in." Vivian pleaded with her eyes.

"Karissa, Tiffany, and Tammie asked her to take them up there to show them around. Tammie wanted to look at some fashion school up there, and Tiffany and Karissa wanted to meet boys or something. They didn't invite me." She said, solemnly, as she looked down into her lap.

"Well, be glad they didn't. Trust me. You're better off safe in your own house." Vivian reassured her.

"You knew about this and didn't bother to tell anyone?" First Lady Grienbachs scolded.

"I didn't want them to get mad at me for telling." She responded quietly.

"You know we do not keep secrets in this house. Now those girls are up there in trouble, and all of this could've been avoided had you spoken up. Go upstairs. I can't look at you right now." The First Lady said.

"I'm sorry!" Generosa cried before storming up the stairs.

"Really, don't be too hard on her. She had nothing to do with it. Cinnamon has a mind of her own. She should've told those girls no. But anyway, I'm so sorry to drop this news on you like this and run. Let me know if you need me to make a formal statement to the police about what I saw or anything."

"No, we don't need you making any statements to anybody. We're gonna handle this from here. Seems like everybody in this house has secrets. Well, we're gonna get to the bottom of them all tonight. You can be sure about that!" The reverend snarled, never taking his eyes off of Gabe.

As John and Vivian made their way out, she could hear the reverend. "Harold, you go call your father to come get you. Gabe, you get down to the basement and wait for me. You wanna dance, huh? We'll see about that!"

CHAPTER 14

The ride to New York was a quiet one that seemed to take forever. *Oh my God, he drives like a grandpa*, Vivian thought, anxious to get to Cinnamon. Unable to sit still, she tapped her fingers along the door's handle. *Roxxy's dead.* Cinnamon's voice played again and again in her mind. Though the reality hadn't set in. She needed to get to the hospital and see for herself.

John let Vivian out at the entrance of King's County Hospital while he drove around to look for parking. After getting the information from the front desk, she took off to the elevators that took her up to the fourth floor where the Intensive Care Unit was. She burst through the double doors calling out, "Cinnamon! Cinni? Where are you, baby?"

"Ma'am," one of the nurses behind the desk began an attempt to assist Vivian.

"Mommy!" Cinnamon sprung up from the hard chair in the waiting area in the hall. She rushed into her mother's arms with a stream of tears flowing.

"Oh my God, Cinnamon. Are you okay? Are you okay?" Vivian asked as she pushed Cinnamon back to arm's length to look her daughter over.

Cinnamon nodded before Vivian pulled her back in close. "Roxxy's dead, Mommy. They shot Roxxy. They killed her." She spoke as if in a trance.

"Shh! Not another word, Cin." Vivian hushed Cinnamon quickly as her eyes darted about the hallway to see if anyone had heard. "Where is she?" She whispered.

"Excuse me, are you family?" A nurse approached.

"Yes, can you tell me where Roxanne Hurrane is? I'm her aunt."

"Oh," The nurse's eyes were apologetic. She switched to a whisper as she gently pulled Vivian away from Cinnamon, walking her towards a small hospital room. "I'm so sorry. We did everything we could, but she was already gone when she got here." They stopped in the doorway. Vivian could see Tracey sitting next to the bed where her sister lay, talking to her corpse. "She's been like this for a while. We can't release the body until we locate the next of kin, but we can't get the poor thing to let go so we can move her to the morgue. One of the nurses tried to escort her from the room, and she had a wild fit, gave her a bloody lip. Maybe you could talk to her?"

Vivian nodded as she inched into the room. Her lip quivered and water filled her eyes seeing Roxxy's lifeless body lay there, eyes closed. "Hi, Tracey" she coaxed.

Tracey's eyes slowly drifted up to meet Vivian's, her hand tightly grasped around Roxxy's. "Hey, Auntie Viv. What'chu doin' here?" She said it casually and almost cheerily.

"I'm here for you ... and Roxxy." She hesitated.

"You hear that, Roxxy? Auntie Viv done came way up here from the boondocks to take us home. So you gotta wake up, sis. You gotta get up." She shook the hand she was holding lightly, then swiftly rubbed her other hand over her sister's forehead. "She don't feel good, Auntie. She won't move. She won't get up."

"I know, honey." Vivian moved slowly towards her niece, sniffling as tears rushed her cheeks.

"She won't get up, Auntie. Why won't she get up?" It was as though Tracey had turned into a little girl overnight, incapable of understanding that her sister was dead. "I keep talking to her, telling her to get up, it's time to go, but she don't say anything back. You think she mad at me again, auntie?"

"No," Vivian's response came out a choked whisper.

"You know when we was younger, my mom used to make me

and Roxxy braid each other's hair. She hated braiding my hair 'cause she used to say it was too nappy, and I didn't sit still good. But how could I sit still? It used to be hurting." She chuckled, a glob of clear snot slowly glided down from one nostril. Her eyes were wild and dazed. "So Mommy would say *'get the comb and go wake sissy up to braid your hair.'* I would go in the room and Roxxy would just lay there, pretending to be sleep. I knew she wasn't sleep, though, 'cause I could see her eyes moving around under her eyelids, you know?" She paused for Vivian's response and Vivian nodded with a tight-lip smile. "So you know what I would do? I would go to the bottom of the bed and tickle her feet until she couldn't take it no more. She would be mad, but she couldn't *really* be mad 'cause she would be laughing 'cause she was so ticklish." She paused again, looked at her sister, and the smile faded as a deep seriousness returned. "You think if I tickle her she'll wake up, Auntie?"

"Not this time, Tracey. I'm sorry." Tracey's bottom jaw began to grind side to side as she clenched down hard, trying to fight back her emotions. It was a losing battle as she broke down, sobbing with her forehead pressed against Roxxy's thigh. Vivian rushed to her side, bending over to pull her close. "I know, honey. I know. I am so so sorry, baby." She rubbed her back and gently grabbed the hand that held Roxxy's so tightly. "Come on, honey. Come on. I know." Reluctantly, Tracey let go of her death grip on her sister's hand, turning to bury her face into Vivian's chest as sobs roared into her bosom.

The nurse returned to the doorway with a sadness even she couldn't fight back. Her eyes welled with tears as she looked on at the scene. She walked over with a box of tissues and placed them on the window sill behind Vivian. "I'll give you a few more minutes." Vivian just nodded in response as she consoled her niece.

It was left up to Vivian to call her sister. She didn't tell Valerie over the phone that her daughter was dead, but was sure that she probably picked up that it had to be something serious for her sister to be back in town. She'd expected the girls home hours before and had heard about the shooting at the skating rink from Petey. In the meantime, Vivian decided to wait to see just how bad things were with Tiffany before calling the other girls' parents. She, Cinnamon, and Tracey took the stairwell down one floor where Tiffany was being treated.

"Why don't y'all have a seat out here. Let me go talk to the doctor." They both slowly sat Tracey down in one of the plastic chairs in the hallway. She still had the same dazed, wild look on her face, evidence that she'd officially checked out. "I'll be back. Okay, honey?" Vivian spoke to her in a soothing voice. Though she knew her comment probably hadn't registered.

Vivian wasn't prepared for the sight that awaited her when she found Tiffany's room. Tammy sat bouncing her knee with anxiety as she looked on at her unresponsive sister. Karissa was slung in the other chair, asleep with her mouth wide open and drool just at the corner of her mouth. "Oh my God," was all Vivian could make out before she covered her gaping mouth with her hand.

Tiffany was barely recognizable. Her pretty, smooth skin was replaced with black and blue bruising about the face. One eye was completely swollen shut. The other flitted about lazily. She was breathing on her own, but still wasn't conscious. Her lower lip was split and right side of her jaw wired shut. Two tiny stitches adorned her eyebrow.

"What ... *happened?*"

"Sister Vivian!" Tammy was surprised to see her. Unsure if Vivian was angry or upset, she immediately started to apologize. "We didn't mean for any of this to happen. We didn't know. I just wanted to visit F.I.T., and they just wanted to see New York. I'm so sorry, Sister Vivian." She began to cry.

"Oh, shh shh, now. I know you didn't. I know." Once again, Vivian found herself consoling yet a third teenager, rubbing her back. "What's wrong with *her?*" She motioned towards Karissa, immediately able to tell that she was on something.

"I don't know. Her and Tiffany were taking some pills from these guys and—"

"Oh my God." Vivian rolled her eyes and slapped her forehead in astonishment. "What am I gonna tell your parents? I can't believe this."

"Do you have to tell them?" Tammy whimpered.

"Do I—*of course* I have to tell them!" Vivian scolded. Tammy looked down.

"Excuse me, miss." Vivian turned to the door to see three police officers. "Are you the parent or guardian?"

"Yes—no. Well, yes, I am Cinnamon's mother."

"Cinnamon?" One of the other officers questioned.

"Yes, she's one of the girls sitting outside. I'm her mother. These are her friends, so I'm the only guardian here as of right now." She explained.

"Do you know how we can get in contact with the rest of their parents?"

"Well, I just called my sister. She's on her way. One of her daughters is sitting outside as well and the other one is ... the deceased." She said, quietly.

"Oh, I'm so sorry for your loss."

"Thank you."

"What about these young ladies? The skating rink was a busy place tonight. So we have several different cases to investigate: the shooting, of course, and this rape and assault." The first officer explained.

"Skating rink? Rape?" Vivian felt confused and upset that she was so out of the loop.

The officer started slowly, "Yes. The girls didn't tell you that the shooting and rape took place at the Empire Skating Rink in Brooklyn?"

"Officer, I didn't even know that there was a rape and no, I didn't know they were at the skating rink. They weren't supposed to be there." Now tears began to well up again as she stared at Tiffany, knowing now that she'd been raped in addition to her beating.

"We'll need to ask the girls some questions."

"Not without their parents you won't. They're all the way in Delaware, so it'll be a while before they get here." Her voice became defensive.

"Okay, that's fine. What about Cinnamon? *You're* here right now. Can we question *her*?" He asked.

"She don't know anything." Vivian quickly replied.

"Well, sometimes witnesses know things that they don't even know they know." The second officer reasoned. "We just want to find out what happened, find out what she saw, so we can catch the people responsible for all of this."

"She's just a girl. They're all just teenagers. She's too traumatized to talk right now. Can't we do this later?"

Reluctantly, the policemen backed off. "Sure, we'll come back tomorrow."

***

Valerie was inconsolable once she found out her Roxxy was gone. Mother, daughter, and son wept together in the hallway outside of Tiffany's room. Vivian had taken care of most of the paperwork, given the state her sister was in. Valerie had a similar reaction as Tracey. Nurses and security had to assist in prying her dead daughter's body from her arms. Now, downstairs, they waited for the other parents to arrive from Delaware. It took awhile for John to locate the group, but he eventually made it up to the floor. He supportively sat nearby, allowing the family to have their grief.

"WHERE IS SHE? WHERE'S MY BABY?" Sister Connie's voice could be heard as soon as the elevator doors parted, followed by Sister Kim and Deacon MoMoney.

John and Vivian both stood to greet them. "Sister Connie! Kim!" Vivian waved them over.

"My God, where are they? Where's our girls?" Sister Connie grabbed Vivian's hands frantically.

"They're here. They're in here." Vivian led them to the room.

"Oh, thank God!" Sister Connie breezed straight past Tiffany's still body to her daughter, squeezing her tightly, exhaling heavy bursts of breath, tears of relief escaping her eyes. A disoriented Karissa stood slowly and expressionless, as she allowed her body to be engulfed by her mother's embrace.

A loud gasp escaped Sister Kim's mouth as she and Deacon MoMoney entered the small space; the deacon purposely avoiding eye contact with Vivian and John. One look at Tiffany, and it was a matter of seconds before Sister Kim's body hit the tile floor. "Dad!" Tammy jumped up.

"Nurse! Nurse! We need a doctor in here!" John called out into the hall once he saw Sister Kim's body lying on the floor.

"Everybody clear the room. Please! Stand back. She needs

146

space." The nurse instructed. Another nurse ran in, holding a small vial in her hand. She bent down and waved it back and forth in front of Sister Kim's nose while the other nurse held her head steady to keep her neck straight. Suddenly, her eyes popped open and she attempted to sit up. "Hold on, now. Just relax. Don't move just yet." The nurse instructed.

The doctor came rushing in as everyone peered on holding their breath. He removed a tiny light from his lab coat pocket. He shined it in her eyes to check her pupils. He did some other checks while she lay on the floor. Eventually, they were able to move her to a stretcher in the hallway where they found an unthreatening knot on the back of her head. She was given some ibuprofen, a small cup of water, and a cold pack for the knot.

After the initial shock and a group prayer, things calmed down some. Sister Kim decided to stay by her daughter's side at the hospital. Deacon MoMoney took Tammy to check in at a nearby hotel. John insisted that he could get a room for Vivian and Cinnamon, and he could stay a few days until they were ready for him to drive them back, but she declined. She wanted to be with her sister, so she and Cinnamon escorted Valerie, Tracy, and Petey back to their Brooklyn apartment. Sister Connie got right back on the road to take Karissa home to Gracious Meadows saying, "Let's get out of this place before we both end up dead." The disgust in her voice was directly aimed at Vivian, and she could feel the blame.

***

Two days passed before Tiffany finally came to. "Praise God!" Vivian exclaimed over the phone. Not wanting to leave her sister's side. She'd been calling the MoMoney's hotel for updates on Tiffany's condition.

"The doctor said she'll be released tomorrow." Sister Kim sounded tired and distant.

"Oh, what a relief. I'm helping my sister with arrangements today, but me and Cin'll try to swing by the hospital later. She's been worried sick about Tiffany. Is there anything we can bring you?"

"No," Sister Kim said, quickly. "It won't be necessary for you to come by."

Sensing a frosty connection through the phone, Vivian asked, "Sister Kim, is everything okay?"

"No, it's not okay," she answered flatly.

"Well I just meant—"

"*I know what you meant.* Look, my husband and I have been talking to Sister Connie and some of the other ladies, and we think it's best if you and your daughter just stay away from our girls. You've done enough."

Vivian choked on air, "*excuse me?*"

Sister Kim's warm tone resurfaced as she chose her next words carefully. "I just mean you and your daughter are used to a ... *different* kind of lifestyle than what we're accustomed to in Gracious Meadows. Our kids don't take drugs and hang out all hours of the night getting in trouble with boys and such."

"And neither does mine!" A vein began to protrude from the side of Vivian's neck. "Do you think we meant for any of this to happen? Cinnamon doesn't take any drugs or run around with boys. She was just homesick to see her family. From what I understand, it wasn't even her idea to come up here. Don't you dare try to blame her. This wasn't her fault! It wasn't anybody's fault!"

Cinnamon glanced up from the kitchen table where she'd been sitting stroking her aunt's hand. Valerie hadn't said one word since they left the hospital. Mostly, she just sat staring into space. Tracey locked herself in her room, only leaving to use the bathroom.

"I'm not going to argue with you about this. I have enough to deal with. Just, please, stay away." With that, Sister Kim ended the call, leaving Vivian to stand with her mouth wide open looking at the receiver.

"I can't believe that woman."

"What happened, mom?" Cinnamon asked.

"Nothing. Nothing for you to be worried about, baby." She walked over and rubbed her back as she looked sadly into her sister's eyes. "Val, you hungry today?" She didn't answer. "You gotta eat something, sis. What if I fix you just a little something? Maybe some wings and grits? I know you like my grits." She spoke as though speaking to a child.

She got busy in the kitchen, heating up some grease for the chicken and boiling water for the grits. She hummed while she worked, uttering little lines of encouragement here and there in hopes of snapping her sister out of the funk she was in. "We need to pick out an outfit for Roxxy to wear on Friday ... Me and Cinnamon looked through the girls' closet last night, and there's a cute pink dress in there that we think will look good."

It was dry and almost inaudible as the small word floated out into the air, "no."

Vivian, surprised and elated, spun around and crouched down to eye level with Valerie. "What'd you say, honey?"

Valerie's gaze was like a spaceship coming in for landing from far away. Her eyes now fixated on Vivian's, "I said ... no."

"No, what?" Vivian smiled.

"Roxxy hates pink. Black is her favorite. She should wear something black."

"Oh, sis, black is so dark and depressing. Don't you want to remember her in something more radiant?" She pushed.

Valerie jerked her hand from Cinnamon's stroke, balling a fist to slam on the table. Startled, both Cinnamon and Vivian jumped. Then she shot out of her chair, letting it topple over as she got in Vivian's face. "I SAID NO! SHE'S NOT WEARING PINK!"

"Oh-oh okay, sis. Calm down." Vivian stammered over her words, her heart thumping from the sudden excitement.

"Don't you tell me to calm down! My baby's dead! *DEAD*! And you wanna dress her up like some Barbie doll."

"Val, I'm sorry. I was just trying to help. I didn't—"

"Trying to help?" Valerie's words slithered from her tongue as her eyes cut to slits. "*Trying to help?*" She repeated. "I don't need any more of your help. Matter of fact ... GET OUT!" She yelled and pointed towards the front door.

"Valerie!"

"I MEAN IT! YOU GET OUT! You know that bullet was meant for Cinnamon. You know it as well as I do. You both know it! Here you come bringing your tail up here when you know you shouldn't be back in Brooklyn." Her glare now fixated on Cinnamon as she inched closer to her face. With every inch, Cinnamon stepped back

149

until her aunt had her pinned against the wall. "This is your fault. My baby's dead because of you."

"Auntie, how—"

"GET OUT! I MEAN IT! BOTH OF YOU GET OUT OF MY HOUSE!

CHAPTER 15

Days turned into weeks and weeks into a month that the Mackey women stewed in their own depression, independent of each other. Cinnamon mourned the loss of her favorite cousin. Vivian mourned the loss of her relationship with her only sister. An unspoken burden weighed heavily between the two, indicative of the guilt they both felt for Roxxy's death.

Despite the first lady's relentless unanswered calls, Vivian hadn't set foot in Greater Saints since their return to Gracious Meadows. Cinnamon was no longer forced to attend bible study either. John came to the apartment several times to persuade Vivian to come to a service. *"Those ladies were just upset. I'm sure they didn't mean any of it. Just come on back, and I'm sure the whole thing will be forgotten."* Still, Vivian's mind was made up. Those women blamed her and her daughter for what happened to Tiffany. Even though Tiffany made a full physical recovery, she knew they would never forgive her.

The only person Cinnamon continued to associate with from the church was Generosa. She still saw her at school, and they continued to eat lunch together. She and Anthony had become something of an item, unbeknownst to the reverend and first lady, of course. Every chance they got, the girls would use each other as alibis to sneak off to dates at the movies or bowling alley with Anthony and Raheem. Anthony was a sweet boy. He'd arrive to their history class with a love letter and a lollipop for Generosa every day. They would exchange notes throughout the day to each other. Generosa saved every single one.

By the end of March, the weather began to change and Spring was just around the corner. There's always something about the weather changing, warming up a little, that makes people go crazy. This year was no different.

The sunny weather caused the ground in Gracious Meadows to begin to soften. Then young girls' bodies began to surface left and right. Five were found in the marsh behind an elementary school baseball field. Animals managed to dig up and scatter the remains of two other girls in a deserted wooded area just outside of the town. One teen's skeletal remains were found minus the skull because she'd been decapitated. The biggest shock was the eight bodies found buried in shallow graves on an old abandoned property inside a small farmhouse. Their bodies had all been dismembered and mutilated. Several of the body parts were found stuffed inside of suitcases. This sent the small town into shock and grief for those who had finally recovered their loved ones. Now they wanted answers. They wanted the person responsible for the heinous crimes.

The girls made plans for that Friday night to go to the mall to meet up with Anthony and Raheem. As usual, the plan was for Generosa to tell her mom and dad that she was going to Cinnamon's house and Cinnamon would tell her mom the same. The foursome strolled through the mall as they window-shopped. Each guy had his arm hung around his girl.

"I'm tired of walking. Can we sit down somewhere?" Generosa asked. She stopped and put her hands on her hips. She seemed out of breath and as Cinnamon looked on, she came to realize that Generosa had put on some weight over the few months she'd known her.

"Y'all wanna get something to eat from the food court?" Anthony suggested.

"Yeah, I want a pretzel." Cinnamon answered, looking at Raheem to cosign. He always insisted on paying for everything when they went out, so it would be up to him to grant her wish.

"I'm hungry. I'll need more than a pretzel." Generosa professed, rubbing her belly.

"Get whatever you want, babe." Anthony responded.

Once the group bought what they wanted, they took a seat in the packed food court. Cinnamon, Raheem, and Anthony each went with a small snack: a pretzel, a cinnabon, nachos. They all looked on as Generosa prepared to go to work on her Chinese orange chicken, side of shrimp and broccoli, and butter pecan ice cream. She was only two bites in before her facial expression changed as her jaws slowed down to chew in slow motion until they came to a complete stop.

"What's wrong?" Cinnamon asked.

"I don't feel so well." She said, slowly. Then, "I think I'm gonna throw up!" She shot up out of her seat to find the nearest restroom, which, thankfully, was nearby.

"I'll go with her!" Cinnamon hurried behind her friend to catch up.

The orange chicken along with whatever Generosa had eaten earlier in the day came spewing into the toilet, splashing the toilet seat. Generosa stood doubled over as other shoppers passed by the open stall with disgust on their faces.

"What'chy'all lookin' at? Mind your business. Never seen a person throw up before?" Cinnamon rolled her eyes and reached in to rub her friend's back. "You okay?"

Generosa took a couple of deep breaths before answering, "yeah."

After she rinsed her mouth out, the two returned to their table at the food court. Once Generosa felt like she was well enough to walk, the group made their way towards one of the mall exits.

"Y'all can wait out front. I'll pull the van around, so Generosa doesn't have to do all that walking through the parking lot." Raheem offered. He was always the designated driver, but he didn't seem to mind. The group would never make it to the front, though.

"GENEROSA!" First Lady Grienbachs was just exiting Bath and Body Works as they passed the front of the store.

"*Mom?* What are you doing here?" Generosa sounded like a frightened child.

"I should be asking *you* that! And what are you doing hanging out with *them?*" She motioned towards Raheem and Anthony but her disapproval was moreso directed towards Raheem. "And Cinnamon? Does your mom know you're here? With boys? With Raheem?" She questioned.

"Uh…" She didn't know how to answer. The boys stood by in awkward silence.

"Y'all know they finding bodies popping up all over this town, and you're out here lying and gallivanting to and fro like you can't be snatched up by some predator any minute!" She scolded. "C'mon. Cinnamon I'm taking you home too. Generosa just wait 'til your father hears about this."

"Bye," Cinnamon whispered to Raheem. Generosa said nothing as she sheepishly followed her mother's orders.

***

Needless to say, Vivian was less than thrilled when the first lady brought her daughter home. Cinnamon was placed on punishment for the next two weeks. In the Grienbachs's residence it was a different story.

"Here I am just trying to have a little me time and who do I see sashaying on by in the mall when she's supposed to be over the Mackeys' house?" The first lady glared at Generosa through slit eyes. She was uncharacteristically pissed with her daughter.

"Oh, really?" Reverend Grienbachs closed his newspaper, sat it on the sofa next to him, and leaned back. His belly protruded through his white tank top as it rested on his thighs. He was calm, *too* calm. This made Generosa even more nervous as she stood in the living room awaiting her destiny.

"And look what else I found in her room!" First Lady Grienbachs dumped out a shoebox full of Anthony's love letters onto the coffee table. "She's been hiding them in her bottom dresser drawer."

"*'Generosa, you truly are the most beautiful woman I've ever seen. I love everything about you, your smile, your voice, your eyes.'* Well isn't that just sweet. You hear that, Moni? Our lil' girl is a woman according to this *Anthony* guy." The reverend taunted. "So you're a woman? You think you're grown? Is that it?" Generosa stared at the matted carpeted floor and shook her head. "Speak up! I can't hear you!" The reverend ordered.

154

"No."

"She must do! Sneaking on the phone, sneaking out and lying about where she's going to go be a little hot momma with her little boyfriend." The first lady chimed in.

"Baby, I told you that lil' chile' Nutmeg, or whatever her name is, was no good. Told you I didn't want our Generosa hanging out with her. Her and her momma ain't been nothing but trouble since they got here. And that mother ... always coming and switching around the church wearing those lil' tight dresses, breasts just hanging all out in your face. I mean that's distracting for any warm-blooded man. I mean I'm a man of God, but I'm still a man." The reverend got lost in his own lustful thoughts for a moment. Then snapping back to reality, he subtly reached his hand down between his legs to make a quick adjustment. "So what do you think we should do?"

Generosa shrugged in response. "I'm really sorry, Daddy."

"Oh, now she's sorry." The first lady hissed.

"Yeah ... she sure is sorry. Sorry and fat!" The reverend spat. "I swear every time I look she's getting bigger and bigger. What'chu been feeding her, Moni?"

"It ain't my fault. She eats everything in sight ... just sickening."

The reverend stood up, unbuckling his belt to slide it through the loops on his pants. "Well ... we'll think of something. You know what time it is. Get down to the basement."

"Please, Daddy. No. Please don't make me go to the basement. I'm sorry. I promise I'm so sorry. I'll never see him again." Generosa pleaded.

"We know you ain't gon' see him again. We're gonna make sure of that." He replied.

"You heard your father! Get your butt down those stairs right now!" The first lady ordered.

Reluctantly, Generosa did as told. Slowly, step by step, she marched down the creaky steps. The smell of urine and feces hit her senses and she almost gagged. She heard the clamor of shackles as a frightened Gabe quickly scurried to his corner and huddled his legs to his chest. His ankles and wrists bound, he sat chained to the wall. He winced from the basement light that hurt his eyes. He'd been down

155

there for the past month, ever since Vivian brought him home from his rendezvous with Pastor Leonards. Left in complete darkness for the majority of the time, except for when the first lady brought down his weekly meal, his eyes had become accustomed to the total blanket of blackness. He was thin and frail and smelled of decay, given only a small bucket to relieve himself. He wasn't allowed to bathe or use the bathroom in the basement. He still wore the same clothes he had on that night, now smeared with his own blood after the pastor had performed unspeakable acts on him, things to *'drive the gay spirit out of him,'* as the reverend had put it.

The two siblings knew all too well the horrors that awaited them once they descended those basement stairs. Over the years, this had become their sanctuary of punishment. The first lady never came down during the punishments. She left that up to her husband to be the enforcer. She only came down after, as sort of the clean up lady. This night was no different. She and the reverend parted ways at the top of the stairwell.

His footsteps were heavy as he made his way down the stairs. Once he reached the bottom, he looked over at Gabe. "I think you still got that devil's spirit in you, boy." He grunted before continuing, "I think you still need a couple more weeks down here to do some praying. Time'll tell." Then he turned his attention to Generosa. "Well? What'chu waiting for? You know the drill. Get out of those clothes!" He commanded. Big elephant tears began to roll down her cheeks as Generosa obeyed her father's orders, shivering from the cool basement air as she did. The reverend found an outlet nearby where he plugged in an old iron in preparation of the task at hand.

***

"I know you don't feel like walking all the way there. Hop in! I'll give you a ride." He said.

"Okay." That one simple word now haunted Karissa. Why had she been so trusting, especially after all the bodies had begun to pop up? She blamed herself for what happened next.

Once inside the van, preoccupied with her head down, digging through her purse to find lip-gloss, was the last thing she could remember. Now that she'd come to, the aching from the back of her head explained her sudden blackout. She'd been hit with something, but what? By who and why?

None of that mattered now as she sat bound and gagged, strapped securely to a chair. Her wrists were duct taped together behind her and her ankles each taped to the chair legs. Her T-shirt had been ripped straight down the front, exposing her extra large breasts. Her eyes bulged as her capturer made his way around to stand in front of her with a wide grin. She tried to scream, but all sound was stifled. It didn't matter. No one would hear her cries anyway down here.

"So glad to see you're finally awake. I was beginning to think we'd lost you already. It's not as much fun torturing a person when they don't know they're being tortured. You know?" He talked as he worked, moving quickly in excitement. He disappeared into another room and returned pushing a table with a metal tray on top. It sounded like silverware, but once the tray stopped in front of her, Karissa could see the table had a variety of medical instruments neatly spread across it. They were shiny and clean, almost brand new. There was one big one that caught her eye, and she began to feel dizzy as if she might faint. It was a saw.

"Oh, no you don't." He chuckled as he pinched her on the arm. "We need you wide awake for this." Karissa didn't say anything but the question mark on her face asked who "we" was. "Well every doctor has to have an assistant, of course." That's when his accomplice appeared from the smaller room.

"Mmm! Mmm!" Karissa's eyes pleaded with the pair as she recognized them both.

"This is—well, I take it by your reaction that you two already know each other." He teased. "Gosh, this is so exciting. Isn't this exciting?" He asked his accomplice.

"*So* exciting!" The accomplice smiled while putting on latex gloves. The duo wore white lab coats, goggles, and blue shower shoes over their footwear. Next they pulled white medical facemasks over their mouths and noses.

BUZZZZ! They were interrupted by an unexpected visitor.

"Oh, who could that be?" Irritation rippled through his voice.

"I don't know." The accomplice replied with a shrug.

"Well, go find out and get rid of them!" Once his accomplice disappeared up the stairwell, he could hear muffled voices. He turned his attention to Karissa, holding up the saw towards the light as if inspecting its nooks and crannies. "How about a right breast removal? Orrr … better yet, how about a full double mastectomy? You know those things are just ticking time bombs anyway, don't you? With all the hormones they're putting in food these days, you'll have breast cancer by the time you're thirty anyway. So far we've only been doing just the nipple, but you have so much to work with here." He tapped the bottom of her breast in an upward motion causing it to bounce.

"Mmm," Karissa shook her head.

"Hmm? What's that? I can't really make out what you're saying with that thing in your mouth. Maybe we should take it out? What do you think?"

Karissa nodded her head feverishly, her eyes begging with reason. "Mmm mmm."

He put down the saw and started towards her then cruelly reneged. "Naaah! From what I hear, you're pretty use to having things in your mouth anyway." Tilting his head back, he laughed hysterically at his own joke. They both could still hear the muffled conversation coming from above. "What is taking so long?" The annoyance grew in his voice.

"MMM! MMM! MMM!" Karissa yelled as loud as she could in hopes that the visitor, whoever it was, might hear and come to her aid.

His hand moved swiftly across her face with an open palm. "Stop that! You stop that right now!" He demanded through clenched teeth, but it didn't deter her.

"MMM! MMM! MMM!" Her body shook as she whimpered in between outcries until he couldn't take it anymore. He grabbed a needle from the tray and filled it with a heavy duty sedative. "MMM! MMM!" Karissa began rocking her chair, making as much noise as she could to draw attention until she felt the deep plunge of the needle to the side of her neck, and she moved no more.

CHAPTER 16

The Mackey women had just sat down to dinner when the doorbell rang, followed by an insistent knock. Cinnamon sat down the glass of wine she'd been sipping and searched her mother's face as though she may be expecting a visitor she didn't know about.

Instead, Vivian scrunched up her face in wonder. "Ugh! I wonder who that could be." Then she got up to answer the door.

Cinnamon continued to eat the barbeque ribs her mother cooked, her fingers red with sauce. A napkin blew off the table as a cool breeze swept in from the front door. She could hear multiple voices, then her mother telling someone to come in. She was surprised to see Vivian followed by First Lady Grienbachs, Sister Connie, and Sister Kim. Cinnamon didn't speak. Instead, she waited for an explanation.

"Cin, Karissa is missing." Vivian said, with her arms crossed. She sounded disinterested, unconcerned.

"Oh," was all Cinnamon said as she slowly chewed the bits of food left in her mouth.

"Cinnamon, we were just wondering if you've seen or heard from Karissa." The first lady moved closer with concern in her eyes.

Cinnamon shook her head, "no."

That's when Sister Connie rushed towards her, grabbing Cinnamon's hands into hers, cupping them together as she crouched on her knees beside the table. "Please. If you've heard from her, I really

159

need to know, Cinnamon." She searched Cinnamon's eyes back and forth for an inkling of hope. Cinnamon, a little startled by Sister Connie's behavior, looked at her mother for help.

"She said she hasn't talked to her, Connie." Vivian said, blandly.

"Please, Cinnamon. She's been missing for two days now. Nobody's heard from her. Nobody's seen her. She hasn't been at school. If there's anything you're not telling me ... I know Karissa can be sneaky sometimes. I know. But if you've heard anything from her, I need to know. Did she go to New York again?" She didn't wait for Cinnamon's response. "Please just tell the truth. I won't be mad. I just need to know where my baby girl is." A tear rolled down her cheek and she sniffled.

Cinnamon shrugged her shoulders in slow motion with a lost look on her face. "I honestly don't know where she is. Maybe..." Cinnamon's voice trailed off as she silently debated on whether she should reveal what she was thinking or not.

"Maybe what? What?" Sister Connie persisted.

Again, Cinnamon looked to her mom for help. "Cinnamon, if you know something now is the time."

"Well, it might be nothing." She paused as she looked around the room. "Karissa was in one of those videos."

"*Videos?* What videos and what does it have to do with this?" Sister Kim sounded impatient.

"You know those *Girls Gone Crazy* videos? She was in one called *Church Girls Gone Crazy.* I was just gonna say maybe she went off to make another video with those guys or something."

"WHAT?" Sister Kim blurted out, astonished by the accusation. "See, I don't even know why we came here. She's obviously mistaken."

"No, I'm not!" Cinnamon snapped.

"How—how do you know she was in a video?" Sister Connie asked, quietly.

"I saw it."

"Oh ... well ... no, she's not making another video." Sister Connie dismissed the idea but didn't seem the least bit shocked by the information.

"How can you be sure?" Vivian asked.

"Because … *I just know.*" She was short. "How did you see it anyway?"

Cinnamon hesitated before answering quietly, "Raheem showed it to me."

"Oh, *Raheem.*" Sister Connie's voice changed quickly to disgust. "It's not bad enough what he did to me. I guess he wants to ruin my daughter's life too." She paused as she stared off into space in her own moment of reflection. "Anyway, that has nothing to do with Karissa's disappearance, you see. I know she's not with any of the guys."

"What guys?" First Lady Grienbachs asked in confusion.

"Never mind," Sister Connie said quickly and focused back on Cinnamon. "Is there anything else you're not telling me? I just need to know where my daughter is." She pleaded.

"I really haven't seen or talked to Karissa, Sister Connie. Not since New York. I'm sorry."

Sister Connie froze, her eyes fixed on Cinnamon's. Suddenly she grabbed Cinnamon's shirt and used her other hand to squeeze her face. "You liar! You're lying! I know you know something! You got her taking those drugs. You had her up there running around with riffraff in New York. You tell me! You tell me the truth right now, you little liar!"

"Hey!" Vivian moved swiftly on her feet to her daughter's aid. She grabbed Sister Connie by the neck, who was forced to release her grip on Cinnamon as she fell backwards on the floor. "Get off of her! She said she doesn't know anything and she doesn't!"

"But she's lying! I just know it!" Sister Connie rushed towards Cinnamon again, but Vivian intercepted, this time grabbing her by her coat.

"Okay, you need to go. I'm sorry about your daughter, but if my daughter says she doesn't know anything, then she doesn't. Now you touch her again and watch what happens." Vivian's nostrils flared as she spoke.

"Okay. Okay. Thanks Vivian. Thanks Cinnamon. It's time to go. Come on, Connie. That's enough." Sister Kim grabbed Sister Connie and ushered her towards the door. Sister Connie didn't say another word. She just clung to Sister Kim and began sobbing as they made their way outside.

"I'm so sorry, Sister Vivian. I wasn't expecting that." First Lady Grienbachs looked genuinely apologetic.

Vivian nodded. "I know ... Poor girl. I hope she finds her soon, especially with everything that's been going on around here. Have you contacted the police?"

"Yeah, the police have finally let Sister Connie fill out a missing person's report, but they haven't done much. They haven't made any progress at all, so we're out here looking ourselves. You understand. If it were Cinnamon, I'm sure you'd feel the same way. I know if it were Generosa, I'd be worried sick."

"I know. I know. Speaking of which, how is Generosa? Cinnamon said she hasn't seen her in school all week." Vivian asked.

"Oh, she's fine. She's been feeling a little ill, so we been keeping her home." The first lady replied. "I should go. Thanks again. I'm sorry about this." Then she hurried towards the door.

"Of course. Take care. And please let us know when you find Karissa."

***

Down at Gracious Meadows Police Headquarters, the scene was frenzy. A special team had been assembled specifically dedicated to the Gracious Meadows' teen girl disappearances. Detective Briggs and Detective Sunil were the two leads of the team, but they hadn't made much progress. Even with the discovery of all the bodies, they still hadn't recovered as many clues as they'd hoped.

"We know our guy is a cutter." Detective Sunil addressed the crowded room of officers as he briefed them on the latest information. "Specifically, he has an obsession with slicing and mutilating the victim's breasts. This is the only detail that links all these cases together, so that's important to remember."

"Have we identified what was used to cut the victims?" An officer asked from the crowd.

"It was hard for the M.E. to identify the exact weapon because of the bodies' decomposition, but they've narrowed it down to some type of switchblade or automatic knife. Possibly a Spyderco or

Benchmade." Detective Sunil replied.

"It's hard to say for sure, though, because there were so many different types of lacerations made to the bodies. Some were made with such precision that we think we could be dealing with some type of doctor or someone in the medical profession. Some of the other cuts were rough and jagged and so haphazardly made, it indicates that we're dealing with an amateur—someone who doesn't plan well, but acts out hastily." Detective Briggs explained.

"Is it possible that we're looking at more than one killer?" Another asked.

"Right now, anything is possible." Detective Briggs answered. "We know we haven't given you much to go on, but we have to work with the details we have. There's nothing we can do for the deceased victims except get justice for their families by finding this maniac. We do that by finding our latest missing girl, Karissa Mills. Finding her alive is key. So what do we know? We know our victim's face." He held up a print out of a recent school photo of Karissa. She looked like a sweet, innocent girl in the picture, wearing a modest dress with sunflowers all over it and her hair swept back into a bun with bangs lining her forehead. "Karissa was last seen wearing blue jeans and a blue and white wind breaker jacket. A witness says she saw her getting into a white van. We have no plate information, but this detail is key as some of our other victims were spotted getting into or standing near a white van. So let's get back out there, re-canvas the neighborhood, and re-interview witnesses and neighbors. Leave no stone unturned. Let's find this girl!" With that, the meeting was adjourned and the crowded room swarmed towards the door, anxious to get back out on the streets.

CHAPTER 17

Pastor Leonards could hear his heart thumping through his chest as he stood before the Greater Saints congregation. The church had never been so silent as they all waited, staring with eyes of judgment and disapproval. Word had gotten around about the pastor and the deacon's sinful rendezvous with the boys of the church. Now, Reverend Grienbachs had them both standing at the altar rendering apologies for their behavior, and Pastor Leonards was up next.

Beads of sweat slid down the side of his bald head. He dared not look at Gabe directly even though this was both of their first time allowed back into the church since the incident over a month earlier. Throughout the service, he did steal side glances of his young boy toy, and something was different about him. He looked broken and empty, his spirit diminished. He had no idea how the reverend punished his son, but his heart went out to him anyway knowing it couldn't be easy living in that house and being a homosexual. It was the guilt that throbbed in his chest, not nerves. It was guilt, not for molesting a child, but for getting his lover into trouble with his parents.

He appeared to pay attention to Deacon MoMoney's apology, nodding in approval and agreement where warranted, but he wasn't really paying attention. Sister Kim looked at her husband from the congregation, nodding along also and interjecting with amen's to show her full support of her husband's repentance. She had a role to play, and that was of a supportive wife and a forgiving Christian. Inside, she burned with hatred and embarrassment, but one would ever know by the painted smile that was glazed onto her face. Once Deacon MoMoney was finished, the congregation lent supportive applause, proof of their forgiveness of his transgressions. A few members gave hugs as they whispered things in the deacon's ear like, "God bless you, brother", "It's okay, Deacon, the Lord knows your heart", "We all fall short of the glory of God".

Next, it was Pastor Leonards' turn. He swallowed dryness and attempted to clear his throat as he gathered his thoughts. "Proverbs chapter twenty-eight verse thirteen reads 'He that covereth his sins shall not prosper: but whoso confesseth and forsaketh them shall have mercy.'" The pastor looked down at his feet as silence fell over the sanctuary. His thoughts battled one another in his head as he tried to decide what to say next. *But I was born this way. I can't help who I am. God made me this way. Why should I have to confess and forsake the true me? And why must I ask for forgiveness from the church? I haven't done anything wrong to the people in this church.* Finally, he broke his silence. "I want mercy, y'all." Light sprinkles of hand claps sounded throughout the church.

"Amen!" Someone shouted.

The pastor continued, "I stand before you today, ashamed of the sins I have committed. But I don't want to be this way anymore. I have spent many many hours in consecration and prayer, asking God to cast out the evil that tried to dwell inside me. The devil *is* a liar and he will *not* make a home in this temple!" He shouted as he pointed to his body. The crowd of onlookers gave a quick roar of support. "We've done a terrible thing," he continued as he glanced at Deacon MoMoney. "I know that, and I apologize to all those who were involved that I may have hurt. I apologize to the reverend and first lady, and I apologize to the members of this church. Without all of your support, I wouldn't be the man of God I am today. That's why I ask for your forgiveness and for your support once more. Please keep me in your prayers as I battle this demon because with your love and prayers I know I can win the fight. I want nothing more than to be the man God wants me to be and to grow in the word, so I can lead others to Christ. So please ... continue to pray for me as I continue to pray for you."

Pastor Leonards was approached in the same way Deacon

MoMoney was, hugs and words of encouragement. "It's okay, Pastor. We love you, and God loves you." "Praise God, Pastor. We're here for you."

After their public humiliation and repentance, it wasn't long before things went back to normal at Greater Saints. Deacon MoMoney went on as usual, collecting offering during Sunday services and aiding the reverend. Pastor Leonards was allowed to keep his position as the Youth Pastor and continue leading the teen bible study. None of the other members, or the reverend himself, dared to mention the scandal. Just like that, all was forgotten. It was as though the whole thing never happened, but when it came to Pastor Leonards, it would soon be found out that old habits died hard.

***

Cinnamon was glad to have her friend back in school, but there was something different about Generosa. Cinnamon watched her waddle her way over to their lunch table, carrying a pile of food as usual. In just a matter of the weeks that she'd been out sick, Generosa appeared to have gained a significant amount of weight. There was something else. She seemed down and drained. She wasn't the most bubbly, outgoing person to begin with, but Cinnamon detected a change in Generosa.

"Heyyy! Girl, I was starting to worry about you! Where have you been? I haven't seen you since that night we got caught at the mall!" Cinnamon rambled in excitement.

"Hey. Yeah, I know." Generosa blandly answered as she failed to make eye contact.

"Are you okay?"

"Yeah, I'm fine. I'm just a little tired, I guess. I've been sick." Generosa replied.

"I know. Your mom told us when she came to my house looking for Karissa."

"Oh?" Something about her wasn't fully invested in the conversation with Cinnamon. She seemed preoccupied with something else.

"Yeah, she's been missing for like two weeks now. They

haven't found her yet, right?"

"No, not that I've heard." Generosa sighed.

Sensing something was wrong, Cinnamon asked, "Generosa, are you sure everything is okay? Are you feeling alright?"

Generosa forced a smile as she glanced up to Cinnamon's concerned face. "Yeah. Really. I'm fine."

"If you say so … I hope you didn't get in too much trouble that night at the mall." Cinnamon chuckled, trying to lighten Generosa's mood, but Generosa grew silent as she stared into her lunch tray. "My mom put me on punishment for two weeks. It's not like I have any friends or do anything anyway, but I missed sneaking to talk to and see Raheem." Generosa remained quiet but began to chew a bite of her pizza slowly. "You know Anthony has been asking about you. I think he missed you too. Have you seen him yet today?"

At that moment, Generosa shot up out of her seat. "I gotta … go." She looked faint, and her forehead began to sweat.

Cinnamon got up too. "Generosa, what's wrong?" She gently grabbed her arm.

"Nothing … I just gotta … Ouuuuuch!" Suddenly she doubled over in pain, dropping her tray to the floor.

"Generosa!" Cinnamon helped her friend by holding her up.

Generosa froze, breathing hard. "I gotta get out of here." She attempted to take another step, but the pain kicked in again. "Ooooh! Oh my God!" She squeezed hard on Cinnamon's arm and before either girl could say another word, they both witnessed the gush of wetness come through the tan pants Generosa wore. It trickled all the way down the pant leg and some even made it onto the cafeteria floor. Students looked on in curiosity as two teachers rushed towards the pair. "Owwww! Oh it hurts!" Generosa cried out in pain, her face distorted. The two teachers quickly wisped Generosa away to the nurse's office, and Cinnamon was left there alone to piece together the puzzle.

***

"Okay, Generosa, I know it's hard, but we're going to need you to get ready to push again. Okay? Can you give us one more big push?"

167

The doctor stationed between Generosa's legs coaxed.

Generosa lifted her head from the hospital bed and gave a nod as her chest heaved up and down. Terrified didn't begin to describe how she felt. By the time she made it to the hospital the contractions were too close and it was too late for an epidural. First Lady Grienbachs made it to the hospital once the school alerted her, and the reverend was still in route. She stood next to her daughter holding her hand.

"Ready? One. Two. Three. PUUUUSH!" The doctor coached. Generosa bore down hard and gave her best effort. She groaned and then let her head loll back in exasperation. "You're doing great, honey. The shoulders are out now. We're almost there, Generosa. One more push. One more push. Get ready. One. Two. Three." She counted down again and Generosa squeezed her mother's hand tightly as she pushed once more.

The first lady leaned in close and whispered in her ear so others couldn't hear, "How could you let this happen? Why didn't you come to me, Generosa?"

Generosa winced as her heart rate increased. Tears ran from the corner of her eyes back into her wild hair. She began to cry, shamed by her mother's words, just as the baby emerged. It was quiet for only a moment. Then, once the doctor gave her bottom a little smack, the baby girl began to chime in on her mother's cries.

"It's a girl!" The doctor exclaimed, holding the baby up to show Generosa quickly, before passing her off to the nurses for cleaning.

First Lady Grienbachs appeared to play the role of the proud grandmother to save face at the hospital. When the nurses asked what Generosa wanted to name her daughter, she told them Angel, but the first lady cut in saying, "*Angel?* Oh no, I think Tabitha is more fitting. Tabitha was an obedient disciple, you know … Tabitha Mary Grienbachs." She instructed while cradling the baby in her arms, a smile spread across her face. The nurse looked to Generosa for her input or approval, but she gave none. She just looked down in disappointment.

Once they were alone, she asked her mother, "Do you think I can hold her now?" She reached out, but the first lady turned her back and continued pacing about the room holding her granddaughter and cooing.

Instead she responded, "No, you should get some rest now. Why don't you lay down? I got her." Generosa, crushed and yearning to have her baby in her arms, obediently complied. She lay down, but she couldn't rest. Too consumed with a sudden overwhelming fear that her daughter would disappear if she blinked, she kept one eye open on her mother, watching her every move with Tabitha.

CHAPTER 18

"I should really get ready to go, Raheem. C'mon." Cinnamon whispered to her boyfriend. The two had finished closing the furniture store, and now sat on Raheem's bed in his apartment upstairs.

Raheem glanced at his small digital alarm clock. "We still have a few more minutes. I'ma drive you in the van. Stop worrying. You know I always get you home in time." He resumed placing wet kisses up and down Cinnamon's neck and massaging her breasts. This had become their ritual on the nights they worked together. They would hurry to close everything up in the store. If there were no customers, and they knew John wouldn't be back for the night, sometimes they would close the store ten or fifteen minutes early to squeeze in some extra time together upstairs. They would go to Raheem's apartment with the pretense of watching TV and talking, but they both knew they would end up making out and doing what the elders called some "heavy petting."

Raheem made his way to Cinnamon's lips and slipped his tongue between to part them. They exchanged saliva, kissing deeply. Soon, Raheem found his hands roaming between Cinnamon's thighs, rubbing his fingers back and forth against her jeans. She began to breath heavily. He took this as a sign and grabbed her hand, placing it between his legs so she could do the same to him. Each time they were together they went further and further, but whenever Cinnamon wanted to stop, Raheem stopped.

Tonight their teenage hormones ran rapid. Raheem leaned back on the bed and pulled Cinnamon on top as the two began to grind against one another. "Why don't you take these off?" He whispered in her ear between kisses as he unbuttoned the front of her jeans and began to slide the zipper down.

"No." She quickly grabbed his hand and sat up straight. "Raheem, you know I'm not ready for that."

He took a deep breath and tried to hide his disappointment. "I know. I know. I'm sorry. Come here." He pulled her close and went back to kissing. *Beep-beep beep-beep*, his pager went off. He snatched it from the small two-drawer nightstand that served as his only dresser. "That's John. Hold up." He patted Cinnamon on the hip, signaling her to climb off of him. Then he grabbed the cordless phone from its receiver and dialed. "Hey … yeah, I'm upstairs … I'm with Cinnamon … uh huh … uh huh … Well, I was about to drop her off anyway … No, they should be there … okay okay I'll check … Gimme like thirty minutes … Well, I gotta drop Cinnamon off first … I know!"

"Everything okay?" Cinnamon asked as she rubbed his chest.

He grabbed her hand and kissed it. "Yeah, c'mon let's get you home. John needs me to bring him a pair of pliers from the warehouse."

After retrieving the pliers, it seemed like Raheem was all of a sudden in a hurry as he drove Cinnamon home. "Why you driving so fast? You better slow down before we get pulled over." Cinnamon cautioned.

"I just don't want you to be late. I'm not try'na have my baby back on punishment again. Those were the longest two weeks of my life." He joked nervously.

"Well, I rather be on punishment for being late or getting caught with you than dead. So slow down."

When they did finally make it to Cinnamon's house, Raheem stopped the van a few houses down as he always did just in case Vivian was around. Normally, he would try to sneak in a couple more last kisses, but this night he almost rushed Cinnamon from the van. "I'll talk to you tomorrow." He said.

"If she's sleep, I can probably sneak and call you tonight." Cinnamon suggested.

"I'm gonna be at John's. I might just end up crashing at his house." He explained.

"Oh … okay." Cinnamon felt like something was up but couldn't tell what; so she planted a quick kiss on Raheem's cheek and hopped out of the van.

He waited impatiently for her to make it to her door. It wasn't even closed good behind her before he pulled off. Neither of the two noticed the black BMW staked outside her apartment. Cinnamon never even detected the glare from the pair of eyes that sat behind the tinted windows just waiting for the perfect opportunity to make his move.

***

Sister Connie hadn't slept well since the day Karissa disappeared. Dark puffiness outlined her eyes instead of the eyeliner she so meticulously wore normally. She mauled at what was left of the nail that used to exist on her index finger as she waited outside the front door.

"Who is it?" A man's deep voice boomed from the other side of the door.

"It's Connie! Dame, open up!" She could hear multiple locks being unbolted. Then the door swung open. Damion's six foot three, two-hundred and fifty pound frame towered over Connie in the doorway. He was a burley, serious man who was easily intimidating without even trying.

"Oh … Connie. What'chu doing here?" He peeked his head out, looking up and down the street into the night air.

Unmoved by his physique, Connie invited herself in, pushing past him. "Is she here? Karissa! Karissa!" She called down the hallway as she walked towards the back to the green room.

Damion was one of the casting directors for the *Girls Gone Crazy* videos. Sister Connie already knew about the video. She was the one who got Karissa casted. She wasn't proud of it and had managed to keep it a secret this long. After Karissa's father left, things just got harder and harder financially. Once she was a teen, she started to fill out. Sister Connie figured they could make some quick money and no one had to know about it. They'd traveled all the way to Miami to shoot that video. It paid good money, and she never thought it would make its way to their tiny town. No one was supposed to know.

Damion was the one to get Karissa the gig in the Miami taping, and he had taken a special, moreso inappropriate, interest in Karissa. Connie knew this but looked the other way because of the money Karissa was bringing home. This forty-two-year-old man would come pick up Karissa, so she could spend the evening with him for what he called a one-on-one photo session. Sometimes these so-called "sessions" would last an entire weekend. Connie never asked Karissa what she did at these sessions, and she never saw any of the photos, but anyone with common sense had to know Karissa was doing more than just modeling for pictures. Connie's only concern was how much Damion was willing to pay for each session. Since he would pay her as Karissa's guardian, Connie didn't ask questions outside of that. She would just say the same thing each time as Karissa left, "Just make sure you have her home in time for school on Monday." Now, grasping at straws to find her daughter, she wondered if maybe the pair decided to cut her out as the middle man. Had Karissa just been with Damion all this time doing some sort of extended session?

"What are you doing? Karissa's not here." His face twisted up in confusion and annoyance by Connie's intrusion. She didn't care. She made her way to the end of the hall and burst through the door of the green room. What she found wasn't Karissa but another young teen who jumped up from the black leather couch that sat against the wall. Unclothed, embarrassed, and startled by this stranger, she did her best to cover herself.

Connie's heart sank quickly, and her hope deflated at the same pace. She slowly backed out of the green room, covering her mouth as she began to weep. Leaning against the wall in the hallway, she slowly sank to the floor. She was losing control.

"Woman, what is wrong with you? I told you she wasn't here." Damion quickly shut the door to the green room.

"I-I … I'm sorry, Dame." She cried. "It's been three weeks. Three weeks. I just don't know where she could be."

"Look, I'm sorry about your daughter. Karissa is young and beautiful. I bet you she just ran off with some young knucklehead or something. But you can't come busting up in here like this." He chastised.

"What would you do if it was your daughter?" She peered up at him with weepy eyes.

A hint of sympathy crept into his eyes briefly. "I don't know." He helped Connie up and walked her towards the door. "I haven't seen her, though, Connie. I swear I haven't, but if I do, you'll be the first to know."

"Thanks," she managed to croak out as she neared the front door.

"She'll turn up. Wherever she is, she gon' run out of money some time, and she'll be back. You know how these kids are, thinking they have all the answers. She's gonna realize she made a mistake and she'll come on home." He assured her. The only thing Connie could do was nod pitifully as she made her exit.

Once back in her car, she sat with her forehead on the steering wheel. She was running on fumes, desperate to find Karissa, and the police didn't seem any closer to finding her. *Think. Think. Where could she be?* She banged her forehead lightly on the wheel as she gripped it tightly.

***

Vivian paced back and forth in her bedroom with the cordless phone in hand. Her palms were moist and her heart beat more rapidly than normal. *It's your sister,* she scolded herself. It was rolling into the second month since she'd left her sister grieving in New York. She didn't even attend her own niece's funeral out of guilt and fear. *'It's your fault,'* her sister's last words replayed in her mind. She was partially right. Still, Valerie was her only sister and she missed her. She wanted to make things right. She couldn't stand the thought of not having a relationship with her.

Her hands trembled as she dialed the number nervously. Petey picked up on the third ring, "Yo!"

"Boy, where you learn to answer the phone like that?" She made a lame attempt to joke.

"Who's this?" He asked, not laughing.

"Who you think it is? It's your aunt."

"Ooooh, hey Auntie Viv. I haven't heard your voice in a

minute. I almost didn't recognize it." His tone changed to a genuinely friendly one. This put Vivian somewhat at ease.

"Mmm mm mm. How you been, Petey?"

"Oh, I can't complain, Auntie. How you and Cinnamon doing out there?" he asked.

"We doing okay. How's Tracey?"

"She's alright. You know it's been hard on her or whatever, but she's tough. She's getting through it." He said, solemnly.

"Yeah…" Vivian hesitated before continuing. "And your mom?"

Petey sighed into the phone, "Not too good, Auntie. Not too good. It's been really hard on her. She don't talk much no more. Most of the time she just stares into space. She won't let us move anything on Roxxy's side of the room. She be acting like Roxxy just gon' up and come home one day. You know?"

The guilt hung around Vivian's neck like a tight noose. Her throat became dry as she tried to swallow the feeling. "You know I would've been there to help if I could. Your mom was just so mad at me."

"Oh, no. You and Cinnamon need to stay as far away as possible now more than ever. We don't need no more family taken out." The line grew quiet. "Oh-oh I didn't mean it like that, Auntie. I just meant … well … I heard…" He hesitated.

"Heard what, Petey?" Vivian asked.

"I heard his peeps is looking for you. Both of y'all."

Vivian mouthed a curse to herself under her breath. "Don't you worry about us, Petey. We'll be alright. Is your mom around?"

"Yeah, she in the room, but I don't know if she gonna wanna talk to you, Auntie." Petey said, cautiously.

"Can you just try to ask her? I just want to hear her voice." Vivian begged.

"Hold on." Vivian heard the sound of Petey putting the phone down. Then he called out to his mother. They had a brief exchange in the background before he returned to the phone. "She don't feel much like talking right now, Auntie. Maybe some other time she might be up to it." He sounded apologetic.

"That's okay. I understand, Petey. I just wanted to make sure y'all were okay. Just let her know I'm thinking about her, okay?"

"Oh, most definitely!" He assured.

"And Petey?"

"Yeah, Auntie?"

"Tell her I'm sorry." Vivian hung up.

Tears welled up in her eyes as she stared at the floor. She and her sister had always been so close. It was killing her that they weren't speaking. Now, to make things worse, she knew what Petey said had to be true. She knew that they'd be after her. She only wondered how soon they would track her down to carry out their revenge.

***

Generosa's apology to The Greater Saints First Baptist Church was much shorter than Deacon MoMoney's or Pastor Leonards's had been. It was almost as though someone had written the words for her, and she just recited them before the congregation. She looked down at her feet as she spoke, wringing her hands nervously as her father's glare burned holes into her back from the pulpit. She only glanced up every so often to look at baby Tabitha who sat on the front pew, cradled in her grandmother's arms.

Since Tabitha's birth, the first lady never let the baby out of her sight—not even for a minute. She was always holding her, feeding her, changing her, or just watching her sleep. Much to the reverend's dismay, the baby's crib was stationed in their bedroom. Generosa rarely got the chance to be alone with the child or even hold her. "You just worry about focusing on your studies—and no more running around with that lil' boy Anthony." That's what she'd been told by First Lady Grienbachs.

Now, as she looked at her daughter bonding and cooing up at her mother, she wanted nothing more than to run over and snatch her baby out of her arms. Still, she continued to address the congregation, "Thank you all so much for your love and support and prayers for me and Tabitha. Again, I apologize for my sinful fornications and just pray that you, my wonderful church family, find it in your heart to forgive me for my betrayal."

Once she was done, Generosa made her way towards the pew

her mother sat in as another church member moved towards the podium to relay the announcements. She extended her arms towards Tabitha but was shooed away by the first lady instead, "You go on ahead in the back with the rest of the kids. I got her." Generosa obediently complied.

Later that evening at the Grienbachs's residence, the reverend seemed to be in one of his unusual moods. Tabitha's constant wailing didn't seem to help either. Gabe busied himself in the kitchen, rummaging through the refrigerator for something to eat while Generosa sat at the table finishing homework. The reverend and first lady sat on the couch in the living room with the TV stationed to the news channel. Karissa's picture flashed on the screen as the anchorman recapped her story. "The teen has been missing for three weeks now. The police say she was last seen getting into a white work van. They believe she may have accepted a ride from someone she knew. If you have any information about Karissa's whereabouts, the police are asking the public to call their hotline at…"

"Me and Sister Kim are gonna go down to the station with Sister Connie tomorrow. This has been so hard on her. I wish Karissa would just come on home and stop putting Connie through this. She has it rough enough being a single mom." First Lady Grienbachs's brow pulled toward the center of her forehead with distaste.

"All these girls are just too fast for their own good these days. And I don't know what they're putting in the water! Got 'em walking around looking like grown women. It's no wonder some man done went and snatched her up. He probably thought she was a woman the way these girls dress and carry themselves these days." The reverend replied. Tabitha cried and flailed her arms and legs about in the bassinet that sat at the floor near the first lady's feet.

"Gerald, I know you're not trying to place blame on Karissa if some maniac out there did kidnap her—or worse!" The first lady tapped the bassinet with the tip of her toe to rock the baby, but it didn't help. Tabitha continued with her shrill screams of discomfort.

"I'm not blaming her. I'm just saying I can see how a man could get the wrong idea. You've seen the girl, Moni— how she dresses and acts all grown! Frankly, I'm surprised something didn't happen to that girl sooner."

"Gerald!" The first lady scolded.

"What? You know I'm right, Moni." He scoffed as he shifted on the couch, trying to get comfortable. He pointed the remote towards the TV to increase the volume as his face twisted in annoyance. "Can't you shut that baby up already? See?"

"See what?"

"This is what I'm talking about. See what happens when these girls look and start to act all grown? Next thing you know, they're shooting out crying babies."

Generosa scrambled to her feet from the kitchen and scooped up Tabitha in her arms. She began to bounce her and walk away when the first lady stopped her. "Where you going with her?"

"I was just gonna check her diaper." Generosa answered, timidly, as she held the baby close.

"Go on back and finish your homework. Give her to me." The first lady held out her arms. Once she had the baby back in her possession she said, "Aint' nothing wrong with her diaper. She just wants her nana. Ain't that right, my lil' suga muga? You just want Nana. I know." She rocked the baby back and forth in her arms as Generosa retreated back to the kitchen. Still, Tabitha continued to whine.

"I'm going upstairs to watch TV." The reverend growled in annoyance as he rose to his feet, his stomach hanging down, peeking through the too small tank top he wore.

"Okay, we'll be up in a few." The first lady answered.

"Well make sure she's quiet when you come up. I don't know how much longer I can take all this crying. I don't know why you had to put that crib in our room anyway, Moni."

"Because I wanted her close by to keep an eye on her. Who else is gonna take care of Nana's lil' pumpkin?" She replied.

"Yeah, well, I got to get up early for a meeting with Pastor Leonards in the morning, and I won't get no sleep with this hollering child. So you do what you gotta do, but I'll do what I have to do to get some sleep tonight. You hear?" He cautioned.

The first lady only sucked her teeth in response, dismissing the pastor's threat as an idle one. "What you meeting Pastor Leonards for?"

"I don't know. He said something about he's been rethinking his position in the church. It sounds like he's thinking about stepping down or leaving."

"Oh…" The first lady got quiet for a moment as she processed the news. "Well, that might be for the best."

Gabe, being in earshot, could hear the conversation but couldn't let his true feelings show. Although they'd been banned from seeing one another, Gabe's feelings never diminished for the pastor. His heart sank at the thought of the man he loved abandoning him. Would he really just leave without saying a word to him? Not even a goodbye? Gabe made up his mind then that he would have to come up with some sort of plan to see Pastor Leonards before he left. Maybe he could change his mind. Maybe he could even convince him to take him away with him.

***

Cinnamon was more excited to see Generosa the next day at school than she ever would have let on. Generosa seemed almost back to herself since the last time she returned to school. Still, something was bothering her and Cinnamon could tell.

"I'm so happy you're back. I missed my lunch buddy." Cinnamon smiled.

"Aww, thanks. I missed you too." Generosa blushed and pushed her hair back behind her ear.

"We have so much to catch up on!" Cinnamon's tone dropped to a more serious one. "I have something to tell you."

"What?"

"Anthony…"

"What about Anthony?" Generosa asked.

"He … he kind of has another girlfriend now, I heard."

"Oh," Generosa looked down into her lap as she fought back tears that began to form.

"I'm sorry, Generosa. Look, forget him! He wasn't all that anyway." She tried to make her feel better. Generosa, too choked up to respond, only nodded and glued on a fake smile to try to hide the hurt. "You know what we should do?" Cinnamon tried to throw some excitement in her voice.

"What?"

"We should have a sleepover, just you and me! I'm finally off punishment. Do you think your parents will let you come over this weekend?" She asked, excitedly.

"I don't know. I don't know about leaving Tabitha." Generosa sounded scared and Cinnamon didn't understand why.

"It'll only be for one night. Can't your mom watch her?"

"Yeah, maybe. I guess I can ask." Generosa said, blandly.

"I mean only if you want to. If you don't want to spend the night, I understand." Cinnamon offered.

"No—no, of course I want to." The genuine smile returned to Generosa's face. "I'll ask my mom tonight.

CHAPTER 19

Things were all a blur as two shadowy outlines moved about around her. She could hear moaning, but Karissa wasn't even sure if the sound came from her. She felt weak and hazy. She slowly blinked back tears due to the bright light that shone directly above.

"Hello, my dear. I see someone is waking up from their nap." The voice said, cheerfully. "Here, you can take this away—and be sure to clean those knives really good."

She could hear the instruments clanking on the table as it was rolled away by one of the blurry figures. She could tell she was lying down, and she had trouble moving. Feeling sluggish and out of control, it took all of her strength to roll her head to one side where her blurry vision fell upon another tray. She could see something on the tray but couldn't make it out.

"Don't worry, honey, you did very well. Part one of the surgery was a great success if I may say so myself."

"Mmmmfff," Karissa managed to slur, her tongue feeling thick and heavy. Unable to form words due to the heavy medication, her facial expression did more of the talking. Sheer panic lit up in her eyes at the mention of a surgery. Her eyes began to dart around the room frantically looking for clues as to what her capturer was getting at. Her focus fell back on the tray.

"Beautiful, isn't it?" He beamed. "Can you guess what that is?"

"Mmmmmfff," She murmured in response.

181

"Well, this," He scooped a mound of bloody flesh into his hand off of a sheet of wax paper. "This is your left breast." He gave it a gentle squeeze as a fresh drop of blood oozed down his latex glove. "And that right there is your nipple." He pointed to a small brown areola, the size of a Hershey's kiss, that sat on ice.

Karissa's eyes shot wide open in horror as she looked down at her chest. Where there once stood two perky mounds of fatty flesh, now only sat one. The right one. On the left, she could see a blood spot coming through her hospital gown and tubes ran from the area out of her sleeve, down into a black plastic garbage. Her body began to jerk from her screams and cries once she realized the depth of the nightmare she was in.

He continued to talk over her screams as though he didn't hear them. "Now, right now we're just draining what's left of the fatty tissues and fluids out of there. Then we can begin part two of the surgery where I'll reattach your nipple." He said with promise in his voice. "Then, if all goes well with that, we can do your other breast!"

Though still heavily sedated and dazed, Karissa managed to moan out, "Whyyy?"

"*Why?* What do you mean '*why*? You girls just don't get it. You all think you can run around, flaunting your bodies and teasing men with your assets. All you do is use us, and you think you're something special. Well you're not. Y'all rely so heavily on your looks and bodies you got no brains, no compassion, no nurturing and understanding for those around you. Well, luckily, you now have me to help you change all of that. See, by removing your breasts you can free yourself from the shallowness that is your existence. You can work on the inside, dig deeper than your outer appearance. Trust me. You'll thank me when it's all said and done. The others didn't make it, unfortunately. Something always goes wrong." He rubbed his chin as if thinking to himself. "But not to worry! You have made it past part one! That's a major improvement. We've never made it this far, have we?" His partner cosigned with a wide smile once back in the room.

Though still unable to move, Karissa's loud sobs shook her body. "Awww there there, now. There's no reason to fret. Hand me the mask. We should let her nap a little more." He said just before lowering the plastic gas mask over Karissa's face. She could feel the cool air blow into her nose and over her mouth. Before she had a chance to let out another whimper, she was out like a light.

***

Sister Connie sat quietly staring into space as Sister Kim and the first lady made small talk. The three ladies waited to speak with the detectives who were heading up the search for Karissa. Every now and then, First Lady Grienbachs would rub Connie's back in an attempt to comfort her. They'd been waiting for thirty minutes before Detective Sunil emerged to escort them back to his office.

"Please have a seat." He said as he rolled his chair from behind the desk to offer to Sister Kim. Sister Connie and the first lady had already taken the two available seats. Now the detective sat on the edge of his desk. Detective Sunil was a beige man who appeared to be of mixed race, possibly Hispanic and Caucasian, but it was hard to tell. His bushy mustache moved up and down on his wide face as he spoke.

"This is what we know. Karissa was last seen walking on Crimson Street at approximately six p.m. She was approached by a man in a white work van. They spoke briefly, and she got into the front passenger seat of the van. Now. Ms. Mills, can you think of anyone at all that Karissa may have accepted a ride from in a white van?" Connie shrugged her shoulders, shook her head, and sobbed into a tissue.

The first lady interjected on her behalf, "We know a lot of people who drive those white work vans. My husband even has one!" She offered.

"Well, let's start with who you know. We'll make a list and rule out everyone we can. What kind of van does your husband have, ma'am?" First Lady Grienbachs went on to describe the work van her husband sometimes used to transport tools and cleaning supplies back and forth to the church. She knew they had nothing to hide and wanted to help in any way she could. The rest of the list included Pastor Leonards, Brother John—who owned three vans, and every other man in Gracious Meadows. It would take forever for the detectives to comb through the list, but they really didn't have much else to go on.

"I think you need to take a close look at Pastor Leonards."

Sister Kim said, sternly. Ever since the scandal with the pastor and her husband, she blamed Pastor Leonards. She believed her husband would have never been involved in such a perverted abomination had it not been for the pastor's influence.

"Why do you say that?" asked the detective. Sister Kim glanced at the first lady before answering. She knew if she told too much, she'd incriminate her own husband, and she didn't want that.

"Well, he just spends a lot of time with the kids. That's all. He's close with them." Sister Kim's mouth turned into a tight, drawn line as she crossed her legs and arms.

"Oh yeah, why is that?"

"What Sister Kim is trying to say is that Leon Leonards is our youth pastor at the church. He leads the teen bible study where Karissa is in regular attendance. I'm not sure if there will be any helpful information he'll be able to provide, but I know you'll have his full cooperation." First Lady Grienbachs said.

"Uh huh, I see. And did Karissa ever mention anything to you about Pastor Leonards?" He directed his question to Sister Connie.

"No, not that I can think of. All the girls just thought he was cute but kind of corny. You know?"

"Did it ever seem like the pastor paid Karissa any extra unwanted attention? Anything like that?"

"No—I don't know." Connie rubbed her head. She was too exhausted to think, and she was sure the pastor didn't have anything to do with her daughter's disappearance.

The detective straightened his back and inhaled. "Okay, well it won't hurt to have a talk with him; see what he knows. We'll continue to be in touch, Ms. Mills, and if anything comes to mind—anything at all, don't hesitate to call or come on down to the station. It may seem like the smallest detail, but sometimes that's all we need." Connie nodded her head and sniffled as she and the other two women rose to their feet.

***

"Thank you for meeting me, Reverend." Pastor Leonards's voice echoed from the church walls. The space seemed much bigger than it really was without the congregation. The pair sat in the front pew.

"Of course, Leon. What is this about?"

"Reverend, I've decided to leave Greater Saints." Pastor Leonards said in an almost painful tone.

"I see … I can't say I'm surprised."

"You're not?" This surprised the pastor.

"No. Considering the mess you've made here, I can't say I'm sad to see you go, Leon. In fact, the only reason why I agreed to keep you here is to save face with the church." Reverend Grienbachs's words were sharp and direct, thrown at Pastor Leonards like daggers.

"I'm sorry?" Pastor Leonards twisted his body to fully face the reverend.

"You heard me. You're a sick pervert, Leon, and you will burn in hell. There's no doubt about that. But what kind of pastor would I be if I exiled you from the church—or worse, because please believe I would love to do worse for the sick things you forced my son to do. But we're supposed to be Christians, true believers of the word. We practice forgiveness and understanding." The reverend explained. "I'm glad you're leaving Greater Saints—"

"Actually, I'm leaving Gracious Meadows altogether. I'm going down to Georgia. I have a cousin down there." Pastor Leonards corrected.

"Even better. When do you leave?"

The pastor hung his head, hurt by the reverend's direct disdain. "My truck is all packed up. I have a buyer for the van later today. So I'll be leaving first thing tomorrow morning."

"Good. Leave the keys on my desk in the study." Reverend Grienbachs stood and walked away without so much as a goodbye.

Pastor Leonards sat for a while with his elbows on his knees and his shiny head in the palms of his hands. He was deep in thought when he heard light footsteps approaching behind him. When he looked up, he saw Gabe's red tear-stained face. He'd been hiding, hovering near the basement steps, listening to the entire conversation.

"You were just going to leave? Without even saying goodbye?"

"Gabe, I'm sorry. I can't keep living a lie. I can't keep pretending that who I am and what I do is something wrong, something to be ashamed of. I love the church but—"

"What about *me?* I thought you loved *me!*" Pastor Leonards froze as Gabe's hand swung from behind his back to produce heavy cold steel now pointed at his nose.

Pastor Leonards spoke slowly. "Gabe, calm down. Just put the gun down. I do love you. I do."

"No you don't! You're just lying!" Gabe's chest heaved in and out as the steady stream of tears flowed down his cheek and snot began to slowly descend from his nostrils.

"Please, listen to me. I do love you, Gabriel. I love you so much. That's why I have to leave. I can't stand it. I can't stand being here Sunday after Sunday, wanting to kiss you, hold you, be with you—but I can't. I have to pretend you don't even exist. Do you know how bad it's killing me inside?"

Gabe took two short paces back and forth, unsure of what to do next. "If you really love me, you'll take me with you." His arm slowly dropped to his side as he continued pacing in front of the pastor.

"I want to. I want to take you away from here more than anything in the world. You have to believe that. But I can't. Do you know what they would do to me? You're underage. If we get caught, they'll lock me *under* the jail!"

Gabe knew he was right, but his emotions wouldn't let him reason rationally. "Then I don't want to live." He quickly pointed the gun to his temple.

Pastor Leonards sprung to his feet. "Gabe, just wait! Please don't do this. You still have your whole life ahead of you. You don't have to do this." He could feel beads of sweat forming along his brow and his dress shirt quickly became drenched with perspiration beneath his arms.

"You have no idea what it's like ... living in that *house* ... with *him*. If you leave, I have nothing to live for. I might as well be dead."

"No. No, you don't mean that. Don't. Do. This. Gabriel, I am begging you." The pastor clasped his hands together. "Okay. Okay. I'll take you with me." He said, suddenly.

"Yeah, right. You're lying again. I'm not falling for it. You don't love me. Nobody loves me. I hate my life. I *hate* it! I don't want

186

to do this anymore." He squeezed his eyes tightly shut and grimaced. The pastor took what he saw as his only chance and grabbed Gabe's arm. The two wrestled to the floor. The teen was stronger than Pastor Leonards expected. "Let go of me! Let go! I wanna die! I wanna die!" Gabe fought hard. *POP!* Suddenly the gun fired one shot and the struggle ended.

***

"I'm surprised your mom and dad let you come over tonight."

"Yeah, me too." Generosa breathily said in disbelief. "I think my mom just wants Tabitha to herself."

"Well, she is the proud grandma! Besides, at least you get to have a break and just chill." *Beep-beep beep-beep.* Cinnamon's pager sounded. She reached over and grabbed it from the dresser, holding it between her index finger and thumb as she squinted at the number. "Oh, that's Raheem." She smiled to herself as she placed the pager back down.

"Aren't you going to call him?"

"No, he knows you're spending the night, and I'm busy. That was just our code we send to each other sometimes to let the other one know we're thinking about them." She bragged.

"You and Raheem seem pretty happy."

"Yeah, we are." Cinnamon gushed. She sat on her bed with her back against the headboard and legs stretched out. Generosa had one leg tucked underneath her and the other dangled from the side of the bed opposite Cinnamon.

The two girls munched on a bowl of popcorn placed on the center of the bed. Music videos flashed across the TV screen, but the sound was turned down low and it was more like the TV watched them as they flipped through some of Cinnamon's magazines.

"You like this?" Cinnamon turned a *Black Hair* magazine around towards Generosa with the cover folded back.

"Yeah, that's cute." Generosa shyly replied. It was a picture of a lady with a swoop bang swept back into a French bun. The back of her hair hung straight down the neck.

"I bet that would look real nice on you."

"Oh, I don't know." Generosa blushed.

"For real. I could do it for you. I know how." Cinnamon offered. Generosa scrunched up her face in response, unsure of herself. "Come on. It'll be fun. If you don't like it, you can always comb it out. I just need a couple of bobby pins." Cinnamon sprung to her feet and shuffled around some things on her dresser. Then she knelt behind Generosa on the bed and loosened her hair from the ponytail it was in. Generosa continued to flip through her magazine. "So what about you?"

"What *about* me?" Generosa replied.

"I mean things are over with Anthony. Is there anyone else you like? You know I'll hook it up." Cinnamon sang in Generosa's ear.

Generosa giggled at Cinnamon's attempt to make her laugh. Then she quickly got serious and looked down. "No, there's no one."

"No one? Really? Out of all those guys at school?" Cinnamon pressed.

"For real. Anthony was the first boy I ever liked … and that liked me too." A single teardrop quickly fell onto a paragraph in the magazine without her permission, blurring the small black letters. Just the mention of Anthony, and a sadness swept over her like an unavoidable tidal wave. She was devastated when Cinnamon told her about Anthony moving on, and she still wasn't over it.

Cinnamon either didn't notice or pretended not to notice Generosa fighting back tears. "Well … we'll just have to find you someone new. Watch after I hook you up with this new doo, all the guys will be try'na holler at you."

"I seriously doubt it." Generosa let out a short cynical laugh as she quickly wiped her eye. "Nobody wants a girl that has a baby. Besides, Tabitha is my main focus now. All I want is to keep her happy, healthy, and safe." The thought of her baby returned a warm smile to her face.

"Speaking of which…" Cinnamon hesitated before continuing, unsure of how to word her question. "How is baby Tabitha's daddy?" Generosa just stared at the magazine with no response. "I just mean I didn't even realize you were pregnant or seeing anyone before Anthony."

"I wasn't seeing anyone."

"Soooo…" Again, Generosa clammed up with no response. "If you don't want to tell me, it's fine." Cinnamon quickly offered.

The pair continued in silence, with the exception of a *Total* video that played on the TV, while Cinnamon finished Generosa's hair.

"There. All done." Cinnamon dipped her fingertip in a jar of gel and softly smoothed back Generosa's edges to finish off the new look. "Go ahead. Check it out." She coaxed Generosa towards her mirror. Generosa turned her head left and right before a big grin of approval appeared across her face. "Uh huh, you like that don't you? Told you I got skills!" Cinnamon teasingly boasted.

"I do really like it. Thank you." Generosa ran her fingers through the back of her hair that lay over her shoulders. "Thank you for being so nice to me, Cinnamon."

"Girl, please."

Suddenly Generosa turned to face Cinnamon. "Can I tell you something?"

"Yeah. Of course." Cinnamon's face turned to worry at the serious look on Generosa's. Both girls sat back down and Generosa took a deep breath before speaking.

"I'll tell you who Tabitha's father is, but you have to promise not to tell anyone."

"Okay," Cinnamon responded.

"Seriously, Cinnamon, you can't tell anyone—not even your mom. I'll be in big trouble if anyone finds out." Now she stared Cinnamon directly in the eye.

"Okay. I promise I won't. You can trust me. Who is the father?"

Generosa took a long pause before answering. "Gabe."

CHAPTER 20

"Go ahead. Tell her what you just told me, Generosa." Generosa, Cinnamon, and Vivian sat around the kitchen table. It took two hours of convincing, but Cinnamon managed to persuade Generosa into telling her mother the information she'd just shared with her.

After a half bottle of red wine, Vivian was awakened from her peaceful stupor by a panicked Cinnamon shaking her. *'Mom! Wake up. This is important!"* She'd whispered frantically. Now the three were surrounded in eerie midnight silence, Vivian barely able to keep her eyes open. Cinnamon rushed about to make her mother a cup of coffee.

"Cinnamon, I don't know. I don't think it's a good idea." Generosa spoke timidly.

"What's wrong? What is it, sweetie?" Vivian did a good job at hiding her impatience as she could sense something wasn't right and her help was needed.

"*Tell* her. Generosa, you have to tell *someone.* It's okay." Cinnamon pushed again.

"I can't," She shut down.

"Honey, I can't help you if you don't tell me what's going on." Vivian gazed into Generosa's eyes pleadingly.

Cinnamon sat a white mug with a picture of Snoopy on it in front of her mother. Then she rejoined the other two at the table. "Generosa ... I know I promised I wouldn't tell—and I won't. If you really *really* don't want me to I won't, but you have to tell *someone.* He can't keep doing this to you. It's not right, and it won't stop unless you talk. My mom will help you."

"You don't understand."

"I won't understand anything if you don't tell me, honey." Vivian tried again. More silence followed.

"Do you want me to tell her?" Cinnamon offered. Generosa shrugged in response. "Mom, Generosa just told me who Tabitha's father is and…" Cinnamon wasn't sure if she should continue. She wanted to help her friend, but she didn't want to betray her trust either.

"*And, what?*" Vivian asked impatiently. "Who is it? That boy y'all was with at the mall?"

Generosa shook her head emphatically, "No. No, it wasn't him, Sister Vivian."

"Well?"

"It's … my brother." It came out a whisper, barely audible.

Vivian had to make sure she heard correctly. "*Who?*"

"It was Gabe, Mom! He's been forcing Generosa to have sex!"

"No! It's not like that, Cinnamon." Generosa's voice elevated.

Vivian looked at Cinnamon, a subtle look that told her to be quiet. "Generosa, it's okay. We're not judging you and your brother. But if you're practicing incest—"

"No! No! No! We don't *want* to do it. Neither of us *like* it." She began to sniffle as her voice cracked. Her head bowed in embarrassment.

"I don't understand." Vivian said.

"It's my dad … Sometimes he's just … just … I don't know. It's like he turns into this other person, a monster."

"Oh, the bi-polar disorder." Vivian said, knowingly.

"*Bi-polar disorder?*" Generosa scoffed in confusion, as though this was the first she was hearing of the news. "He's just crazy. When Gabe or me do something bad, we both have to get punished. He takes us in the basement and makes us … *do* things."

"Do things like what?" Cinnamon interjected.

"Cinnamon, maybe you should let me talk to Generosa alone." Vivian suggested.

"No! She's *my* friend. I want to know what's going on!"

191

Cinnamon objected.

"Yeah, but I don't think you need to be hearing this."

"Mom, stop treating me like a baby. With everything I've already been exposed to, I'm pretty sure this won't ruin me." She cut her eyes at her mother and Vivian read the subliminal message clearly as she shifted uncomfortably in her seat. Her daughter was right.

"It's okay, Sister Vivian. I want Cinnamon to stay. Please." Generosa was more comfortable having her there.

"Okay, honey. Go on."

"My dad makes us get undressed, and he makes us ... touch each other and do things to each other."

"Generosa, listen to me. This is very important. Did the reverend force you and Gabriel to have sex with each other?" Vivian asked, already knowing the answer. Generosa looked into her lap and nodded in shame. "Oh my God. Oh my God." Vivian began to chant. She felt a fire rising in her chest. "I'm calling the first lady right now—"

"NO!" Generosa's head jerked up quickly, her eyes wide and wild.

"Honey, it's okay. Your mother needs to know what's going on. She won't be mad at you."

"You don't get it, do you?" Generosa looked at Vivian in a way that suggested she had an extra head. "She already knows."

"What do you mean she knows?" Vivian was confused.

"She knows, Sister Vivian. She knows what goes on in the basement. She pretends not to know, but I know she does."

"How do you know if you've never told her?" She asked.

"Because ... this is not the first time I got pregnant." Her eyes fell back into her lap as a knot rose at the base of her throat. Her body shook slightly as she began to weep.

Vivian scooted her chair next to Generosa's and hugged her tightly with one arm, before releasing to rub her back. "Oh my God, child. I had no idea you had another baby."

"Me neither. How come you never told me?" Cinnamon questioned.

"I don't ... not anymore." Cinnamon and Vivian exchanged puzzled looks. Everything that came from Generosa's lips now seemed

192

to flow as unsolved riddles. "He's gone. I had a baby boy a year and half ago, Isaiah. I hid that pregnancy too, but when I finally gave birth I told my mom that my dad had been forcing Gabe and me to have sex and…"

"*And, what?*" Vivian found herself asking again.

"He was having sex with me too."

"Who? *The reverend?*" Vivian was beyond speechless. She began to chant again, "Oh my God. Oh my God."

Generosa nodded quickly. "I told her, and she told me I was a liar and a sinner, but I know she knows I was telling the truth because I heard them arguing about me. Then, after Isaiah came out with Down syndrome, I think she really knew. The family kept the baby a secret. After that, he stopped having sex with me, but he still made Gabe do it while he watched. And whenever Gabe couldn't … *you know* … he would call him a gay sissy and beat him all night then leave us both chained up."

"*Chained up?*" Cinnamon's and Vivian's shock both came out in unison.

"Please, Sister Vivian, please. You can't tell. You don't know what they'll do to us. You just have no idea." Generosa pleaded desperately.

"Okay, just calm down and let me think." Vivian gnawed on her bottom lip then took a sip of her coffee. The rage inside her wanted to drive right over to the Grienbachs's house and blow both their brains out. *Calm down, Viv. Calm down*; she spoke to herself. *We don't need another situation on our hands.*

"Where is Isaiah?" Cinnamon asked.

"He's gone." Generosa answered.

"Gone?" Generosa nodded. "What do you mean *gone?* Gone where?"

Generosa shrugged and grabbed a napkin from the holder. She blew her nose and tried to get her breathing under control before answering. "About two weeks after he was born, he disappeared."

"Disappeared how?" Vivian asked.

"They won't tell me."

"Who won't?"

"My mom, dad, even Gabe won't tell me—if he knows. I think

he does." Generosa almost sounded like she was talking to herself for a moment, lost in her memory.

"So this baby—*your* baby, Isaiah—just up and disappeared into thin air? How is that even possible?" Vivian sounded doubtful.

"All I know is my mom took him to the basement bathroom to give him a bath and he never came back up. That was the last time I saw him. I kept asking and asking *Where's Isaiah? Where's my baby?'* But they just ignored me. They just pretended he never even existed, and I guess after a while, I forgot he ever existed too … until baby Tabitha came." All of a sudden Generosa's mood changed. "Sister Vivian, you gotta help me! I don't want Tabitha to disappear too. My mom won't let me near her. She keeps the baby with her at all times. I just know something's gonna happen to her too. I just don't know what to do."

"Okay, just calm down. Everything is gonna be alright. I promise. Nothing is going to happen to Tabitha." Vivian continued to rub Generosa's back to sooth the teen before rising to her feet. She continued to speak as she poured the remainder of her coffee into the sink. "Why don't you girls try to get some sleep tonight. First thing in the morning, we'll head down to the police station."

"Sister Vivian, please, my mom and dad can't find out I told anyone about all this. You don't know what they'll do to me. They're not the people that you think they are." Generosa was still terribly frightened.

"Don't worry. They won't find out. The first thing we have to do is get you and your brother and Tabitha out of that house. Maybe we should call DSCYF first." Vivian wasn't too sure of the plan herself, but she knew something had to be done. It had to be done sooner rather than later. "Cin, why don't you fix you guys some warm milk. That should help Generosa get some sleep. In the morning we'll all have clearer minds. One thing's for sure, you can't go back to that house."

If only there had been some way for Vivian to ensure that. Hours later, just before the sun had the chance to make an appearance, the trio was jolted awake by heavy banging and the door bell insistently ringing.

"What in the…" Vivian hissed as she marched down the hall to the front door. Her robe billowed behind her as she hurried to tie the belt around her waist in an attempt to conceal her curvy body.

Sister Kim's fist was raised mid-air ready to pounce on the door again when Vivian swung it open. "Vivian! Where's Generosa?" She asked frantically as she pushed passed Vivian into the living room without an invite or a hello.

Her face twisted in an annoyed scowl, Vivian answered with attitude, "She's in Cinnamon's room sleep. Well, at least she *was* sleep. We were *all* sleep, but she probably ain't no more."

"Tell her to get dressed, get her things, and come on!" Sister Kim ordered.

"Hold up. What's going on?"

"It's a family emergency." She answered as she paced back and forth impatiently.

"What kind of emergency?"

"Look, it's a private matter, Vivian. The first lady sent me to come get Generosa. Now will you please go wake her up?" Sister Kim pressed.

"She's not going back to that house. I'm taking her down to the police station."

"Police station? For what?"

"I'm sorry, but I can't tell you that." Vivian wasn't really sorry.

"You can't tell me?" Sister Kim sucked her teeth and breezed past Vivian towards Cinnamon's room. "I don't have time for this today." She didn't bother to knock, but it didn't matter. The girls were already awakened by the commotion. "Generosa, come on. Get your stuff. You're coming with me."

Generosa looked back and forth between Vivian and Cinnamon with cold in her eyes. White crust formed a trail towards the side of her right eye where she'd been crying throughout the night while she lay. "Wh-what?"

"Come on, girl. It's an emergency. It's your brother. We've got to get to the hospital right away." Sister Kim said.

"*Gabe?* Is he alright? What did they do to him?" Vivian stood close to Sister Kim's face now, afraid for the boy.

"What did *who* do to him? I already told you. It's a private family matter."

Generosa scrambled to her feet and began arranging her

overnight bag in a hurry. She threw quick glances at both Cinnamon and Vivian to let them know they shouldn't say another word. She was worried about her brother and needed to get to him right away, even if it meant risking her own well being. "I'll call you later." She said, quickly, to Cinnamon after her things were gathered. She didn't bother to change out of her pajamas.

Vivian stopped her at the bedroom door and grabbed her by her shoulders. She stared directly into Generosa's eyes, looking for reassurance that Generosa was okay to leave with Sister Kim. Her eyes ping-ponged back and forth between Generosa's as she spoke. "You call us if you need anything at all. You hear? *Anything*. I mean it, Generosa. And don't you worry about anything. Everything is gonna be alright. You have my word." She hugged her tightly and Generosa nodded in understanding before Sister Kim wisped her way.

***

"Thankfully, it was just a flesh wound. The bullet merely grazed the left side of your torso, Mr. Leonards." Leon sat up in a hospital bed as the doctor filled him in. "The blood clotted with no problems right away and we only had to do a few stiches. So you'll be free to go in just a few moments here." Pastor Leonards jerked up his right arm and coldly stared at the doctor. The handcuffs securing his wrist to the bed clanked. "Oh ... I'm sorry. I meant you'll be discharged from the hospital. I guess the police will have to take it from there."

Hours passed before detectives Sunil and Briggs showed up to interview the pastor. Detective Briggs spoke first. "Mr. Leonards," his voice boomed. "We've spoken to Gabriel."

"How is he? Is he okay?" Pastor Leonards's genuine concern was evident all over his face.

"Well, he's really torn up about what he did to you." The detective revealed. "It seems like he really looks up to you." Pastor Leonards wasn't sure how much the detectives knew. He sat in silence and allowed Detective Briggs to continue in an attempt to draw out as much information as he could. "We understand that you're moving?"

"That's right." Pastor Leonards kept his answer short.

"And you and Gabriel are close." He suggested.

"I guess you can say that. I have a good relationship with all my kids."

"Your kids?"

"My kids at Greater Saints First Baptist Church. I'm the youth pastor there, so I try to be a pastor who they feel they can come to, talk to, confide in. You know, that sort of thing." He explained.

"I see. So why don't you go ahead and tell us what happened at the church today, Mr. Leonards?"

"Should I have my lawyer here for this?" he asked.

"You can if you want, but what do you need a lawyer for? We know that Gabriel is the one who had the weapon, and he shot you. We just need to get your side of the story."

"Well, why am I still handcuffed to this bed then?" Pastor Leonards jangled the cuffs again.

"That's just procedure. You know, a precaution. We weren't sure which of you was the aggressor, so we have to cuff you both until we find out what's what." Detective Briggs tried to make the whole thing sound breezy and casual. Pastor Leonards rolled his eyes in response. "Now, what happened today at the church?"

The pastor took a deep breath before answering, still unsure if he should talk without a lawyer. "I went to the church today to talk to Reverend Grienbachs. That's Gabe's dad, as you probably already know." Although Detective Sunil hadn't said a word yet, both men had out their pads jotting down notes. "I was giving my resignation from the church."

"Oh?" Detective Briggs paused to look up from his notes.

"Yeah. I'm moving to Georgia, and I just went by to talk to the reverend and hand in my set of the keys to the church."

"And why are you resigning? Do you have another job lined up in Georgia?" The detective asked.

"Not yet. I have a cousin down there who's agreed to let me crash with him for a short while until I do find a job."

"So no job offer. Why just up and move to Georgia? Why all of a sudden? From what we've heard, you've done some excellent work at the church. You even helped head up the fundraiser to raise reward money for one of the missing girls in Gracious Meadows."

"Yes, all of that is true. I do love working for the church. It's just that…" He hesitated.

"Just that what?"

"Some of my personal lifestyle choices don't really coincide with what we teach at Greater Saints. Lately I've found it harder and harder to keep going through the motions when I don't necessarily agree with everything, so I made a decision to leave."

"I see. Mr. Leonards, is it true that you own a white work van?" Detective Sunil spoke up for the first time. Detective Briggs set him up nicely to trap the pastor in a corner.

"Yes, but not for long. I have a buyer lined up for it. I was supposed to meet him today, but this happened." He pointed to his ribcage.

"Pastor Leonards, Karissa Mills is in your bible study group. Isn't she?"

"Yeah?" He didn't see where this was going.

"How would you describe your relationship with her?"

"The same as with the rest of the kids. Like I already told you, I'm their *pastor*. I like to think of myself as a mentor to these kids."

"Uh huh, I see." Detective Sunil stared stone-faced at the pastor. "Well, can you tell us your whereabouts on the day she went missing?"

"I don't know. That was weeks ago." The pastor twisted up his face. "What is this about? You think I had something to do with Karissa's disappearance?"

"You tell me."

"Absolutely not. I would never hurt her or any of the other kids. That's just crazy. Just ask the church members. Ask her mother, Sister Connie." He grew defensive.

"Oh, don't worry. We will, but right now we're asking you." Detective Sunil wasn't ready to let up just yet. "First there's this sudden rush to move to Georgia and you're also selling your van. Why sell your van?"

"I don't know. I don't really need it. I really only use it to bring supplies to and from the church and since I won't be working in the church anymore…" His voice trailed. "Besides, it would be kind of hard for me to get both of my vehicles down to Georgia right now along with the moving truck. Plus, like I said, I'll be crashing with my cousin for a while until I get on my feet and there's really nowhere for me to put two vehicles. It just makes sense."

"So if we search your vehicle we won't find anything that may suggest Karissa was in that van with you?"

"No, you won't find anything, but I think I want a lawyer now. If you're not going to release me, this interview is over until my lawyer gets here." The pastor leaned backed, winced as he crossed his arms, and glared at the detectives.

Detective Sunil flipped his notepad closed and clicked his pen. "Good, because a search warrant is being obtained for the van as we speak. I hope you're right."

***

Generosa's heart felt like it would thump right out of her chest as she walked down the corridor of the psychiatric ward in the Gracious Meadows Correctional Hospital. She left Sister Kim behind in a waiting area as she went to join her parents in Gabe's room.

"Oh, honey, you're here." First Lady Grienbachs remained seated next to Gabe's hospital bed. Her eyes were bloodshot like she'd been crying. Still, she managed to give a pleasant smile. She seemed out of it.

Reverend Grienbachs stood on the other side of the bed. Every now and then, he paced the floor, occasionally pulling up his slacks by the belt to meet his oversized stomach.

Generosa's eyes darted around the room. "Where's Tabitha?" She asked in a panic.

The reverend diverted his eyes to the floor. The first lady answered, "Your brother is laying here in this *crazy* ward and all you can think about is yourself? Generosa, you know better than that."

"I'm not crazy." Gabe sat up, visibly upset with his hands crossed in his lap.

"Well, you must be! Tryin' to shoot folks. Talkin' 'bout you want to kill yourself. And for what? All for some perverted fairy? This is not the way we raised you." The reverend spoke harshly.

Generosa remained quiet, looking from afar as she hovered near the doorway. She could see in Gabe's eyes that something was wrong. He wasn't himself. He seemed delayed. The reverend continued to reprimand his son until a nurse interrupted. "Excuse me. The lawyer is here to see you, but we can't let anyone else back here."

"We should go talk to him, Gerald. Generosa, you stay here and keep your brother out of trouble for a few minutes." The first lady instructed.

Once they were alone, Generosa slid the chair the first lady had just been sitting on closer to the bed. "Gabe, what happened?" He stared out the window, gnawing on his bottom lip, but said nothing. "Talk to me." Generosa put her hand on top of his, but he flinched away. "Gabe, please just tell me what happened." His jaw tightened and a single tear slowly rolled down his cheek. "Is it true? Did you really try to kill Pastor Leonards *and* yourself?" She pressed.

Gabe's voice was dry and his breath stale as he opened his mouth to speak. "I ... I didn't—I wasn't really gonna kill him. I just..."

"You just *what?*"

He looked lost and still refused to meet his sister's eyes. "I only wanted to talk to him. He was gonna leave me, Generosa." He swallowed hard. "I love him so much. He can't leave me here ... with them. You know."

Generosa grabbed his hand firmly. "I know. Don't worry. We're gonna fix this, Gabe. I'm getting us some help."

"Help?"

"Yes." She lowered her voice to a whisper and glanced at the door to make sure no one was coming. "I told Cinnamon and Sister Vivian what he does to us, and they're gonna help us."

"YOU DID WHAT?" His back stiffened and now his eyes looked directly at Generosa's. "What'd you do that for? Why would you do that?" He panicked.

"Don't worry. We don't have to be afraid anymore. We can't keep living like this. They're gonna find a way to get us out of that house once and for all. You, me, and Tabitha." Gabe put his forehead in the palm of his hand. "Gabe."

"Yeah?"

"Where is Tabitha? Do you know?" She asked her brother.

He shook his head, "I don't know. I haven't seen her since yesterday morning."

Generosa was uneasy. She didn't like what she heard. "Gabe."

"Yeah?"

"I told them about Isaiah too."

Gabe clearly became even more uncomfortable. He shifted on the bed, and his eyes found their way back out of the window. "What about him?"

"You know," Generosa whispered forcefully.

"Generosa, I don't—"

"You know! Look at me!" She demanded as she pulled his face to align with hers. "Gabe, please. Please, just tell me. What happened to Isaiah?" Her eyes watered as she begged her brother.

"What difference does it make? He was retarded anyway. Just let him go. I don't want to talk about him ever again." Now he was uncomfortable and agitated.

"I deserve to know. I deserve to know. He was mine!" She begged. "Look at what they've done to us. It's not right, and you know it's not right. I don't want whatever happened to Isaiah to happen to Tabitha. Please tell me where he is."

Now he chewed on his bottom lip hard while trying to decide what to do or say next. He took a deep breath before answering.

CHAPTER 21

"I just can't stop thinking about them." Cinnamon leaned up against Raheem's shoulder on his tiny twin bed. The two cuddled while attempting to watch *Batman Forever* on his small television.

A day had passed since Generosa dropped the bomb on her. She wanted to go to the police immediately, but Vivian wanted to wait until she knew more about what was going on with Gabe. Vivian was out on a date with a man she'd met at work. *"How can you go on a date at a time like this?"* Cinnamon had asked her mother earlier that day.

"There's nothing we can do right this moment, so why shouldn't I go get wined n' dined?" True to form, all Vivian thought of was her new prospect. Cinnamon wondered which category this new guy would fall in. That was the extent of their conversation before Vivian sauntered off wearing a revealing number.

Now, here was Cinnamon almost doing the same. Even though going over to Raheem's wasn't a real date, she still didn't feel right doing nothing. She had only shared with Raheem that Generosa and Gabe were in trouble, but she wouldn't go into detail. She didn't want to betray her friend's trust. Raheem didn't seem too concerned. He was really into the movie even though he'd already seen it when it was out in the theater.

"You need to relax. Your mother's right. There's nothing you can do right this second. So..." He pulled her close and gave her a quick peck on the cheek. She sighed in response. "Com'ere," he turned her face towards his as he made his move. For a moment, Cinnamon found herself lost in his kiss. Raheem was a great kisser. Though, it wasn't as if she had a lot to compare him to.

They began their usual routine. He kissed her neck and slowly slid his fingers beneath her T-shirt. She caressed his teenaged biceps and it wasn't long before he'd completely removed her shirt. Instead of unsnapping the back, he hurriedly yanked down the front of her bra to get to the goods. She wasn't nervous. This wasn't the first time they'd gotten to this point. Squeezing, pinching, and rubbing the right, he licked, kissed, and lightly nibbled on the left. He grabbed her hand firmly and planted it on his zipper. She responded accordingly, undoing his belt buckle, then button, and finally the zipper. Then she slipped her small hand inside.

They carried on for a while like this until Raheem decided he wanted to take things to another level. "Lay back," he instructed. She complied obediently. Then he unzipped her jeans and slid them completely off.

"Raheem," she whispered.

"Shhhh, don't worry," he kissed her lips to quiet her. Then he proceeded to pull her panties down before making a trail of kisses down her stomach and beyond. It wasn't long before he had Cinnamon moaning heavily in pleasure she'd never felt before. Once he felt satisfied with his work south of the border, Raheem came up for air and continued to kiss Cinnamon's neck. Grinding skin to skin, Raheem was tired of waiting. "I want to feel you, baby."

"I want to feel you too, but—"

"But what?" He cut her off impatiently. "It's been three months. I want to take things to the next level. Don't you love me?"

Cinnamon had been forewarned by her mother that these words would come sooner or later and that she shouldn't feel fooled or pressured, but right now none of that advice mattered. Her body craved the attention. "You know I love you, Raheem." She whispered in between kisses. He didn't have to say another word. He just looked into her eyes with his sincerest expression. "Do you have protection?" Her mother's words rang in her head. If she didn't remember anything else when that "special moment" arose, she was to *always make him wear a condom.*

"Yeah. Hold up." He lifted himself from her body and shuffled a few things around in one of his milk crates. Then he licked his lips and waved the gold foil back and forth between his fingers. He tore off the corner with his teeth. Cinnamon lay still as she watched him roll it on. She could feel her heart rate increase with fear of the unknown. He knew this was her first time. "Don't worry, baby. I'll be gentle. I promise." He said.

She parted her rigid thighs for him to enter. *Beep-beep beep-beep*, her pager went off. "Wait!" She pressed both palms into his chest.

He let out a loud sigh of annoyance. "Just check it later."

"No! It might be my mom. You know I'm not supposed to be over here. What if she's looking for me? Let me just see." Raheem unwillingly allowed his body to fall on its side as Cinnamon jumped up from the bed to rummage through her jeans to find the pager. "Can I use your phone?"

Raheem rolled his eyes, "Go 'head. Is it your mom?"

"I don't know." Cinnamon's hands quivered as she dialed the number. She wouldn't let Raheem know, but she was relieved by the interruption. The phone didn't have to ring one full time before someone answered. Before Cinnamon could utter a word, she heard a timid voice.

"Cinnamon! It's me, Generosa." She whispered anxiously into the phone.

"Generosa, what's wrong? What happened to Gabe?" Cinnamon rattled off questions.

"Gabe's in trouble. It doesn't look good. He's in the psychiatric ward at Gracious Meadows. He shot Pastor Leonards."

"Oh my God!"

"What? What is it?" Raheem asked in the background.

"I'm sorry. I didn't mean to interrupt, but I needed to talk to you. I need your help." Generosa sounded desperate.

"Of course! What's the matter?"

"Gabe told me about Isaiah. I know what they did to my baby." Generosa's voice sounded strained and unsteady.

"What happened? Where is he?"

"Cinnamon, please just listen. I haven't seen Tabitha all day. I haven't seen her since before I came to your house yesterday. It's happening again. I keep asking my mother where she is, but they won't say a word. I can't let the same thing that happened to Isaiah happen to Tabitha."

"Okay, slow down. Just stay calm. We'll be right over." Cinnamon's exchange over the phone only lasted briefly. She assured Generosa she'd be there as soon as possible before ending the call.

"What's going on?" Raheem asked.

"We gotta go. Now!"

"Go where? We not gon' finish what we started?" Raheem didn't try to hide his disappointment.

"Not tonight. I'm sorry, Raheem, but Generosa needs my help. Something's not right. I need you to take me over to her house. Please." She dressed quickly as she talked.

Raheem let out a long burst of frustrated breath as he rubbed his hands up over the back of his head and down over his face. "Okay."

Once they were both fully dressed again, Cinnamon waited anxiously by Raheem's door. He hit the power button on the TV and grabbed his keys. Then he grabbed Cinnamon around the waist and pressed her against the door with his body before laying a light gentle kiss on her cranberry lips. He ran his thumb over the bottom lip then looked deep into her eyes. "Cinnamon, you know I love you, right?" She nodded. "I'm sorry if I tried to move things too fast tonight, but just know I'm willing to wait until you're ready—as long as it takes. Okay?"

Cinnamon gave a small smile and nodded again, "okay."

The ride was quiet to the Grienbachs's house. Dusk was setting in and the sun was saying its goodbyes for the evening. The sky was gray except for a settling line of orange. Cinnamon's mind raced with horrid thoughts about what Generosa could have possibly found out about her baby, Isaiah. Did they give him up for adoption without Generosa's permission? Had they been hiding him somewhere? Had he been a dumpster baby? Thrown away like trash? The thoughts ran on and her legs shook side to side nervously.

"Baby, relax. Everything will be fine. I told you that whole church is bananas. I bet you it's nothing." Raheem put his hand on Cinnamon's thigh in an attempt to calm his girlfriend.

"You don't understand. Everything she told us yesterday is really crazy ... and *sick*. She sounded really worried on the phone, Raheem." Still she tried to relax. She slid her legs forward to try to stop the shaking. When she did, she felt her foot land on top of something small, a rock maybe. When she looked down, it twinkled in the van's dark interior each time they passed a lamp post, catching Cinnamon's eye. "What is that?"

"What?"

Cinnamon reached down and picked up what turned out to be an earring. She turned it in her fingers up towards the window to get a better look from the outside lights. "Whose is this?" She didn't try to hide the anger in her voice.

"What is it?" Raheem tried to steal a glance while keeping his attention on the road.

"It's a girl's earring, Raheem. Now who does it belong to?" Cinnamon's voice was stern with jealousy.

"*Earring?* I have no idea."

"Sure." Cinnamon rolled her eyes.

Raheem sucked his teeth. "Cinnamon, I swear I have no idea whose earring that is or how it got in here. I really don't. Maybe it's been in here for a while—since before John started letting me use the van."

"Uh huh," Cinnamon continued to study the small stud. As they turned onto the Grienbachs's block, a sudden epiphany sent shockwaves to her heart and it began racing. The stud was a small '*k*' like the same earrings Karissa had stolen from the store in Brooklyn.

Raheem pulled over a few houses down from the Grienbachs's. "Cinnamon," she jumped when he reached for her hand. Her expression was a frightened one. "What's wrong?" He glanced down at her balled up fist then back to her face. "Cinnamon, I thought you trusted me. I'm telling you, you're the only girl in my life. I haven't had nobody else up in this van, for real." Cinnamon sat frozen, scared and confused as to how the missing teen's earring could have wound up in her boyfriend's van. Raheem sucked his teeth again, "Let me see the earring."

Cinnamon clenched her fist tighter. "Just forget it." She unlocked the door and pulled the handle, but Raheem pulled on her arm.

"Wait for me."

"No, it's okay. I should go alone. I'll call you later." She tried to get out again, but Raheem tightened his grip.

"You sure?"

"Yeah"

"Alright, well let me at least get a kiss." He said as his fingers loosened their grasp. Reluctantly, Cinnamon leaned over and gave the most passionless and quickest kiss she could manage to fake in that moment.

"Please, baby. Don't be mad. I'm telling you the truth. Be careful and make sure you call me when you get home tonight or at least beep me, so I know you're okay." He instructed.

"Alright." Cinnamon couldn't look at Raheem. Instead, she leaned into the door to push it open and hopped down from the van's passenger seat. Once Raheem pulled off, she made her way towards the house. From the outside, there appeared to be only one light on in the house, one of the upstairs bedrooms. Generosa had given her strict instructions to just wait near the back door. No one was to know she was there. Cinnamon followed directions and scurried to the back while her eyes darted about to make sure no one saw her and possibly mistook her for an intruder.

She shifted back and forth from one foot to the other with her hands shoved down in her pockets. Her shoulders were hunched up near her neck to keep warm. After dark, the temperature cooled and the light hoodie she'd worn out earlier in the day wasn't fit for the weather. She had no idea she'd be waiting there for thirty minutes. During that half hour, all she could think of was Karissa and the earring. She took her hand out of her pocket and eyed the small jewelry in the palm of her hand. She pinched the back of the stud and examined the 'k'. This was definitely Karissa's earring and the thought of it sent chills up her spine, causing her to shiver. Had she been dating the killer all along? Kissing him? Hugging him? *Dang*, she'd almost had sex with him too.

She thought back to all of their late night conversations shared on the phone after Vivian had gone to bed. Then she thought about what everyone had told her all along. *'Stay away from him.' 'He's a rapist.'*

The voices played over and over in her head. Maybe everything she'd been told was true. Maybe he really had raped Sister Connie and now ... *had he killed Karissa? Had he killed all those other girls too? The knife,* suddenly that small detail landed in her mind like the spaceship in *Independence Day.* The knife, the earring, the accusations, it was all coming together like one bad dream. Cinnamon's breathing became heavy, and she felt dizzy. Her eyes watered and her blood boiled like hot lava pulsing through her veins.

Just then the screen door creaked open, startling her. She jumped and dropped the earring in the grass, then grabbed her chest once she realized it was Generosa. "Cinnamon, it's me." She whispered. Cinnamon bent down to retrieve the earring, then stepped back, her breath caught in her chest. "Are you okay?"

"Yeah ... yeah, I'm fine."

"Hurry. Come in, but be quiet. They're in their room watching TV." She whispered as she opened the door wider to let her in. The door creaked again, and the two teens froze to listen and make sure the coast was clear before heading in the kitchen. Everything was dark and silent inside. Cinnamon walked close behind Generosa so as not to bump into anything in the unfamiliar surroundings. They paused again once they made it to the top of the basement steps when they heard Reverend Grienbachs belt out a loud hearty laugh. Generosa opened the door and Cinnamon closed it tightly behind her. Then they made their way down, stepping ever so lightly as they went. Cinnamon had motioned towards the light, but Generosa shook her head no. She didn't want to take any chances. Once they made it to the bottom, Generosa whispered, "Hold on. Stay right here." Cinnamon's heart thumped loudly as she stood in the darkness and waited for Generosa to return from the dark.

She heard a click and a dim light shone. Generosa waved for her to join her in the corner of the basement furthest from the stairs. "Isaiah is here. He's down here somewhere."

"What do you mean? A baby can't live in a basement."

"No, he's not alive, but his body is here somewhere." Generosa's voice had a sadness but also a determination to it.

"How can you be sure?"

"Gabe told me at the hospital. He told me everything. They

killed my baby, Cinnamon. They killed him." She said, her voice rising slightly.

"How?"

"I'm not really sure. I think they drowned him. I told you my mom took Isaiah down to give him a bath that night. I thought it was weird she didn't just bathe him in the kitchen sink like we usually did. I should've known…" Generosa paused as her mind drifted back to that awful night. "Anyway, I went upstairs to get my clothes out for church the next day, and my dad had Gabe helping him to do some work on the furnace down there. Gabe said Daddy went into the bathroom with my mom and Isaiah to pee. Gabe stood near the door waiting for Daddy to come out, so he could grab some tissue for himself. When he did, he said both of my parents had a weird look on their faces and he saw Isaiah turned on his stomach in the tub … floating. He said my mom quickly grabbed him up and covered his entire body with a white towel—even his face. He said he saw my baby's foot just dangling from the towel. It wasn't moving, Cinnamon." She turned to Cinnamon with a lost, sad look in her red, watery eyes. She sniffled quickly, "Anyway, he said my dad hurried him away from the door and shut it. That was the last time he saw Isaiah. Gabe is positive they never left the basement with my baby. I know he's dead, but I just need to see with my own eyes. I need to know for sure. I know he's down here somewhere. I need your help to find him. It'll be evidence for when we go to the police to tell them everything." She had it all planned out.

"Okay. Where do we look first?"

They quietly scoured the basement from corner to corner. They moved shelves, opened boxes, climbed on ladders. At one point, they thought they may have found the missing newborn behind some loose bricks. But once they removed them, all they found was a stack of old pornographic magazines from the 70's and some video tapes.

"Generosa," Cinnamon whispered from her corner of the scavenger hunt. "I have to pee. I can't hold it."

Generosa pointed towards the bathroom. "Don't turn on the fan and don't flush the toilet." She was cautious not to alert her parents.

Cinnamon nodded as she made her way across the floor. She sat down and relieved herself with her head cradled in the palms of her hands. Although she was there to help, her mind was still reeling from her thoughts of Raheem. She wondered if she should tell someone about the earring and the knife. *I have to do something*, she thought as she looked up to grab some tissue. When she did, she had a feeling of déjà vu. Her eyes landed on the small door below the sink again. *But it's so small*, she thought. After wiping herself and tossing the used tissue in the toilet bowl, her reflexes took over. Without thinking, she flushed the toilet. She gasped immediately and washed her hands quickly.

Generosa was on the other side of the door in no time whispering, "*Cinnamon!*"

Cinnamon opened the door. "I know. I'm so sorry. I forgot that quickly." Both girls froze and looked up towards the ceiling. It was hard to tell if the reverend or first lady had gotten up from two floors below. They remained silent and still for at least five minutes, their hearts thumping practically in sink. The adrenaline was too much for Cinnamon. She was the first to break their silence, "I think I—"

"*Shhhh,*" Generosa still erred on the side of caution. She waited an additional minute before exhaling the breath she'd been holding in fear. "I told you not to flush." She reprimanded angrily.

"I know. I'm sorry, but I think I found Isaiah."

"Where?" Generosa's whisper was a little louder now, her anticipation taking over.

Cinnamon slowly held out one finger and pointed. "There."

Generosa moved quickly. They switched spaces with Cinnamon standing by the door and Generosa on her knees. She tugged on the door and jumped back when about three small larvae fell out onto the floor. She resumed cautiously, only using the tips of her fingers with her pinky in the air. The air fresheners still hung in place where Cinnamon had seen them before. Generosa yanked them down hastily. That's when she came to the small piece of plywood that was nailed in place.

"Shoot! I need something to get this off."

Cinnamon quickly disappeared and shuffled things about out in the basement. She reappeared holding a rusty hammer. "Here. Be quiet."

"I know," Generosa's breathing was heavy as she worked to pry the wood off. There was a snapping sound and a corner chunk of the wood flew onto the floor. She dug deeper with the claw of the hammer, *crack*. The wood split in half, leaving only a quarter left to be removed, but the girls' suspicions looked to be confirmed already. The orange cardboard of a tiny Nike shoebox peeked through the open space. Once she had all the wood gone, the chips scattered at her knees on the tile floor, Generosa's hands trembled as she worked to fit her fingers in the narrow space. Using her nails around the border of the box, she worked the box out little by little. The box was light in weight. She sat it gently on the floor and looked up at Cinnamon.

"Open it."

Both girls prepared themselves for what they might find as Generosa slowly slid off the lid. Their gasp was heard in unison. Cinnamon stood frozen, her hands clasped over her mouth and eyes wide. Generosa collapsed into a quiet sob with large elephant tears falling right into the box. Just as Gabe had described, there was a small white towel and one tiny skeletal foot with a thin layer of deteriorated skin that peeked from beneath it. Generosa pulled the towel back to discover tiny bones protruding from what looked like thin brown tissue paper. The body was badly decomposed. Tiny sprouts of hair were matted to the skull. Most of the skin had disintegrated, but there was no mistaking. It was the full skeleton of a baby—Generosa's baby, Isaiah.

"What do you think you're doing down here?" A calm, clear voice boomed from behind them, a shadow loomed over the bathroom, startling both girls. Cinnamon jumped and turned to see the tall frame of Reverend Grienbachs.

CHAPTER 22

Just as Pastor Leonards knew, the police found nothing during their search of his van. His lawyer came to his aid as soon as he made the call and he was released in less than twenty-four hours. The police had nothing to hold him on and, after the search turned up nothing, Detective Sunil wasn't so sure they had their guy after all. "He just doesn't seem to fit the profile," is what he'd told his partner. It came out during questioning that the pastor preferred the same sex. Their guy, Sunil felt, hated women, but was definitely a heterosexual male. Something about the pattern and obsession with the women's breasts told the detective that their perpetrator was one who was unlucky with the ladies or possibly inadequate sexually. Either way, Pastor Leonards was home free.

Leaving Gabe in the fragile condition he was in, tugged at the pastor's conscience, but he stayed clear. He wasted no time leaving Gracious Meadows, not even to finalize the sale of his van. After popping a few caffeine pills he picked up from a Shell gas station, Pastor Leonards burned down Route 13 and never looked behind him.

***

"I told you already. My daughter is home. I can't." Vivian leaned into Martin, her latest romantic interest, as she spoke. The three glasses of wine she enjoyed during their dinner left her feeling loose and happily buzzed. He held her close around the waist and pressed his lips firmly against hers once more to muffle her words. Giggling into his mouth, she melted into their kiss. Neither of the two even noticed the same black BMW parked across the street about three car lengths down. Then again, Vivian hadn't noticed that same vehicle for the past three nights that it had been there.

Martin's hands roamed below Vivian's waist, groping her behind. She wanted nothing more than to let him in. She couldn't remember the last time she'd been with a man and her body yearned for the attention. She didn't want this to be the way she introduced Martin to Cinnamon for the first time, though. *Cinnamon, this is Martin, the date I was telling you about. Martin, this is my daughter, Cinnamon. Okay, we'll just head off to the bedroom now!* She played the ridiculous conversation in her head and giggled aloud once more.

Martin leaned away from Vivian, "what?"

"Nothing. Really, it's nothing, but I should go now."

"Uuuuuuuugh," Martin let out an exaggerated huff of disappointment.

Vivian gave her best, most innocent puppy dog face. "I really had a great time tonight, Martin. Thanks for dinner."

"You're welcome," he shoved his hands into his pants pockets. Then he leaned in and kissed her on the cheek. "I'll call you."

"Okay."

Vivian watched Martin walk down the steps and towards his car before opening the front door. Then she locked it behind her. She let her body fall back against it, closed her eyes and tilted her head back before letting out a sigh. "Cinnamon!" She called out into the empty apartment. When she received no response, she squinted at her watch. It was almost a quarter to midnight. "Cinnamon!" *Now she know better than this*, she thought. She threw her purse down on the table, flipped on the light switch and marched down the hall, her heels clicking loudly against the wood. She was baffled to find an empty room when she turned on the light to Cinnamon's room. Everything was quiet and still, neatly in its place.

Cinnamon never broke curfew. Something wasn't right and Vivian felt it immediately. She hurried to the phone to page her daughter, but before she could lift the cordless off the stand, it began to ring. "Hello?" There was a pause on the other end, then *click*. The person hung up. Vivian stared at the phone for a moment then proceeded to enter in Cinnamon's pager number.

After changing her clothes and rolling up her hair, Vivian paged Cinnamon again and sat waiting by the phone. She got up to get some coffee to take the buzz from the wine off when the phone rang again. Again, the person hung up. Whoever it was called a third time. Vivian answered, "Cinnamon? Is that you?" There was silence on the other end. "Whoever this is, stop calling here and playing on this phone. Now is not the time. Grow up and get a life!" This time she ended the call before they had a chance to hang up.

The coffee did its job, and now she sat at the kitchen table bouncing her leg on the ball of her foot. She clicked on the phone to make sure the line was open. When she confirmed a dial tone, she placed it back on the charger. She'd paged Cinnamon five times within the last hour and half with no response. The last two pages were sent with an urgent *9-1-1*. All the worst thoughts began to race through Vivian's head, especially with a serial killer on the loose. She sprinted to her room to get dressed. She wouldn't sit and wait any longer.

***

"You couldn't just leave it alone. You had to go snooping." Reverend Grienbachs paced back and forth across the living room floor. The girls sat quietly, terrified by the Reverend's calmness. Generosa sniffled with her eyes wet, looking at the floor. Cinnamon contemplated bolting for the front door, but she knew she wouldn't make it. "So ... what do you have to say for yourselves?" The reverend took a few more paces. "What do you think we should do about this uh—situation?"

"I don't know, Daddy. I ju—"

SLAP! The reverend's hand was loud and heavy across Generosa's face. The sudden pop caused Cinnamon to jump. "*You just what?* Huh?" He mocked his daughter. This time she knew better than to respond.

First Lady Grienbachs had been immediately informed of the girls' mischief by her husband. Now she slowly plunkered down the steps one by one, her robe open and barely hanging on. Her loose fitting clothes were disheveled and three sizes too big. She looked tired, unkempt, and annoyed by the disturbance.

"Well well what do we have here?" She glared at Cinnamon. "Will you quit that sniffling!" She barked at Generosa. "Pull yourself together for goodness sakes!" Generosa tried to gain control of her emotions. Her eyes were red and swollen from all the crying and her face matched the same crimson color from the slap. "You just couldn't leave well enough alone. Could you?"

"What do you think we should do?" The reverend asked.

The first lady ignored his question. "You really are such a pretty young lady. You know that?" She gently stroked the side of Cinnamon's cheek. "Why couldn't you just be a good girl and mind your business, sweetie? You just keep on getting *my* good little girl in trouble. Every time I try to give you the benefit of the doubt, you just let me down." She purposely pulled the edges of her mouth down to mock a frown and sighed. Cinnamon yanked her face away in response.

"She's a feisty one too, just like that momma of hers." The reverend chuckled.

"Ugh. Honestly Gerald, is that all you ever think about? Need I remind you why we're in this situation in the first place?" Her response caused a straight face of embarrassment to quickly appear. She rolled her eyes and turned her attention back to the girls. "Your mom *is* pretty loose, though. Isn't she?" She cackled and taunted Cinnamon.

"Don't you talk about my mother!" Cinnamon hurled in response. "You know she's gonna be looking for me. There's nothing you can do. We know all about what's been going on here, and she's already told the cops." She lied, wishing it were the truth. Now more than ever she wished her mother had just went straight to the police once Generosa had told them everything.

"Oh yeah? And what's that? What do you think has been going on?" The first lady hissed.

"I know all about what the reverend has been doing to Generosa ... *and Gabe*. He's been abusing them and forcing them to have sex with each other. He got Generosa pregnant before and now we have the body to prove that you *killed* that baby! It's just a matter of time before we find out what you've done with Tabitha. Where is she?

You kill her too?"

"Hmmm looks like you've been watching too much TV, missy." That was all the first lady said.

"Mom, please. Please tell me where Tabitha is. I know you've done something to her." Generosa quietly dared to speak up.

The first lady leaned down and into Generosa's face so that her warm breath could be felt on her nose. She squeezed her face with one hand so that Generosa's cheeks bulged and her lip hung down to show the bottom row of her front teeth. "You better shut your mouth. We expose you to these worldly sinners for all of five minutes, and you've forgotten your commandments already. Maybe you need some time in the basement to refresh your memory. *Honor thy father and thy mother.*" She shoved Generosa's face, thrusting her head back towards the couch. Then she spun on the heels of her fluffy slippers and took her turn to pace the floor a few times. "You don't know what you're talking about anyway. Tabitha is just fine. That's all you need to know, and I don't want to hear her name in this house again. Maybe if you weren't waltzing around flaunting your goodies all the time, we wouldn't be in this predicament."

"How can you say that?" Generosa whined, her bruised feelings apparent. She was met with another slap, this time from her mother.

"That'll be enough of that now!" Spit flew from the first lady's mouth. She was silent as she paced. Then she spoke to the reverend as though the two girls weren't in the room with them. "She's right, you know. Her mother will come looking for her, and she *will* be relentless. You know how those loud mouth New Yorkers can be. We don't need the attention or the questions."

"So what, then?" The reverend seemed as clueless as ever. It was clear who ran the show now.

"Go grab the keys. You're going to the police station."

"*The police station?*" The sound of that plan clearly made the reverend nervous.

"Yes. Didn't you just hear? Our baby granddaughter is missing. Something terrible might've happened to her. We must report her abduction immediately." She said with a sinister smirk.

The reverend grinned and nodded emphatically. He liked the plan so far. "And what about her?" He nodded toward Cinnamon.

"Leave that part up to me. You take Generosa to the station downtown. I'll deal with *her.*" With that, the foursome parted ways with their respective partners in tow.

The first lady stayed close until they made it into her car just in case Cinnamon tried anything. Once inside, she locked the doors, started the engine and backed out of the driveway. Kirk Franklin's *Melodies from Heaven* played softly on the radio. The tempo of the song matched First Lady Grienbachs's calm mood. She stared straight ahead as she drove, saying nothing. Cinnamon stole glances out the corner of her eye as she wondered what the first lady had in mind. She felt her pager vibrate. When she and Generosa were in the basement, she'd switched it to vibrate, and it hadn't stopped going off the whole time. She knew it was probably her mother.

"My mom is probably out looking for me by now." She spoke.

The first lady took her time before responding. "I'm sure she is." She had an eerie, smug smirk painted on, her eyes still glued in front of her.

"Where are you taking me?"

"Don't worry. You'll see … Everything is going to be juuuuuust fine." She turned the corner and drove two blocks before coming to a red light.

Cinnamon didn't like her vibe, and she wasn't about to sit and wait to see what would happen next. She saw her only opportunity and took it. Giving her best shot, she cocked her fist back and came full force to the side of Lady Grienbachs's jaw, knocking her head into the driver side window.

"Wh-what are you doing?" The first lady fought back, using both hands to wrap around Cinnamon's neck while still trying to keep her foot on the brake. She squeezed hard and Cinnamon clawed and scratched at her face. The street was empty as their fight continued. Cinnamon could feel her breath leaving her body as she struggled for air. She was seeing stars as the pressure behind her eyes increased with the first lady's grip. She knew she had to do something. She stretched her arms as far as they would reach and jabbed each of her thumbs into the first lady's eyes. The first lady let out a shrill scream of pain, causing her to release her grip. Cinnamon wasted no time. She raised her body up and grabbed both sides of the first lady's head, bashing it into the driver window. She pushed hard and repeatedly. Even once she noticed a spot of blood developing on the window, she kept slamming. She didn't stop until she heard the window crack. First Lady Grienbachs moaned in agony. She was still conscious but way out of it. The pain was too much and caused her to unwillingly forfeit their fight.

Cinnamon reached over her and hit the button to unlock the doors. She escaped the vehicle with haste. Her legs moved swiftly beneath her, carrying her like the wind. She never looked back. She didn't stop until she came to the intersection of where John's Furniture Store was. Doubled over with her hands resting on her knees and panting, she looked at the building. She glanced up to see Raheem's bedroom light still on upstairs. *I thought he would be at John's house,* she thought. She was afraid, but she was desperate. Her home was too far to walk and so was the nearest police station.

As she stood catching her breath, and weighing her options, a pay phone caught her eye. She lazily strolled across the street to the pay phone. Her breath was loud and heavy as she moved. She made a collect call to her house, but after the operator put her through, the phone just rang and rang before going to the answering machine. "Mom?… Mom? It's Cinnamon. I need you to come get me. I'm at John's store. If you're there, please pick up … Okay, well, if you get this, please come get me." Feeling defeated, Cinnamon sadly hung up the phone. She knew her mom well enough to know she was probably out looking for her by now.

With no money to page Vivian, Cinnamon had no choice but to ask Raheem for help. She studied his van parked out front then headed towards the store. There was a side entrance to take the stairs up to his apartment. When she turned the corner of the building, Cinnamon noticed a light coming from one of the warehouse windows. She crept over and peeked in. She could see the back of a white lab coat moving around the room methodically. She couldn't tell who it was, but she watched the person move about the room, taking things to and from a small tray that sat on one of the shelves. They walked back and forth to retrieve different items from different parts of the warehouse. Cinnamon had only been in the warehouse a handful of times to check for things in stock, but she had never noticed any of the items this person had stashed and stored around the place. Then she watched as the person carried the tray to the far corner of the warehouse, squeezed behind one of the storage shelves, and disappeared down what looked like stairs to a basement. *I didn't even know there was a basement*, she thought. She never saw it when she was in there, and she never saw any of the warehouse guys use it.

Her curiosity was peaked, and she couldn't help but to find out where the secret stairway led. She waited a few minutes and looked behind her to make sure the coast was clear. She made her way to the back door of the warehouse. To her surprise the door was already unlocked, and she gently eased it open. Then she slipped through and eased it back, but didn't shut it all the way. It was cool and frighteningly quiet in the warehouse. It didn't seem as scary during working hours when employees were moving in and out of it. She walked slowly along the wall towards where she saw the white lab coat disappear. She could hear muffled voices below and her heart began to race. One voice was a girl's, but she couldn't make out what they were saying.

Just as she neared the door, she heard a male voice suddenly get louder as the person approached the stairs. Cinnamon quickly dashed behind a shelf that held boxes of assemble-yourself coffee tables, the wind from her body causing a purchase order to blow off one of the shelves onto the floor. The boxes were stacked high enough to hide her, but her heart thumped loudly and she wondered if the lab coat would hear. The person trotted up the stairs and burst through the door in excitement.

Cinnamon could tell from his back that it was a man; a man who seemed to be in a jolly mood as he sang through a medical face mask. "Our Gooooood is an awesome God we praaaaaise from he—" The person suddenly stopped. She could hear him pick up the purchase order. "Hmmmm, how'd you get on the floor?" He read over the purchase order before taking a slow look around. Cinnamon held her breath on the other side of the shelf. She could hear him walking around, checking the warehouse until he came to the open door. "Humph, that's strange." He pulled the door shut, making a thud that caused Cinnamon to jump. She clamped her hands over her mouth to muffle her breathing. "Hellloooo? Is somebody in here?" He sang. After standing in the middle of the floor in silence for thirty seconds, he shrugged his shoulders, shuffled some things on a shelf, hit the light switch, and headed into the furniture store, closing the door behind him.

Cinnamon stood frozen with her hands over her mouth for ten minutes before releasing her breath. Her heart still pounded on, but she was pretty sure the lab coat had left. She slowly eased herself into the dark from behind the shelf. She took slow, light steps toward the secret door while listening for lab coat to return. She turned the handle and slowly creaked the door open. It looked like a dungeon, dark and dank except for a very dim light that peered from underground space. The steps were wooden planks, unlike the other steps around the property. They made noise each time she descended even though she stepped carefully. With each move she paused to listen up the stairs for white lab coat. As she neared the bottom, she could hear the sniffles and moaning of a girl. She could also smell something horrible. It smelled like rotting flesh, blood, feces, vomit, and urine.

Then she saw her. "Oh my God."

"Mmmm! Mmmm!" Karissa, startled and afraid, huddled in a corner away from Cinnamon. She was clearly frightened beyond measure. Her mouth wasn't duct-taped shut anymore. Someone had manually pierced her mouth closed with a lip ring that ran through both lips. They were swollen and there was still dried blood around the piercing. Her ankles wore handcuffs with a long iron chain attached that ran to the wall, anchored somehow into the brick. Her wrists were bound together in the same way. The filthy hospital gown she wore had a huge brown stain on the front that Cinnamon guessed was blood. Half of her head had been shaved and the other half was wild and matted with dirt. She looked as though she'd lost fifteen pounds. She wasn't the Karissa that Cinnamon remembered.

"Karissa," Cinnamon whispered. "Is that really you?" Karissa didn't respond. She just looked at Cinnamon with wild, scared eyes. "It's me. Cinnamon." Cinnamon moved forward and the sudden movement sent Karissa into a frenzy.

"MMMMM! MMMM!" she screamed through her seamed lips as she swung her shackled hands back and forth to ward off Cinnamon from coming any closer.

"It's okay. It's okay. I'm not here to hurt you." Cinnamon held her hands up in a surrender position. Still, Karissa eyed her suspiciously. "Everyone's been looking for you for weeks! Sister Connie is worried sick."

Cinnamon paused and looked around at the scene. Karissa sat hunched up on a dirty twin size mattress that lay on the floor. Next to the mattress was a bucket that she could guess what was in it. In the middle of the floor was a hospital bed. Next to that bed was a tray with lots of odd medical instruments that Cinnamon had never seen before. The room was depressing with its dirt floor and no windows. There was another small room, but she didn't want to know what was in it.

"Who did this to you?" She turned her attention back to Karissa, who sat like a wild tiger who'd just been captured. She didn't respond. "Was it Raheem?" Karissa gave a strange, confused look as though she wasn't even sure who Raheem was anymore. "We gotta get you out of here." Cinnamon looked around for anything to unbind Karissa but found nothing.

As she searched the room for the key to the handcuffs, suddenly Karissa's eyes widened even more and she began hopping around on the mattress like a leap frog. "Mmmmm! Mmmm!" She looked alarmed, but Cinnamon didn't understand right away.

Then she heard the lab coat return just above them. Cinnamon's heart began to race immediately. She whirled around, but there was only one way out. Then she heard his footsteps coming down the stairs quickly. She could see the horror in Karissa's eyes, but she wasn't sure if it was for her or herself.

"What's wrong, pumpkin?" Cinnamon could see the back of the lab coat as he spoke to Karissa. She'd dashed underneath the stairs and prayed he wouldn't turn around. He looked left and right, then up at the ceiling as if listening for something. "Were you down here talking to someone?" Karissa whimpered and shook her head in response. "You suuuuuure?" He slowly walked over and caressed the hair that was left on her head. "You wouldn't lie to me now would you?" Karissa cried in response. "Good!" He said suddenly and loudly as he stood up straight. "Then we can get started."

"Mmmmm! Mmmm!" Now Karissa screamed through her sealed lips hysterically. Whatever was about to get started, Cinnamon gathered she'd already experienced and was terrified to experience it again.

"Calm down, my sweet. Relax." He spoke softly now. "I'll just be a few minutes. I still have to finish getting everything prepped." He disappeared into the other room.

Cinnamon could hear him humming as he bustled around the room with instruments clanking. She knew when he came out of the room, she'd be spotted immediately. It was now or never. She mouthed the words to Karissa "I'll come back for you." Karissa said nothing but shook her head, begging Cinnamon not to leave her there. Cinnamon held her finger to her lips to make sure Karissa didn't make a peep that might blow her cover. She crept from behind the stairs, looked towards the door to make sure lab coat was occupied, then made a mad dash up the steps. Once again, she was on the run. She'd made it to the warehouse door before she heard his voice mumbling below.

"Who was that?" He demanded from Karissa. He wasted no time waiting for an answer from the mute teenager. He made a beeline for the stairs, taking two at a time. He made it up to the warehouse just in time to see the exit door close. "Shoot!" He cursed himself and smacked the side of his head repeatedly while trying to decide what to do next.

Cinnamon ran in the middle of the street. No one seemed to be out on the road. She ran the route she knew home, but home was still at least five miles away. She kept running until she was out of breath and tried to assure herself that no one had followed her. She kept glancing over her shoulder with the eerie feeling she was being watched. Her pager vibrated repeatedly as she ran. Finally, she slowed down to see who it was. It was Raheem. She barely had time to hear the van come up behind her. She jumped when the headlights bore down on her from behind, causing her to drop the pager. *SCREEEECH!* The lights were too bright to see the driver, but whoever it was hit the accelerator quickly with full force. Cinnamon bolted down the street, but she never had a chance. In seconds the bumper of the van rode only feet behind her running ankles. That was the last she remembered before feeling the impact.

"Cinnamon?" The driver got out and called to her. He walked over and nudged her body with his foot, *"Cinnamon."* He got no response. Satisfied with his deed carried out, he got back in his van and took off.

CHAPTER 23

"The good news is Mrs. Grienbachs has decided not to press charges."

"*Press charges?* I'm telling you my daughter did not attack her. There has to be some other explanation."

"Look, I know this is hard for you to hear, but teens run away from home all the time. We're all just lucky that Mrs. Grienbachs tried to do the right thing by driving her home."

"She's lying." Cinnamon could hear the voices floating around in the background, but she couldn't interject on the conversation for some reason. Her tongue felt heavy, stuck. Her mind felt scrambled like a colorful kaleidoscope. She had a hard time focusing.

"You weren't there, Miss Mackey." An officer spoke calmly to the worried mother. Vivian sighed in frustration and held her head. "I have children too. I know how hard it can be to accept that you don't know everything about them."

"You're not listening. Cinnamon did not run away from home." She said through clenched teeth.

"Ma'am, I've known the Grienbachs for almost fifteen years. They're good people. Every year they hold a bake sale at the church to donate to the department for equipment they know we need. Mrs. Grienbachs would never hurt your child." He insisted.

"Yeah, well, did you know that your precious upstanding citizens have been abusing and molesting their own children?" Vivian shot.

The officer stuck his thumbs through his back belt loops and bounced forward on the tips of his toes as he let out a chuckle. "And where did you get this lil' tidbit of information?"

"Her own daughter told us!"

"Look. PK's tend to make up all kinds of lies. Sometimes it's for attention. Sometimes they want to feel and show that they can be *down* too." He reasoned.

"Down with *what?* Since when is child abuse and molestation a teenaged trend?" Vivian couldn't believe what she was hearing.

"To tell you the truth, I'm more concerned with *that.*" He pointed to the stud earring Cinnamon had in her pants pocket when she was undressed at the hospital. All of her personal effects sat in a plastic bag on a chair, except for the earring. The officer singled it out after recognizing it from the description given to the entire force of what Karissa had been wearing when she was last seen.

"What about it?" Vivian asked, confused.

"I have reason to believe that is the earring of one of the missing teenagers, Karissa Mills."

Vivian swallowed in response. The accusation sent a chill through her. "I'm sure there's some explanation for it." *What the heck is she doing with that?*

Cinnamon's eyes began to flutter. She felt far away, but something was pulling her back. It was the sound of her mother's familiar voice. Her body twitched and interrupted their conversation.

"Oh my God, Cinnamon? Cinnamon?" Vivian cupped her hands around one of Cinnamon's as she leaned over her face. "Baby, it's me. It's Mommy. I'm here. Wake up, Cinnamon."

"Mm-mm-mommy?" Cinnamon's eyes finally fluttered open.

"Oh my God! Nurse! Nurse! Get the doctor! She's awake!" Vivian called into the hallway. The police officer moved to the side as a nurse made her way in. "Thank God! Oh, Cinnamon, thank God you're awake. I've been praying for the past two days nonstop."

It took a few blinks before Cinnamon's eyes adjusted around the room. It was easy for her to gather that she was in a hospital room, but she was still trying to piece together the fragments that explained how she'd gotten there. The doctor came in shortly after the nurse.

"Well, hello, Cinnamon!" Dr. Bergs was a tall, lanky, cheerful woman with a wide smile. "So glad to see you awake, sleepy head. We were starting to worry." The nurse finished taking Cinnamon's vitals, then moved aside to allow the doctor to take over. Like all doctors, Dr. Bergs whipped out her flashlight. "Now, Cinnamon—that's such a lovely name for a lovely girl by the way, I want you to follow the light with your eyes."

Cinnamon did as instructed, looking up and down, then right and left. It was when she looked left that her eyes fell upon Karissa's earring that sat just inches away. She shot up in the bed, causing the doctor to jump back. "Karissa! We have to help Karissa!" She yanked her mother's arm, then winced from the pain of her own broken arm.

She'd been in an unresponsive state for the past two days with a concussion, but the doctor didn't think it was serious—and it wasn't. Unbelievably, she'd managed to escape the hit and run with only a broken arm and a minor cut on her ankle that was stitched up. Hours passed before another driver came down the street and found her still lying where the driver of the white van had left her. The good Samaritan called the ambulance and eventually Vivian was tracked down and notified after being out all night looking for her daughter.

She was frantic. Even though her head throbbed from the sudden rush of blood when she sat up, she was focused on one thing only. They had to get to Karissa.

"What is it? What's wrong, baby? Do you know who did this to you?"

"Yes! It was Raheem, and he's got Karissa too."

The police officer stepped forward. "Karissa, the missing teen?"

"Yes! Yes! He has her down in the basement. Mom, we have to do something! We have to help her." She pleaded.

"Okay, just calm down. Tell us what happened." Vivian spoke in a soothing voice while the doctor, nurse, and officer stood waiting to hear the tale.

"I found her earring in Raheem's van when he dropped me off at Generosa's house."

"You were out riding around with him after I told you I didn't want you seeing him?" Vivian's voice changed from gentle to stern in a heartbeat.

"Let her finish." The officer interjected.

"I found that earring on the floor of the van. Plus he has a knife! I saw it. He keeps it in the glove compartment."

"So how do you know Karissa is in somebody's basement? I'm not following." The officer asked.

"I saw her. After I escaped from First Lady Grienbachs's car, I didn't know where else to go, and I was afraid she'd come looking for me." Cinnamon's story was all over the place.

"*Afraid?*" Vivian questioned, then glared at the officer so as to say *See, I told you so.*

"Yes, mom. I snuck into their house to help Generosa look for her baby. After we found the dead baby—"

"*Dead baby? What dead baby?*" Now she had the officer's undivided attention.

"Let her finish," Vivian demanded. By now, he took out his pad and started to jot notes.

"Generosa's first baby."

"I didn't know she had a baby." He mumbled under his breath.

"That was the first one. Her second one is missing. That's why she called me to come over to help her find out what happened to the first baby because she was afraid that whatever happened to *it* would happen to the new baby, Tabitha."

"Yes, okay, I did hear that a missing report was filed for the child just before…" His voice drifted as he looked at Vivian, unsure if he should drop the bomb shell on Cinnamon in her fragile state.

"Before what?" Cinnamon asked, anxiously.

"Baby, there's been an accident."

"What kind of accident? Is Generosa okay? What happened?" Cinnamon fired off her questions of concern. Vivian looked down as tears welled up in her eyes. She shook her head silently and Cinnamon began to cry. "I don't understand."

"It looks like the tire on the pastor's truck had a blow out. It sent the vehicle veering off the road, flipping several times, before it landed down in the marsh bank. Then…" The officer trailed off again.

"What? Then what?" Cinnamon was impatient to know.

"Cin, the truck caught on fire. The whole thing incinerated." Vivian said.

"So? She got out, right? Tell me she got out."

The officer shook his head, "I'm sorry."

"What do you mean?"

"It was a pretty bad blaze. Even with two fire trucks, it was hours before they could put it out." He explained.

"So?"

"Any human remains would've been completely dissolved in the fire. I'm sorry."

Cinnamon's face became wet in moments. She wrapped her casted arm around the front of her body as she rocked back and forth. "No, no, no, no. This can't be happening. I was just with her."

"I'm so sorry, honey." Vivian rubbed her back.

The whole room was silent in grief until Cinnamon suddenly blurted, "That baby isn't missing. They did something to that baby. I'm telling you."

"Who did?" The officer asked.

"The Grienbachs! I know everyone thinks they're so wholesome and good people, but they're not. I don't know how I'll prove it, but I think the first lady did something to baby Tabitha."

"Cinnamon, I've already told your mom that I've known the family for a very long time. I know you're very upset, and you were practically in a coma for the past two days. They have you on medication. You're probably not thinking clearly and—"

"I'm telling you, I'm not mistaken about anything. Those people killed Generosa's first baby, and they probably did the same to Tabitha!" She grew agitated.

"Cinnamon, calm down. Just breathe." Her mother coaxed. "You said y'all found a dead baby?"

"We did, Generosa and me. We found Isaiah in the basement bathroom at her house. He was in an orange shoebox and wrapped in a white towel. Gabe thinks they drowned him."

"Gabe?" The officer questioned.

"Yeah, the Grienbachs's son. Generosa's brother. He's the one who told her where to look for the baby."

"Isn't he in a psychiatric facility for shooting someone and threatening suicide?"

"Yes, but—"

"Okay, I've heard enough."

"Listen! You have to believe me! I'm telling the truth!"

The officer sighed before he responded. "Okay, you have my word that I will make a visit to the house and look into this. In the meantime, we need to get back to Karissa. Now you said she was in a basement too? The Grienbachs's basement?"

"No, no, no. She's in a secret basement at John's Furniture Store. It's on Main Street."

"Secret basement?" he questioned.

"Yes. There's a hidden stairwell behind one of the shelves in the warehouse. All the time I've worked there I had never noticed it or seen anyone else use it."

"So how do you know Karissa is down there?"

"I saw her!"

"Cinnamon, you went down there by yourself? What is the matter with you? Anything could've happened." Vivian scolded.

Cinnamon ignored her mother's inquisitions. "She's down there. One of her breasts is cut off. Her lips have been pierced shut and her head is shaved."

"*Shaved?*" Vivian's face twisted as she imagined the young girl's new look.

"Yeah. Raheem did a real number on her. She's handcuffed to the wall down there and she doesn't even look like the same person— but I'm sure it was her. She looked terrified." Cinnamon's mind wandered back to the ghastly sight. "Mom, we have to go back there and get her! We have to save her. There's no telling what he'll do. Look what he did to me!"

"So you saw the person who hit you?" The officer asked.

"No, but it was a white van just like the one Raheem drives. He almost caught me in the basement. That's why he ran me down. He tried to kill me."

The officer stepped out into the hallway and radioed his walkie talkie. If they were going to save Karissa before she ended up like the others, they had to move fast.

***

Raheem was hunched over a pair of dingy white Nikes, brushing them with a toothbrush and a concoction made of bleach, water and cleanser when the sudden bang on his apartment door startled him. The sneaker slipped from his hand and landed on the floor.

"RAHEEM JAMESON! THIS IS THE POLICE! OPEN THIS DOOR!" They demanded on the other side.

His heart began to race as he jumped up. He looked at the door. Then he looked out the window. *Fire escape. There's no way I'm going back to jail.* He hurriedly slipped his sockless feet into the sneakers that were half clean. Then he headed out of the window. He'd made it one flight down before the police burst through the door using a battering ram. Not realizing just how tiny the space would be, three officers waited in the hall while the other three crammed into the room.

One officer stuck his head out of the open window. "We got a runner!" He announced, then spoke into his walkie talkie, "All units, he's headed down the fire escape on the north side of the building. Suspect is wearing gray sweatpants and a white tank top."

Raheem's feet hit the pavement with a spring, allowing him to easily catch his balance. Just as he turned to run, the barrel of a nine millimeter firearm pointed at his nose froze him in his tracks. "Police! Freeze! Get down on the ground!" Raheem cursed at himself as he put his hands up and knelt down to the ground.

"Where is she? Where's the girl?" An officer demanded.

"Wh-what girl? I don't know what'chu talkin' about, man." He sounded convincing.

"Make this easier on everybody. Just tell us where she is, Raheem. Where is Karissa Mills?"

"*Karissa?* Look I don't know what's going on, but I have no idea. I haven't seen that girl."

"Fine. Don't talk. We have warrants to search the entire premises anyway—and your van." The officer taunted.

"Search all you want. You won't find anything."

"You sure about that? Not even in the secret basement?"

"Basement? What are you talking about?" Raheem did a good job at acting confused.

"Just quit already. Your girlfriend already gave you up. You thought you killed her, didn't you?"

"*Killed* her? Wait, *what*? Cinnamon? Is she alright? Where is she?"

As their exchange took place out front, John pulled up to the store. Officers tried to hold him back until he explained that he was the owner of the property. Then he saw Raheem being detained on the ground. "Raheem! Officers, what's going on here? He hasn't done anything."

"John Mitchell?" One of the officers asked.

"Yes?"

"We have a warrant to search this property and a van owned by you that is driven by Mr. Jameson here." John glanced over the warrant quickly, realizing he had no power to do anything.

The officers' radios could be heard crackling with a voice coming through. "We got something. We found the stairs. We're going in … She's here! … Hello? Honey, can you hear us? She's not responding! Get the paramedics down here immediately!"

John and Raheem looked at each other helplessly. Then all of a sudden John said, "Raheem, what did you do?"

"Nothing! John, you gotta believe me. I didn't do anything, man!" Raheem wrestled on his belly, but the officers kept him subdued.

When the paramedics finally emerged from the building with a gurney carrying Karissa's tattered body, it was too much for John. He gasped and turned his back, placing his hands atop his head. Raheem lifted his face from the pavement just enough to catch a glimpse of her face before she was wisped away. She was totally incoherent as the paramedics worked on her feverishly.

"Raheem Jameson, you're under arrest for the kidnapping and assault of Karissa Mills. You have the right to remain silent…" Two officers hoisted him to his feet and read him his Miranda rights as they escorted him to a police cruiser.

"John! John, call my lawyer. John!" He called out as he bent his neck to lower his head into the car. John looked over at him through the car window but said nothing. Instead, he looked up to the sky as if praying while running his hands down over his face as he exhaled.

***

"I feeeel liiiike gooooing hommmme, I feeeel liiiike gooooing hommmme," Sister Cathy sang into the microphone, her soulful voice projecting out. Sniffles and weeping could be heard throughout the sanctuary at Greater Saints First Baptist Church that morning. It was a dreary, cloudy day outside the doors. The ceiling fans rotated above and cardboard fans waved back and forth in the hands of the congregation to fight off the humidity. It was a quiet, sad scene. There were no caskets. Instead, two easels stood side by side at the front of the church. One had a large picture of Reverend Grienbachs and the other a picture of Generosa, caught in a rare moment where she was smiling. The first lady sat on the front pew dressed in a black suit with a lace black veil covering her face. She didn't cry or make a peep. Her expression was blank as Sister Kim hugged her tightly and wept into a tissue. There were very few family members that had turned out for the memorial service. Still, the small church was packed with friends and people of the community who knew the family.

"We don't have to do this. We can turn around and go right back home if you want." Vivian spoke gently to Cinnamon. Both women wore black dresses with patent leather heels. Cinnamon couldn't fit her cast through the sleeves, so her jacket hung around her shoulders.

"No, I want to. I want to pay my respects to Generosa."

The two quietly entered the church and got in the viewing line. They immediately noticed Gabe standing in the back corner. He wore a dark suit but his hands and feet were shackled. Two prison guards stood on either side of him. Cinnamon offered a small smile, but it was as though he looked right through her. His eyes told a story of heavy sedation. Mother and daughter briskly walked to the front, clutching to each other for support. Vivian felt like it was her first time in the church all over again with the whispers and stares they received. This time she held her head high and marched on with her daughter.

Once at the front, they stood in front of Generosa's picture and shared a moment of silence. They didn't stop to offer words of condolence to the first lady. As they walked past, both First Lady Grienbachs and Sister Kim glared at them. The police officer from the hospital had followed his word and filed a report to look into Cinnamon's story. The first lady had given her full cooperation, allowing them to search their entire home. They turned up nothing. The skeletal remains of baby Isaiah were gone, and they found nothing to suggest that any abuse had taken place at the residence. There was nothing they could do.

There was standing room only left and the duo settled in a slim space along the back wall where they remained on their feet. Cinnamon hadn't noticed, but Tammy stood two persons away. She saw Cinnamon first. "Hey," she leaned forward and whispered.

"Oh, hey, Tammy."

"How you been?" She wiggled her way past the man standing between them and made herself a space next to Cinnamon.

"Okay," Cinnamon shrugged and lifted up her casted arm.

"I heard about what happened with you ... and Raheem."

"Yeah," Cinnamon didn't feel much like talking about Raheem. She didn't want to hear the *'I told you so's'*.

"I just wanted to tell you that I'm really sorry. For real."

"Thanks," the girls paused for a moment to pay attention to the service, but there seemed to be more Tammy wanted to say.

"I don't blame you for New York. I thought you were real cool, and the only reason I haven't talked to you in a while is ... well ... because of my mother, you know?" She sounded genuinely apologetic.

"Yeah, I know ... I thought you were pretty cool too, Tammy." Cinnamon gave a smile to comfort Tammy's apparent nervousness. "I still do."

"I just wanted you to know."

"Hey, where's Tiffany?" Cinnamon asked as she scanned the room.

Tammy's expression changed to a sad one. "She's not here. She don't leave the house much anymore ... actually, she doesn't leave at all since..."

"Oh ... I'm sorry," Now Cinnamon's tone matched hers.

"Yeah..."

The memorial was carried out in traditional fashion, with the exception of the two brass urns that sat on each side of the pictures. People gave pleasant remarks. A friend of the reverend gave the eulogy, and a pastor from another church gave a brief sermon. "Let's remember to keep the Grienbachs's family in our prayers. In addition to the tragic loss of the reverend and Generosa, First Lady Grienbachs's granddaughter, Tabitha, is still missing. Let us all be there for the family in their time of need."

"Can you believe that cute lil' baby is missing now?" Tammy whispered as her forehead wrinkled. "I wonder if Raheem took her too."

"She's *not* missing," Cinnamon hissed through clenched teeth. Just the sight of the first lady sitting there, pretending to grieve over her granddaughter, caused her blood to boil.

"What do you mean?"

"Never mind," she answered quickly. "It was good seeing you, Tammy." Cinnamon turned sharply towards her mother who seemed to already read her mind.

"You ready to leave?" Cinnamon nodded.

They strolled slowly towards Vivian's car and Vivian looped her arm through her daughter's. "Are you okay?" Vivian asked.

Cinnamon shrugged as she looked down at the black tar. "I guess ... I just can't believe she's gone ... Now we'll never know what happened to Tabitha."

"I'm so sorry, Cin. I know Generosa was one of your only friends down here. I'm gonna miss her too." Cinnamon clung to her mother's waist with her one good arm, pulling her in closer. "My poor baby, you've been through so much this year. I really thought this time would be different. I really thought a fresh start here in Gracious Meadows would be our ticket." She pushed a strand of hair away from Cinnamon's face.

"It's okay. It's not your fault, Mom. How could you have known these people would be so crazy, and everyone tried to warn me about Raheem. I should've listened."

"Speaking of which, you know we still gotta get you down to that station—but we don't have to do that today if you don't feel up to it."

"No, let's just get it over with. I'm ready to put all of this behind me."

The district attorney's office was building a strong case against

Raheem for the abduction of Karissa. They added on two more charges including attempted murder and endangerment of a minor. Detectives Briggs and Sunil were pushing hard to connect him to the other Gracious Meadows murders, but hadn't successfully connected the dots yet. That's why they really needed Cinnamon's testimony for Karissa's case, especially *without* Karissa. Doctors predicted she would be in recovery for a while. In addition to being diagnosed with major Post Traumatic Stress Syndrome, she was also diagnosed with temporary aphasia—a speech and language disorder caused by damage to the brain. Although she was conscious again, she hadn't said a word since they found her. The doctors attributed her condition to the level of shock she experienced, and it was hard to say if she'd ever speak again.

Because she was still a minor, Cinnamon wasn't required to testify at the actual trial. Instead, everyone agreed that she could do a video-taped testimony. This was a relief to Cinnamon because she wasn't ready to face Raheem in person. She didn't want to see him. He was a monster in her eyes now and the sense of shame and gullibility she felt over ever dating him was overwhelming. During the ride to the police station, she replayed all of their conversations together and reminisced about the time they spent together. She tried to remember something—*anything*—that might suggest she'd been wrong and he wasn't a sadistic killer, but she found nothing. Everything pointed to him. He'd reached out several times through letters given to his lawyer proclaiming his innocence to Cinnamon, but she threw each letter away before ever reading them.

CHAPTER 24

"Do you ever hear voices or do you ever feel like you're a different person? Like someone else is inside of you?"

"Like a split personality?" Raheem questioned and Detective Briggs nodded. "Oh, you're asking if I'm crazy." He said, flatly. "No. No voices and no other personalities that make me do things. I'm *not* crazy."

"Well then tell us who your partner is!" Detective Sunil slammed his hand on the metal table. He'd grown tired of going around and round in circles with Raheem. Detective Briggs, Michael Goldstein—Raheem's lawyer, and Raheem were all tired. They'd been through this line of questioning several times within the past weeks since he'd been arrested. Here they were again, back in the interrogation room.

The detectives tried, unsuccessfully, to get Raheem to name his accomplice. "Raheem, we know you didn't act alone—unless it was a multiple personality of yours. You already said it wasn't so..." Detective Briggs was the calmer of the two detectives.

"So? What?"

"So help us out here, and maybe we can talk the D.A. into cutting you a little slack, maybe knock your sentence down a little. I mean you're already going away for Karissa's attempted murder. Are you really ready to let your partner just walk away scot-free?"

"I already told you. I ain't got no partner 'cause I didn't have anything to do with this." He insisted.

"I hear you, and I want to believe you. The problem is the evidence we have says otherwise." Detective Briggs said.

"What evidence?" Raheem's palms sprung from the sides of his head where he'd been holding them with his elbows planted on the table.

"The knife! The patterns!" Detective Sunil's voice was loud and agitated again. "There were two very distinct, different types of puncture marks on Karissa—as was the case with the other bodies we found. Now are you ready to stop yanking us around or what?"

"I. Don't. Know ... WHAT YOU ARE TALKING ABOUT!" Raheem flew up out of his chair, causing it to topple over to the floor behind him. He had had enough.

"Okay, that's enough. My client has cooperated as much as he can. He has nothing else to say." Michael finally chimed in and ended the line of questioning.

The truth was, the coroner's office couldn't say definitively whether there were two perpetrators or not. While it was true that they found different wound patterns, it was still possible that one person could've worked alone to make the different punctures. There really was no way to prove otherwise. Whether there was another murderer roaming the streets of Gracious Meadows or not, Raheem's fate had been sealed. With Cinnamon's testimony as arsenal, once the judicial system was done, Raheem would be an old man before he'd ever have the chance to see the light of day as a free man again.

***

"I'm glad they got that monster off the street." Vivian sipped through a bended straw from a glass of ice tea. A month had passed since Raheem was convicted and sentenced to thirty-two years in prison for the abduction and attempted murder of Karissa. Now, the Mackey women sat in a booth seat at *Charlie's*, a small restaurant specializing in American food.

Cinnamon stuck a golden crisp fry in her mouth, then wiped her greasy fingertips with a napkin. "Yeah, me too ... Mom?"

"What's up, babe?"

"Can we not talk about Raheem anymore? I want to forget that he ever existed."

"Sure, of course." Vivian made a motion zipping her lips and tossing away the key. "I'm just happy the streets are safe again. There haven't been any abductions in months, but you're right. We should focus on something more positive." She glanced out of the window. It was a lovely hot August day. The sun shone brightly and flowered trees swayed from a stifled breeze. "You know what we should do? We should go on a shopping spree!"

"A shopping spree?" Cinnamon didn't sound convinced with the idea at first.

"Yeah! Why not?" Cinnamon shrugged in response while she took a sip of her cola. "*Cinnamon.* Since when do I have to beg you to go shopping?" Vivian made an exaggerated puzzled face and laughed.

"You're right! I don't know what's wrong with me. Let's go before you change your mind!" Cinnamon turned giddy at the second thought of the idea. With that, Vivian paid the bill, and the ladies slid out of the booth to be on their way.

The shopping spree turned out to be a great idea. The ladies returned home with fists full of shopping bags. They'd shopped until closing time, and the mall had to put them out. The sun had since set. Still, their spirits were lifted for the moment, and they were chatty, just like girlfriends. Vivian slammed the trunk close after retrieving the last of the bags, and the pair headed towards their apartment.

"Ooowee! Now that's clean right there. Cin, what you think about that car?"

"It's cool, I guess."

"You *guess?* Girl, that's a 750 iL right there! Soon as I finish saving up, that's the kind of car we gon' be riding in next. Just watch!" Vivian was impressed as they slowly strolled past the shiny black BMW, taking it all in with admiration.

"I wonder whose it is. Maybe Cara's?"

Vivian sucked her teeth. "Girl, Cara don't make that kind of money managing apartments. Whoever's it is got some loot." They took one last look then headed up the stairs and inside the apartment.

Cinnamon flipped up the living room light switch as she usually did, but nothing happened. "Hmmm, I think the bulb must be blown out." She put down her bags and headed down the hall to turn on the other switch, when she suddenly let out a scream. The scream was short and snuffed out in a hurry.

Vivian dropped her bags and moved quickly down the hall, "Cinnamon?" Her heart thumped and panic rippled through her voice. She didn't know what hit her, but she went down without the chance to fight.

Vivian could hear the sounds of whimpering and voices talking, but they seemed far off into the distance as she slowly came to. Her temples pounded, causing her to squint, and her vision was blurry. Baby blue, silky fabric dangled up and down in front of her. Someone had picked through their shopping bags and a piece of lingerie had been pulled out.

"Gotta give it to ya. You still have good taste, baby. Hope you wasn't plannin' on getting sexy tonight for anyone because obviously there's been a change of plans." His voice sent a pulse of terror and fear straight through her body. *It can't be.*

It was Cinnamon's whimpering that finally brought her fully to, reminding her of where she was. "Come on baby, wake up. There you go."

The fresh new white Nike Air Forces caught her attention first. Then her eyes traveled up the legs of someone wearing a black and white track suit. Her gaze finally landed on the hideous scar that she knew all too well. Her eyes popped wide open and she tried to scream, "Mmmm! Mmmm!" but her attempt was futile. She and Cinnamon sat side by side, gagged and bound to kitchen chairs. The chairs had been positioned to face the couch.

"Go ahead and take the bandanas off—but if you even think about screaming for help, I'll blow your brains out with the first peep." He sat coolly on the couch, hunched over and leaning forward with one hand draped over the curve of a wooden cane for support, and the other pointing an automatic .45 in their direction. A tall, dark, burly man with a big bushy beard who was dressed in all black removed the bandana from Vivian's mouth first. Then he moved to Cinnamon to follow suit. "Be careful, Benny."

Both men shared a chuckle, "Yeah, lil' momma almost bit my whole hand off last time." Cinnamon's face scrunched in confusion until she made the connection. He was the man who tried to grab her at the fair.

"Feisty. Just like her mother."

Vivian's voice was barely audible as though she questioned the fact that she was even saying his name again. "Vic—" He cleared his throat, cutting her off. She looked down in submission immediately, "I mean, Vicious—"

He cut her off again, "*Vicious* what?"

"That was you I saw at the diner! I just knew it!"

He laughed, "Baby girl, I been following you for months now. Thought you'd just mosey on down here and get ghost on a brother? Thought we wouldn't find you?"

"Please don't..." She couldn't bring herself to beg for her life.

"Please don't what?" He cocked his gun for effect. "Please don't ... kill you?"

"I thought you were—"

"Oh, you thought I was *dead*, huh? Dead like your niece, huh? Benny what was ol' girl's name? The one from Brooklyn?"

"Roxxy."

"Yeah, Roxxy. You thought I was dead like Roxxy?" He smiled proudly.

Cinnamon suddenly stopped crying and looked up, "You killed Roxxy?" She asked softly.

"You killed Roxanne?" Vivian repeated the question, but with anger rising in her voice. "You son-of-a—"

Vicious pressed the gun beneath her chin, "You were saying?" Vivian leaned her head back away from the barrel as a single tear slid from the corner of her eye. "That's what I thought." Vicious relaxed back on the couch. "Yeah, she was an unfortunate casualty, got in the way; just like that lady at the fair did, too. That bullet had your name on it, missy." He spoke to Vivian.

"You ... you ... you *animal*!" Vivian spat.

"*Me? I'm* an animal? You hear this, Benny? *I'm* the animal." The two men exchanged smirks. "You and that lil' rug rat there just thought you could kill me and take off with my money, and *I'm* the animal?" He ran his tongue along the back of his teeth, making a suction sound as though trying to dislodge a piece of food. "Well ... you thought wrong. As you can see I'm very much alive, and I'm back to get what's mine."

ABOUT THE AUTHOR

Just Jewel is an author, poet and blogger born and raised in New Jersey. She attended Essex County College where she obtained her Associate's Degree in Business Administration while holding several positions within the insurance industry.

God Bless the Church Folk is Just Jewel's second novel and third published written work. She currently resides in Southern California, and the author is positively passionate about writing! Visit Just-Jewel.com to learn more about what she has in store next.

Think Into Existence Ink

T.I.E. Ink Titles

God Bless the Church Folk by Just Jewel
Heroine Chronicles by Crissy Jetson
The Mini Poetry Project Vol. I: A Collection of Random
Expressions by Just Jewel
Two Way Mirrors by Just Jewel

ON SALE NOW!
WWW.TIEINK.COM
PO BOX 12174 * EL CAJON, CA 92022 * 619-663-4449

www.ingramcontent.com/pod-product-compliance
Lightning Source LLC
Chambersburg PA
CBHW022006170626
46808CB00001B/311